BOUND BY SECRETS AND SIXERS

NIDHI CHOWDARY

Made with ♥ on the Notion Press Platform
www.notionpress.com

Contents

Contents

Acknowledgements

Writing this book has been a journey of love, imagination, and countless moments of inspiration. I want to express my deepest gratitude to everyone who has supported me along the way.

This book would not have been possible without the unwavering support and belief of my family. Your encouragement has been my greatest strength, and I am forever grateful.

To my brother, and friends, thank you for being my biggest critics and my go-to expert for all things cricket. Your insights and patience in clearing my endless doubts mean the world to me.

And to my readers, your love, motivation, and enthusiasm inspire me to keep writing. Thank you for being a part of this journey and for believing in these stories as much as I do.

Prologue

In the world of flashing cameras, roaring crowds, and the endless chase for records, he was a star—shining brighter with each run, each victory. The cricket field was his stage, the game his art, and the world, his adoring audience. Every glance, every cheer was his, as he lived a life few could even imagine—a life of fame, glory, and endless applause.

But beneath all the bright lights and camera flashes, she existed in the shadows, unnoticed, hidden, and ever-watchful. She was a secret—one whose presence wasn't celebrated, whose victories were always wrapped in layers. She worked in silence, protecting the nation, safeguarding its secrets, and maneuvering through the dangerous twists of a world in silence. She was a woman of mystery, dedicated to a cause bigger than any personal desire.

Their worlds collided by chance, as fate often works in mysterious ways. A mission brought them together—a mission that would force them to spend three months side by side.

This is a story of love, dedication, and passion—not just for each other, but for the nation they both served in their own way. It is a story of two people from different worlds, united by fate and driven by a love that burns brighter than the most celebrated victory.

Please don't expect this to be a suspence or thriller, it is not. It is a romantic love story filled with heart-fluttering romance that will leave you blushing and giggling. It is the story of two souls finding love in an unexpected setting, and sticking together till the end. It's more about their love than about their professions.

CHAPTER ONE

Shaurya, the Captain of Indian Cricket team, was running in the garden of the hotel they were staying, his pods plugged in. His tee shirt stuck to his body like a second skin, the sweet seeping through the thin layer of clothing.

Even after 3 laps around the garden, his breath was regulated, and he looked relaxed. Drops of sweat cascaded from his damp hair, and rolled down from his forehead, sliding from his sharp pointed nose, falling onto the ground from his chin.

With his jaw clenched and puffy muscles adorned with droplets of sweat shining under the morning sun, he was no less than a dream to the girls around. Every girl in the park kept their eyes fixed on him, as most of them came to the park only to get a glimpse of him.

But he was unfazed by the attention fixed on him. His eyes remained rooted on the path in front of him, his entire concentration on the track in front of him.

"Looks like our captain is again the centre of attraction," Akshith, the vice-captain and the all-rounder batsman teased as he lunged forward to match steps with Shaurya.

"Don't worry. Now that you are here, you can have your share of attention," Shaurya replied in a cool tone, with a roll of his eyes. Akshith chuckled at Shaurya's comment but didn't counter.

After jog and a relaxing shower, the team gathered for breakfast, which mostly consisted of the nutrients and carbs they needed according to the diet-chats crafted by their nutritionists.

The bus took them to the stadium where their last match of the series was scheduled to take place. The coaches and the captain assessed the field and the pitch conditions and the humidity. The team then gathered to discuss their strategy for the match.

The head coach briefed them about the field conditions and the team they were going to play against before explaining them their roles. Once he was done, the batting and bowling coaches took their turns in providing inputs to the team. The captain was the last one to put forth his points.

As the players moved to the nets to warm up, the technicians started setting up their equipment. The teams started with basic stretches, jogs and field drills. They practiced a little in the nets, getting accostomed to the batting and bowling conditions of the pitch. After a little practice in fielding like catches, throws and agility drills, they moved back to their respective dressing rooms to get ready for the match.

The gun sounds puerced the eerie silence of the dark night where the little sparks from the guns when the bullets got fired was the only source of light. Both the parties involved relied on their hearing ability and the night sights attached to their guns to take down the enemies, protecting themselves simultaneously.

"Where the fuck is this backup team?" A grunt is heard from the microphones as Rakshith chided to his team about the backup team being late for their aid.

"They will be here soon, Rakku baby. Now stop getting irritated and concentrate on killing those bastards before they put a bullet into your skull," Bhavin commented making Rakshith utter a series of curses as he moved behind another wall. The remaining officers connected to them only shook their heads, habituated to the their banter.

"Bhavin I swear if you call me.."

"Guys, wait. I think someone is here," Another voice cut off Rakshith mid sentence, alerting the team. Shika turned back, clutching her gun with both hands. She shot the man before he could shoot Nithin. With a nod, both of them continued to walk in different directions.

"The backup team will join us in 90 seconds. Let's grab some kills by then, shall we?" A smirk danced on their lips as they moved swiftly, using doors and walls as thier covers. They killed 3 more people before the backup fall in. Together, they killed 20 terrorists, emptying another terrorist base.

"Let's see what they are here for," At Rakhith's words the team started searching every inch of the house, carefully examining and noting down every detail they came across.

They managed to get their hands on a few maps, with few cities marked in red, two cell phones and a few bundles of currency along with a few guns.

"Looks like they were planning something hazardous in these cities," Bhavin muttered inspecting the bodies of the terrorists, searching their pockets.

"And now they can't," Ananya affirmed with a smirk, her eyes fixed on the maps sprawled in front of them. "Do you think we can get more information from these cell phones?" She turned to Rakshith expectantly.

"We can always try our luck," Rakshith shrugged taking the phone from her. They sealed the phones and continued with their search.

"Guys!" Nithin exclaimed, grabbing the attention of others. "There," He pointed to the roof. With a round of shots, the peice of roof fell to the ground along with a packet. They confiscated the packet and moved out.

Once they reached their base, they started examining the proofs they collected. Ananya put on the gloves and carefully opened the packet they collected from the roof. Ananya took out of the picture of a man along with some code written on the back of it.

The team moved to her to get a closer look at the picture. "Now who is this Beggar?" Shika wondered out loud, her eyes fixed on the picture in Ananya's hands. The man seemed to be in his 40's, his eyes blood red and his lips a dark shade of purple. His hair was messy and clothes were torn.

"He must be smoker." Ananya concluded, passing the photo to Rakshith who called in Veer to enquire about the man in the picture.

"Do you think he is a local?" Shika asked once Rakshith joined them back after a brief chat with Veer.

"Don't know. But we have to get him soon," Rakshith replied with a sigh. Soon the photo was circulated to all the army bases, agents and police. The teams started searching for the man in the photograph.

"Guys, it's time to leave!" At Rakshith's announcement, they swiftly packed their things and shuffled into the car waiting for them. Upon reaching the airport, they took a flight to Delhi.

"As we have already reported everything, can we just go home? We will go to office in the evening," Bhavin fake yawned to show how sleep-deprived he was. The remaining members rolled their eyes at his drama but they all wanted to rest for a while too.

Due to the case, they couldn't have proper rest for the past 10 days. They had to keep an eye on the actions of the informers to get to terrorists hide out.

"Though he overacted, I agree with him, guys. I feel too tired to hear Kulkarni's sir's lecture now," Shika muttered resting her head on Nithin's shoulder. Nithin smiled at his girlfriend and wrapped his hand around her shoulder, with a gentle kiss to her temple.

"Okay. Please pick me up on your way to office then," Ananya mumbled, gathering her hair in fists and tieing it with a rubberband.

Exchanging nods, the team stepped out of the airport. They haven't even reached their car when Nithin's phone went off, draining the color from their faces.

"Jai Hind Sir," The three words were enough for them to understand who was on the other end and also the fact that they weren't going home but to office. After hanging up the call Nithin turned to his team with a sigh and they silently got into the car.

"I should have slept in the plane instead of listening to your stupid rant," Ananya accused Rakshith with narrowed eyes, her voice grumpy.

"It was the other way around, Anu," Rakshith said in a bored tone, trying to find a comfortable position to doze off, even for a bit. He finally scooted down and placed his head on a grumpy Ananya's shoulder and dozed off.

They reached their office after a 40 minute drive and Ananya shook Rakshith awake once the car entred the building. The team shuffled out aand headed to their wing.

"Jai Hind Sir!" They coroused as they stood in front of Mr. Kulkarni, their head officer.

"Good morning, team," Mr. Kulkarni greeted them with no expression on his face, making them all roll their eyes internally.

"What good happened this morning?" Shika muttered under her breath which was audible to all of them as she wasn't as low as she thought. They pressed their lips together to stop the smile that threatened to break out.

"I know you are all tired because of the last few days. I will have others handle the mobiles and retrieve data. The photo is already circulated to other agents and to police. Hopefully, we will get our hands on that man soon too. You all can rest for a week. I'll see you after a week and don't party like animals," Huge grins broke out on their lips listening to him. They all nodded their heads eagerly.

"You may leave now. But keep your phones on," They were all out of his sight as soon as Mr. Kulkarni completed his words. The old man shook his head at their madness and moved to the control rooom where another team was already working on the mobile phones to retrive the data and was checking the matches for the man in photo from the data they had.

"The chief called us to office just to ask us to take a leave? He could have informed the same in the call too, right?" Bhavin almost whined. Almost.

"He just wanted to make sure we were all fine without fatal injuries," Ananya explained, her head falling onto Rakshith's shoulder who was sitting between her and Bhavin on the back.

Seeing Ananya, Bhavin too rested his head on Rakshith's shoulder making him sigh at his friends but he didn't say anything to them and let them rest.

Ananya, Bhavin, Rakshith and Vikram, all of them went to the same college. Ananya was junior to the boys by an year but an event made them friends and they always remained so, except for Vikram and Rakshith.

Nithin and Shika joined them during their training and from then, they were all a team, a family in all their missions.

"That man, he would die but never accept that he cares for us," Shika's comment earned a laugh from her friends. She was right though! Mr. Kulkarni was and is very proud of his team and their achivements but never confessed it in front of them or praised them in front of them. But he does praise them in front of his collegues and higher-ups.

"Guys, there is a match this evening. Let's watch it together?" Nithin suggested, averting his eyes to the mirror for a moment before turning his attention to the road.

But he got a little too excited and his voice startled the two sleeping people at the back.

"What the hell, Nithin? Who shouts like that?" Ananya chided moving away from Rakshith's shoulder. But Bhavin didn't opt for words to repramid him. He went a step ahead and spanked his head making the poor man yelp.

"Sorry!" He replied sheepishly, matching his gaze with them through mirror. "But let's watch this match guys! Please!" He pleaded making Ananya and Bhavin exchange doubtful glances before tehy turned to Rakshith.

"Okay," Rakshith agreed after thinking for a minute making the group hoot in excitement.

Nithin dropped everyone off after the team decided to rest for the day and meet in the evening to watch the match together.

CHAPTER TWO

"Boys, time for the National Anthem," Dhruv informed his teammates. The players quickly slipped into their jerseys and moved out of the dressing room. The children were already waiting for them and they grinned widely, their eyes filled with excitement as they gazed at their favorite players. Each player held a child's hand as they moved through the stands, into the grass.

The crowd erupted into loud cheers upon noticing the players stepping in, their heads held high and chests puffing with pride, carrying their nation's name on their jerseys and the zeal to win in their eyes.

The flags of both nations fluttered proudly in the hands of spectators. The cameraman did an excellent job of jumping onto the flags in the crowd and then onto the faces of the captains of the respective teams.

The players of both teams stood in horizontal lines, their national flags behind them and the children in front of them. The Australian National anthem was played first, a mark of respect and recognition to the home ground. When the Indian National Anthem started, the players and the Indian fans sang along, their heads held high and voices filled with pride.

The teams started another round of practice, with a few stretches and warm-ups as they waited for the toss. The host called both the captains to come forward for the toss.

"Shaurya, do you want to go for it today?" The host asked Shaurya, a warm smile plastered on his lips. Shaurya glanced at the opponent captain for a second and then nodded his head with a smile of his own.

"What's your call, William?" The host turned to William. He took a brief moment to think and replied with a "tails". Shaurya flipped the coin into the air.

Though the camera was focused on the ongoing toss, it also captured the little banter going on behind Shaurya. The young players, Naksh and Likhith were fighting for a pair of gloves.

"Looks like Naksh wants to use Likhith's gloves for the match," The commentator exclaimed with a chuckle making Shaurya turn to the youngsters. With a shake of his head, he turned to the coin on the ground.

"By the way, it's heads. What's your call, Shaurya?" The host asked, forwarding the mic to Shaurya.

"We'll bat first," Shaurya answered after a brief pause.

"India won the toss and chose to bat first," The host announced as Shaurya took off his cap and put it back on after adjusting his hair.

"William, what are your thoughts on bowling first?" The host turned to Williams.

"We are prepared for both scenarios. This pitch looks good, we are confident in our bowlers to make early breakthroughs." William replied confidently.

"Excellent. Any changes to your lineup for today's match?" The host posed his next question.

"Yes. We've made a couple of strategic changes to our bowling lineup, bringing in some spinners to add variety. We are hoping they will give us an early breakthrough as we are going to bowl first," William explained, his posture relaxed.

"What about you, Shaurya? Any changes in the batting order?" The host asked the next question. Shaurya shook his head with a smile.

"We are sticking to our game plan and backing our top order to set a strong foundation for us," He replied coolly.

"Thank you, captains. Best of luck to both of you," The host wished them both. The captains moved to their respective teams after thanking the host.

The teams moved to the dugouts and the Indian openers secured their pads while the Australian team moved to the ground to set their field placements.

"Bhavin, where are you guys? The match is about to start!" Nithin exclaimed through the phone as his teammates hadn't reached yet.

"We will be there in 5. Who won the toss?" Rakshith, who answered Bhavin's phone enquired.

"India,"

"Then we'll be there in 2," he cut the call and turned to Bhavin. Bhavin increased the speed, getting the hint.

The friends settled on the floor after locking the doors, their backs pressed to the couches behind them, snacks and drinks sprawled in front of them.

As the openers stepped into the field, the crowd erupted into a round of cheers, songs blasting from the DJ. The camera zoomed to a few placards displaying funny comments and quotations before moving to the players to capture their reactions. The teams smiled at a few while the others made them crack up into bursts of laughter.

The bowler was given a chance to pick a ball from the box in Empire's hand and soon, the match started.

Though the batsmen struggled in the first two overs, they started hitting boundaries and sixers from the third over. The bowlers changed their styles and tactics to control them. They tried googlies and yorkers but the batsmen played carefully, making sure not to give in and fetch the singles and doubles whenever possible.

At 70, India lost its first wicket as the ball fell into the hands of a long-on fielder. The captain stepped in, carrying the responsibility of setting a respectable target in front of the opponents to not burden the bowling unit. Another wicket fell quickly and the second opener made his way back to the dugouts after getting stumped.

It took a few balls for both the new batsmen to get a grip on the field and Dhruv started aiming for long shots and boundaries. Shaurya stepped back, letting Dhruv take the lead, helping him with comfortable singles and doubles.

But when Dhruv got out, the wickets started to fall quickly. Though the other batsmen and Shaurya managed to secure a few big hits, the fall of wickets made it hard for them to build a strong partnership with Shaurya. Despite the occasional big hits, the fall of wickets became a cause of distress among the spectators.

"Yaar! Why are these people so desperate to go back to the dressing room?" Nithin chided, irritation clear in his tone.

"Can't they stick in the crease for a while? They should at least try to stand at the non-striker end but no, they aren't doing that even!" Bhavin added, his lips twisted in displeasure.

"Why don't you guys go and play then?" Ananya chided her friends, not liking the way they were talking. The fall of wickets is irritating her too but she doesn't want to talk ill about the players because of that.

They all turned their attention back to the screen opening the lids of their cokes. Shaurya hit a sixer when Ananya was taking a sip from her coke and Shika turned to her with starry eyes, a grin etched on her face.

"No! He hit sixers when I wasn't drinking too!" Ananya explained, her eyes widened in horror as she already figured out what was going on in her friend's superstitious mind.

"Try again. If he doesn't score this time, I will accept that it was a coincidence," Shika pleaded, displaying her puppy eyes. Having no other option, Ananya brought the tin to her lips and Shaurya struck another boundary as she took a sip of the cold liquid.

"See! I told you. He's scoring when you are having coke. It is butterfly effect. Come on, Anu, have it." Shika encouraged, her voice chirpy and enthusiastic as she pushed the tin to Ananya's lips to have another sip.

Ananya turned to others for help but they just shrugged, grins etched on their faces as they steered their concentration back to the match. The third time Ananya took a sip, Shaurya bragged a comfortable two.

Though Ananya tried to use it and get rid of the coke, Shika argued he scored 2 because of her taking a sip.

For the next 5 overs, Shika made Ananya drink 5 cokes, literally pouring the liquid into her mouth.

"Mr. Shaurya! I am stuck with this stupid because of you," Ananya glared at the man through the screen, who was completely unaware of her presence and the glare she was throwing at him.

The Indian team managed to put a decent score of 210 in front of the opposition by the end of their batting.

During the break, the teams rehydrated themselves and discussed their strategies while the friends sitting in Shika's living room discussed their choices for food and placed an order.

Shaurya and his team stepped into the field as Ananya grabbed the food from the delivery agent after paying and thanking him.

As the bowler took his place beside the stumps, Ananya placed their snacks on the table in front of them. With a nod from the Umpire, the first ball was delivered and paralley, the first slice of pizza was lifted by Bhavin.

Shaurya's strategic field placements and the reverse-swing and off-swing deliveries from the bowlers made it hard for the opposition to score, restricting their batting. As they grew irritated due to the increasing required run rate, the slower ones played a crucial role in taking the wickets.

When William and Mark managed to establish a partnership of 75 runs, the match turned interesting. Shaurya, determined to break their partnership, changed the bowlers and field placements.

While the bowlers and fielders struggled to break the partnership, Shika somehow concluded the slice of pizza in Rakshith's hand was the problem. She snatched the pizza from his hand and stuffed it into Nithin's mouth making both the men stare at her with weird expressions while Ananya and Bhavin burst out laughing at her act.

After a few more strategies and changes in field placements, Siraj finally took the wicket of William making Indian fans sigh in relief. In the consequent over, Akshith managed to stump Mark, drastically reducing the scoring pace of the Australian team.

With both the established batsmen out of the crease, the Indian team gained the advantage and they utilized it fully by not letting any batsman stick for more than a few overs.

The final wicket fell for the first ball of the 19th over, concluding the match. The Australian team managed to score 195 runs by the time they lost their last wicket with 11 balls in hand.

The Indian fans burst into a series of cheers and hail while the team celebrated with shared hugs and pats on the backs. After the handshake between the players of both teams, they moved to their respective dugouts. The evening concluded with post-match presentations, honoring the players with exceptional performance in the match.

CHAPTER THREE

The cricket team started with their cool-down routine, aiding the minor injuries they encountered during the match and relaxing their muscles. After aiding their needs, they again gathered to discuss their performance and areas of improvement. The coaching and support staff, with the assistance of technology, assessed their performances and briefed the players about the same along with the areas each of them need to work on to play better.

The social media and technical teams worked together and uploaded the match details on the official social media handles while the players moved to their bus as there were no press meets scheduled for any of them.

Upon reaching his room, Shaurya made a beeline to the bathroom and took a relaxing shower to loosen his sore muscles. Once done with his bath, he dialed his mother and enquired about her health and dinner.

It was a habit he carried on over the years. Though he was traveling, he made sure to call his mother at least once a day and enquire about her well-being. After talking to his mother for a while longer, he wished her good night and got ready to rest, the exhaustion of the day finally catching onto him.

It was the next evening and the team gathered for dinner. The light-hearted conversations filled the air, mixed with teases and chuckles of the players as they teased each other.

"Shaurya Bhai, now you have become the Captain too. When are you going to get married?" Siraj asked, his voice full of teasing.

"Arey Chotu, let me adjust to the captaincy first. And why are you suddenly interested in my marriage?" Shaurya arched a brow, his face countered in mock suspicion.

"Just like that," Siraj shrugged.

"But he is right, Shaurya. If not marriage, you should at least get a girlfriend now. You are already 28 and you won't be aging backward," The head coach commented with a chuckle. Shaurya's friends burst out laughing at his words but Shaurya just shrugged his shoulders with a growl.

He was still learning how to handle the team and carry out his duties as a captain without making the senior players feel disregarded and youngsters demotivated, providing all of them with equal chances.

"I know you want to master the art of handling the team but that's not how it works, captain. Every year, new members will join the team and the performance of you guys will alter. Each of you has your own strengths and shortcomings. A few of us will retire, a few may improve in terms of performance and a few may lose their touch. The team you have been handling for the last 6 months has evolved to this and it won't stop here. We have to become adaptable to the upcoming changes. " He shared his wisdom.

"And Shaurya," The coach paused, his lips curving into a teasing smirk. "Unlike other fields, we will be retired in our late 30's or early 40's. Then, you have to spend all your life with your partner. So, make a careful choice, my boy. It's hard to find a great partner. If you miss the chance, you have to bat and bowl on your own," Though his words were teasing intended to pull Shaurya's leg, they made Shaurya think.

Should he start considering seeing someone? He never paid attention to those things believing things would happen when the time was right but now he couldn't help but wonder if he should give it a shot.

"Let the right girl enter and I bet Shaurya will be running after her like a puppy," Akshith's playful jab broke Shaurya's trance making him glare at his best friend. But Akshith being Akshith, didn't take Shaurya's glare seriously.

The team's manager stood in the middle and called out for attention." As we don't have any matches for the next few weeks, if you all agree, we can stay back for the next 4 days. You can go sightseeing or anything you want to do before flying back to Mumbai." A cheer echoed once he was done with his announcement and the players started discussing the places they wanted to visit.

The friends who dozed off at Shika's place after the cricket match gathered at the dining table. After a breakfast filled with lots of fun and teasing, they parted ways to reach their respective adobes. Bhavin dropped Ananya at her place and left for his own.

As soon as Ananya stepped in, she was wrapped in a tight hug. Her younger brother, Vansh, squealed in excitement on seeing his sister after two weeks.

"I missed you," Both of them blurted at the same time. Vansh was six years younger than her and was the captain of the U-19 cricket team. They are each other's best friends and role models.

"What's your score?"

"Did you get any injuries?" Again they both spoke at the same time and burst into fits of laughter. They both settled at the dining table and Vansh explained his match exaggeratedly while Ananya listened to him with utmost concentration.

"If both of you are done hyping each other, go get these things from the supermarket," Rashmi, their mother ordered placing a list on the dining table.

"Mumma! We just returned from our hectic work," Ananya whined, not ready to step out. Vansh bobbed his head, agreeing with his sister.

"You can laze around for the entire week from tomorrow. Now go and buy these. I have an appointment in an hour," Rashmi ordered in a no-nonsense tone. Rashmi being a nutritionist prefers organic vegetables over the regular ones in the stores.

They both drove to the supermarket once Vansh changed his clothes.

"Di, I want new spikes," Vansh gazed at his sister who was busy picking up fresh vegetables her mother jotted down in the list.

"Okay. You added them to your shopping list or want to go shopping?" She turned to him, an apple in her hand.

"I added them to my wishlist. I will share the link with you," He said, hugging his sister in happiness. From the time Ananya started working, Vansh stopped taking money from his parents. He was more comfortable using his sister's money.

"What about your ICT trails?" Ananya enquired as they rummaged through the racks, searching for the groceries on the list.

"The selection committee visited our Zonal league matches and coach sir thinks I might get selected in ICT in the coming months. But let's see," Vansh sighed by the end.

"You are my hero baby. Whom will they select if not you?" Ananya wrapped her hands around Vansh's bicep, dragging him through the racks as she ranted about how great a player he was and how he shouldn't think negatively.

Ananya was always his personal, favorite critic. She motivates him when he starts doubting his capabilities and criticizes his mistakes when he gets too comfortable or cocky.

"Do you want to eat double ka meetha?" She raised a brow at her brother when they reached the rack filled with bread and dairy products.

"Sure. I don't have any matches in the coming month and you will exercise with me, right?" He asked. With a nod of her head, Ananya grabbed the bread packets and gave them to Vansh who threw them into their shopping cart.

"Thank god. I was getting late for my first appointment," Rashmi grabbed the cover from Vansh and started searching for something. The siblings wanted to roll their eyes at their mother but controlled the urge to do so.

"You were waiting for us? Why Mumma?" Ananya asked, a little skeptical.

"Not for you. I was waiting for avocadoes on the list. They are for Mrs. Singhania. If not for them, I would have asked your Dad to bring the groceries on his way back," She walked away taking the avocadoes while the siblings stood there, stupefied.

"We just wasted our time to shop for someone else?" Vansh asked with a scowl on his face. The siblings groaned audibly but knowing they can't do anything about it, they both moved to Ananya's room.

CHAPTER FOUR

A week flew by and it was time for Ananya to join her job back. After testing for a whole week, she felt more than ready to resume her role of being the secret savior, changing roles and chasing thugs.

"Di, please drop me at the stadium on the way," Vansh requested as they settled to have breakfast. Ananya agreed happily. Once Vansh grabbed his cricket kit, they were ready to depart.

Though Ananya usually travels by car, upon Vansh's request she took out her scooty. She used to drop Vansh off at his practice on her scooty during the initial days of his career when Ananya was in college.

As they passed through the familiar lanes, the siblings recalled the memories of those foggy winter mornings filled with their banters and those uncountable cups of chai Vansh and his gang used to have with Ananya's money.

By the time they reached the stadium, the senior Indian Cricket team was already busy with their practice. A few from Vansh's team were also doing their usual stretches as they waited for others to join them. Vansh pushed his helmet into Ananya's hands and took off running after a quick hug to her.

Ananya shook her head at her brother's antics and was about to start to her office when she remembered Vansh's phone was in her pocket. With a sigh, she parked her scooty to a side and took off her helmet.

Ruffling her unruly hair, she made her way towards the middle of the stadium where her brother along with a few of his teammates stood surrounding someone. The man was nearly 6 ft tall with a lean but attractive physique.

As Ananya scanned her surroundings, she felt a little self-conscious as everyone around her was dressed in sportswear while she was in her jean top, her hair tied in a sleek pony and a watch resting on her wrist.

While Ananya was busy thinking how out of place she looked, she bumped into someone. "Ouch!" The person exclaimed, his hand flying to his forehead as he rubbed his head to soothe the pain.

"I am sorry. I...I didn't see you coming," she quickly apologized stepping back, creating a respectable distance between them. The man stared at her for a moment, expecting her to recognize him but Ananya just stayed silent expecting a reply to her apology.

"That's okay," The man mumbled, still wondering why she wasn't squealing or even asking for an autograph or picture with him like his other fans. Leaving the man to wonder, Ananya made her way to Vansh.

Shaurya was surrounded by the young talents of the country who swarmed around him as soon as they spotted him. When he was busy giving a few game tips to the junior team, they heard a voice calling out for the captain of the U-19 captain, making them turn to the source.

"Vansh!" A girl dressed in a white button-up shirt and blue faded jeans called out, her eyes fixed on the man she came for but Shaurya's eyes remained on her, taking in her features, carefully observing every curve and contour of her face.

"Hi, Di!" The junior team chirped, their excitement palpable as they waved hands at the familiar figure standing in front of them. She was their regular spectator and refreshment sponsor when they were playing for Delhi and back in the academy.

"Hi, Boys!" Ananya's face lit up with a smile as she waved back at them. "Did I interrupt?" It was then she noticed the man with them was none other than Shaurya the captain of the Indian Cricket team. Her lips parted in disbelief and surprise but she quickly schooled her expressions and smiled at him. A small, friendly smile, her lips curving a little.

Ananya has always been a fan of Shaurya's game and his aggression on-field but that was it. She never paid any interest in his personal life nor did she want or expect to meet him one day. She liked the way he played and that was it for her. She wasn't crazy about him. She follows him on social media too but never actually pays attention to what he posts or what others say about his posts.

"I am so sorry if I had disturbed your talks. I just came to give Vansh his phone," She apologized when none of them replied to her earlier question.

"That's alright, Ms..." Shaurya paused, waiting for her to introduce herself.

"She's Ananya Di, Vansh's sister," An over-excited Siddarth blurted out before Ananya could. Shaurya turned his eyes to Siddarth for a second to acknowledge his words and then darted his gaze to Ananya with a smile.

Vansh took his phone from Ananya and thanked her.

"Nice to meet you, sir." She smiled at Shaurya who returned the gesture with a warm smile of his own. She then turned to her brother and his friends. "Bye, guys! Come home if you guys are free on Sunday," She smiled at the boys and ran from there making Shaurya chuckle at her hurried takeoff.

"She's always busy," Vansh commented under his breath. "She's a fan of yours, sir," He said to Shaurya.

"Doesn't seem so," Shaurya mumbled, his eyes tainted on the way she left.

"Well, she is a weird kind of fan," The boys shared a laugh at that remembering one of their regular teasings with Ananya while Shaurya stared at them confused.

Ananya walked into her office, humming to a random song she heard on her way. Her friends arrived earlier and seemed to be indulged in one of their usual banters. Shaking her head at their madness, she sat beside Rakshith who was staring at his teammates who looked similar to a bunch of monkeys rather than the officers they were.

"Any information regarding the man in that photo?" Ananya asked Rakshith. Rakshith turned to Ananya and shook his head with a sigh.

"No idea. Kulkarni sir is yet to come," he told her. They entertained themselves with the silly banter between Bhavin and Shika with Nithin trying to control them until Mr. Kulkarni entered the room.

"Jai Hind, sir!" They all chorused, straightening their backs. Kulkarni returned their greeting and turned to the door as if he were expecting someone to join them. The team shared confused looks but remained silent.

When they saw Vikram entering, their heads whipped towards Rakshith, their eyes wide with disbelief and fear. Vikram and Rakshith have been an inseparable duo since they were in school. Until a girl entered their lives and broke their friendship. While Vikram and Rakshith completely avoided each other after that, Ananya and Bhavin tried their best to be there for both of them when they needed their friends.

"Someone please tell me it's not what I think it is," Shika whispered to Ananya and Nithin, her voice tinged with desperation and fear. She still remembers the last time they handled a case along with Vikram and the team had to walk on eggshells the entire time due to the feud between their leaders.

Vikram stood in front of the team but his eyes remained fixed on Rakshith who stared back with equal intensity. The tension in the room was palpable as the men stared at each other, their eyes blazing with fire and something none of them could decipher.

"We caught the man in Sikkim," Kulkarni's voice broke the heavy fog that settled over the room, grabbing the attention of them all. "He wasn't ready to open his mouth at first but after tasting our hospitality for two days, he finally gave us what we needed," his voice cut through the silent environment and the team listened to him with complete attention.

"Their target is Mr. Mishra and from the information we got, they already set the plan into motion," He paused to let the team process the information.

"Which Mr. Mishra, sir?" Vikram asked the question they all wanted to ask. They could think of 3 Mr. Mishras who could be the target of them.

"The head coach of ICT, Mr. Atul Mishra. As you all know, Mrs. Mishra is a cabinet minister and his abduction will create both political instability and the cricket fans will create a ruckus if something of that sort happens," They nodded their heads, understanding the gravity of the situation.

"Does the government know about it?" Rakshith asked after a slight pause, his voice tentative.

"Yes. I just had a meeting with higher-ups and we have a plan," Mr. Kulkarni replied, his voice oozing with confidence.

"Till the time we catch the people assigned for the task, you people are going to guard the team. You will be introduced to them as journalists. We have already talked to the president of BCCI. We'll assign a few more officers to assist you," He explained the plan.

"I want you to keep a close eye on everything happening around the team, especially the coach. You have to be very careful in assessing every person interacting with the team to protect them from all the possible attacks," He commanded, his voice full of authority.

"Why the whole team, sir? Can't we just focus on Mr. Mishra or better isolate him until we catch them?" Bhavin was the first to raise a question.

"That's not an ideal thing to do. What if they have a change of plans or go for an easy target while we get busy guarding the coach?" Vikram countered.

"What about the times when they don't have any matches or tours? What will we do then?" Rakshith pointed out a loophole. No matches means the team won't be together and they can't guard them in the disguise of journalists at that time.

"Their schedule is packed for the next 3 months. Let's hope we catch those thugs before that. If not, we have to come up with other plans," Mr. Kulkarni answered.

"Will the cricket team consent to this? I am sure they wouldn't want a bunch of reporters trailing behind them, staying with them." Ananya put forth her point. As much as she knew about the team, and the way they work, they would never allow a bunch of strangers, mainly the media to travel with them and risk their privacy.

"We have a solution for that. They would straight away reject the idea if you approach them as regular journalists. We got the orders ready from the PMO stating you are a team selected by the sports ministry to document the sports and the daily routine of the stars to encourage young talents and to motivate them. Though they might have objections to this, they won't be able to go against the order passed by the PMO." Though the team was apprehensive about how the players were going to react, they knew it was important to do.

"So, we are going to make a document of the sport and the routine of the players?" Vikram asked.

"Pretty much. Try to keep it as realistic as possible. No one should suspect a thing. Take their interviews, record their practices, mingle with them, try to get them comfortable with you guys, and win their trust. Do whatever it needs to keep them alive without raising doubts," Kulkarni ordered to which the team replied with a 'Yes sir'.

"You will get your fake ids by evening and from tomorrow you are going to join them," Kulkarni sir walked out after that, leaving the team to plan and discuss their strategies.

CHAPTER FIVE

Once Mr. Kulkarni was out of sight, Rakshith and Vikram indulged in another staring competition. Ananya and Bhavin shared a look and sighed, not understanding how to make them reconcile.

"Will you both stop staring at each other like long-lost lovers?" Nithin was the first to break the silence, his voice tinged with irritation. Both men looked away, their faces turning red in embarrassment.

"Vikram, Rakshith, you both had an ugly fight in the past. But can't you let it go? Now that we are all a team, can you both be..." Ananya paused, trying to find the right word. "more cordial?" She finished, her hopeful eyes locking onto Vikram and then moving to Rakshith.

"I won't let my personal issues affect our work," Both of them said in sync and a scoff followed. Ananya sighed at their indirect declaration of their intentions to keep their cold war going.

"They were either twins or star-crossed lovers in their past lives," Shika muttered to Bhavin who was staring at his friends with a stoic face. Bhavin shook his head at Shika's utterances but couldn't keep the small smile from gracing his lips.

After concluding neither of the stubborn men was ready to let go of their feud, the team decided to focus on the task at hand and started formulating strategies to keep a close eye on the coach and the players without getting caught.

By the end of the day, a colleague of theirs handed over their fake ID proofs to them, and after a brief discussion about their roles and backup plans, they departed to their respective adobes to get ready to slip into another facade.

Shaurya stepped out of his bathroom, a towel hanging around his hips and his body glistening with the tiny droplets of water. Wet strands of hair fell messily onto his forehead, dripping with water. With deft fingers, he grabbed his phone from the dressing table, drying his hair with his free hand.

"Good evening, Shanu," He greeted his team manager, his tone polite but laced with curiosity as he grabbed his shorts and t-shirt from the closet.

"Good evening, Shaurya. I have some news. Not a good one and I need you to keep your calm while I explain this," Shaurya could already feel something was wrong from the way Shannu spoke.

"Okay," Shaurya agreed, slipping into his clothes.

"So, a few people are going to join us for like 2-3 months. It seems to be an order from The Prime Minister to make a documentary kind of thing on various sports and the players to let the people know more about it and to encourage new talent. The team will be traveling with us, recording some practice sessions, taking a few interviews, and will make a report on the team's activities," Shannu explained calmly while Shaurya's jaw clenched in irritation.

"Are they going to visit us or will they stay with us?" Shaurya asked, his anger and irritation barely contained.

Shaurya doesn't hate the media, he feels grateful to them instead for keeping him and his fans connected. But there are instances where the media forgot their boundaries for their ratings and views which caused him and his fellow teammates a lot of problems. Besides, meeting someone to give an interview is one thing but sharing space with a bunch of unknown faces, and being conscious 24x7 is a completely different thing.

"They will stay with us. The BCCI president and coach tried to negotiate but all we got in reply was 'Everything is for the best interest of the nation'," Shannu recollected.

"So, we are going to spend 2-3 months with journalists who can easily access our personal space and can use it against us in the future?" Shaurya's anger was barely contained, the nerves on his neck popping out.

"Not exactly. They are not regular journalists. They work in the PMO and they also signed the NDAs. So, hopefully, it's less risky," Shannu tried to assure, but his voice lacked conviction. He wasn't sure himself.

"I'll try to be cordial to them until they stay away from our personal lives and concentrate on their work. If they try to cross the boundaries, I won't take accountability for what happens to them," Shaurya warned. He can't exactly go against the orders issued by the PMO and BCCI. All he could do was to hope for the journalists or whatever they call themselves to be humane enough not to make the personal lives of the players their gossip materials.

As the line went dead, Shaurya let out a groan, his fingers running through his hair. He and his team already have enough public attention and now this new documentary seemed to be an added burden.

Ananya was in her room, packing for the upcoming mission when Rashmi knocked at her door. Ananya turned to her mother, who stood leaning against the doorframe, hands folded below her chest.

"Where are you heading this time?" Rashmi asked with a raise of her brow.

"To find a son-in-law for you," Ananya joked, a giggle falling out of her lips. With a roll of her eyes, Rashmi stepped in, grabbed the frock from Ananya, and started folding it.

"I will find a groom for you. You just come home on your own feet," Rashmi's comment, laced with an underlying worry and fear made Ananya sigh. She wrapped her hands around her mother's shoulders and kissed her cheek with a giggle.

"I will, Mumma. Don't you worry," Ananya assured squeezing Rashmi's shoulders and then kissing her cheek again, making Rashmi smile at her daughter.

Once done with packing, the mother-daughter duo made their way to the dining table where Vijay and Vansh were waiting for them to have their dinner. The family started with their dinner with a few words being exchanged between them from time to time.

"Papa, I am going on a mission tomorrow. I will be back in a few months," Ananya informed her father, who nodded his head, without asking any further questions. He knew it was confidential so restrained himself from enquiring further.

Ananya didn't miss the way Vansh's smile dropped upon her announcement. She knew it would upset him. It wasn't something new.

After dinner, Ananya served two scoops of ice cream in glass bowls and walked to Vansh's room. Vansh was sprawled on his bed, his feet pressed to the wall and his eyes glued to the ceiling as if he was lost in thoughts.

Placing the bowls on the table, Ananya settled beside her brother. "Are you upset?" She asked, placing her hand over his.

Vansh shook his head in denail, not meeting her eyes. Ananya stared at her brother, her eyes pleading him.

Vansh sat up with a sigh, running his fingers through his messy hair.

"It's just for 2-3 months Vanshu! I will be back before you realise," Ananya tried to persuade him.

"What if you get into some trouble over there?" He mumbled in a choked tone. It was never easy for him to see his sister play with her life with a smile. As much as he is proud of her selflessness and courage, a part of him is always worried for her safety.

Maybe that is how the family of every solider and officer out there feels while sending their loved ones to risk their lives to safe the nation.

"Nothing will happen to me. I have superpowers, you know?" Ananya giggled, trying to lighten the gloomy atmosphere. Vansh rolled his eyes when she flexed her barely existing biceps to prove her point.

"I am not a kid anymore," He replied, his tone clipped. Ananya understood the fears of her family, she felt guilty for hurting them but not even once she thought of quitting her job. It was her passion, her life.

"Just a few more years, Vanshu. I promise I will spend all my time with you after that," She grabbed the ice cream bowl and forwarded a spoonful of ice cream to him.

"You have to keep this promise of yours, Di," Vansh's voice quivered as he tried to hold the tears threatening to spill.

"Of course, I will. We will take your wife and my husband too," Ananya winked at last making Vansh chuckle.

The talks continued till late night with the siblings pulling each other's legs and teasing each other about their future spouses.

When Ananya was animatedly explaining something about her recent bet with Bhavin, Vansh, with a mischevious smile, smeared some ice cream on her nose making Ananya stop her rant abruptly.

She stared at her brother for a moment, blinking her eyes and then she touched her nose. When she felt the cold slimy ice cream on her fingers, her eyes widened in shock and anger.

"Vansh ke bachhe!" And just like that, the siblings chased each other around the bed, their laughter filling the room.

"Vansh, Anu! Get up! What should I do to these dogs?" Rashmi, who came to wake her children up chided seeing the mess they created around the room. The pillows and sheets were thrown randomly with the siblings deep asleep on the bed, their limbs sprawled all over the bed.

On hearing their mother's yelling, Ananya sat up rubbing her eyes.

"Good morning, Mumma!" Ananya grinned, unaware of the glare her mother pointed at her.

"How many times did I tell you to tie your hair? It looks no less than a bird's nest and then you complain about hair loss," Rashmi chided, her fists pressed against the curves of her hips.

Understanding the situation, Ananya silently slipped out of the room. She proceeded with her morning routine and got ready within the next 2 hours.

The family had their breakfast together and Ananya walked out with her bag after bidding farewell to her parents and brother.

"Good morning!" She chirped, slipping into the backseat after Rakshith loaded her bag into the trunk. Vikram nodded his head in acknowledgment while the others greeted her back.

"You could have greeted back, Mr. Grumpy," Ananya exclaimed with a roll of her eyes, staring out of the window. Vikram heard her but chose to ignore her words.

They reached the airport after a 35-minute drive and made their way to the lobby where the cricketers would be joining them. A few staff members of the cricket team were already present there and the men started interacting with them while the ladies found a seat for themselves at a little distance.

"They complain about us being talkative and start talking with any person they spend more than 5 minutes with," Shika exclaimed with a roll of her eyes, pointing towards Nithin who was laughing at something one of the men said.

"You know the best part, they will discuss their entire life starting from birthdays to salaries with strangers and will call us out for sharing things with our best friends and parents," Ananya added with a scowl.

"Hypocrites!" Both exclaimed at the same time and shared a laugh before moving to others as the cricketers started to join them in the lobby.

CHAPTER SIX

As soon as the players stepped out of the team bus, the paparazzi swarmed like bees to honey. Flashes flickered madly, the shouted requests for poses and smiles, the chaos of clicking shutters, and the press bodies in motion created a whirlwind of excitement and frenzy.

Some players obliged, pausing to strike poses, while the others simply walked past, throwing a brief polite nod toward the cameras.

The players exchanged quick greetings and updates. Shaurya slipped off his shades and scanned the area, his sharp eyes briefly noticing the few unfamiliar faces standing with the team. A frown made its way onto his face as he noticed a familiar face amid the unknown.

"Good morning, everyone!" The manager's voice cut through the chaos of chatter, drawing the attention of the team. "Let me make a quick introduction," He pointed to the unfamiliar group standing with them, prompting a few murmurs and, exchanged glances among the team.

"They are the people I mentioned yesterday. They are from the Prime Minister's Office and will be traveling with us for the next 3 months," Though his tone was even, the irritation could be clearly seen on the faces of the players as they processed the information.

Without acknowledging the displeased looks of the players, the man added, "They've already signed the NDAs, so you can rest assured of your privacy being invaded and misused."

His words failed to assure the team as they continued to exchange those annoyed glances. But they forced smiles towards the people standing in a corner. They returned the smile awkwardly.

The manager then started introducing the crew to the team one by one and when he was about to introduce Ananya, Akshith, the all-rounder cut him off.

"Wait, you were the girl at the stadium yesterday," Akshith stepped forward, pointing a finger at Ananya, his eyes narrowed.

"Yes," Ananya answered with another awkward smile.

"What are you doing here? Don't tell me you are some crazy fan stalking one of us," Akshith's voice was laced with a mixture of irritation and accusation. Ananya's eyes widened in surprise and shock upon hearing his accusation.

"You are mistaken, sir. I am not stalking anyone of you," She tried answering politely, controlling her irritation.

"Stop lying and confess already," Akshith deadpanned. "Or do you want me to call the security and ask them to escort you out?" He added, folding his hands.

"What? I really work in the PMO." Ananya declared, her irritation increasing with every passing moment. "See for yourself," She shoved her ID into his hands and Akshith grabbed the card, his eyes narrowed in suspicion.

"Well, I'm still going to keep an eye on you," he said, his voice quieter but no less condescending. "And trust me, my eyes are very sharp."

Ananya merely rolled her eyes, clearly unimpressed. She cast a quick glance at her fellow agents, who were trying—and failing—to stifle their giggles. She could feel the heat of embarrassment rising in her chest but pushed it down, determined not to let this man get under her skin.

"Why are you so rude to her? Maybe she is here to do her work, not everyone is a mad fan of you Akshith bhai," Siraj, one of the players muttered, not realizing that Ananya could hear him perfectly well.

"Rude? I'm not being rude. She's the one who bumped into me yesterday. I think she's here for me," Akshith whispered, his tone dripping with self-assurance, clearly oblivious to the eye-rolls his statement was eliciting.

Ananya, unable to hold back any longer, let out a sarcastic laugh. "Oh, please," she snapped, her voice cutting through the small huddle of players. "Trust me, you're not as special as you think you are. And if I were here for someone, it definitely wouldn't be you."

Akshith's smirk flattered at Ananya's words and the team shared a laugh at that. Before the duo could indulge in another fight, the announcement was made and they moved to the gate.

Onboard, the team settled into their seats, the hum of the plane's engine filling the cabin as it prepared for takeoff.

Ananya tied her hair in a messy bun and pulled out a book from her bag. Shaurya, seated in the row beside hers, found his eyes drifting toward her more often than he'd like to admit.

There was something about her—her boldness, her sharp wit, the way she held her ground against Akshith—that intrigued him.

He shifted in his seat, a small smile tugging at his lips as he continued stealing glances at her till their flight landed in Lucknow, their first destination.

Once the players settled into their respective suites and freshened up, they gathered in a hall. The coach explained to them the playing styles and pitch conditions with the help of videos, and analysis from the previous matches.

On the other hand, the agents gathered in another room, with the maps and blueprints of the hotel sprawled on the table in front of them. They analyzed the whole building, and marked the blindspots and exit points, checking for any security loopholes or threats.

After a while, Ananya stood by the pillar near the pool, observing the people around, trying to find any unusual movement. Shaurya walked in, his phone pressed against his ear as he gave instructions to someone over the call.

His focus on the conversation kept him oblivious to her presence and when someone jumped into the pool from behind, he was startled.

Shaurya's foot slipped on the damp floor. In a reflex, he reached out to steady himself, his fingers closing around Ananya's arm. The sudden pull made her lose her footing as well, but her instincts kicked in, and she grabbed the pillar with her free hand.

Shaurya held onto her hand tightly as he regained his balance. In the process, his phone slipped from his grasp and fell into the pool with a soft plop.

"Are you okay?" Ananya asked, her voice laced with worry.

"Yeah. But my phone..." He trailed off, looking at the pool. Ananya let out ah "Oh,"

"Can you hold it for a minute?" Shaurya asked, untieing his watch. With a nod, Ananya grabbed his watch, and before she could ask him what he was up to, he jumped into the pool with a splash.

He resurfaced after a minute with his phone. Droplets of water slid down his face, clinging to his lashes before sliding down his sharp features and falling back into the pool. His damp hair clung to his forehead, while his shirt, soaked and transparent, clung to his chest outlining hard lines of his body.

He stepped out of the pool and grabbed a towel fro the nearby poolchair while Ananya continued to stare at him, her eyes following every little movement of his.

"Judging by the way you are staring at me right now, I think Akshith was right to doubt your intentions,"

The teasing lilt in his tone snapped Ananya out of her trance. Her cheeks flushed a deep shade of pink, and she quickly averted her gaze, clearing her throat.

"He...he was just sprouting nonsense," Ananya managed to push the words out.

"Oh," Shaurya mused, clearly enjoying the reaction he got from their new host. He felt a little disappointed when she didn't get excited the first time. Now seeing her flushed made something stir in his heart, a feeling he couldn't name but made him happy.

Ananya hurried away, chasting herself while Shaurya stood by the pool, watching her retreat, with a smile tugging at his lips.

CHAPTER SEVEN

Ananya

We have already checked all the hotel's entries and exits and talked to the staff. The cameras are installed, and we have established secure lines for information transfer. I have also met Shaurya and made a fool of myself.

Wait, why am I thinking about him now? I mean, yes, he was handsome, no denying that, but why am I remembering him now? What's wrong with me?

I paced around my room like a restless cat, my mind replaying our earlier interaction over and over. I was in the blink of losing my mind when a knock interrupted my thoughts.

When I opened it, Shika stood at the door with a bright smile. Though confused about her unusual happiness, I smiled in return and stepped aside to let her in.

"The team invited us to join them for dinner," she announced, flopping onto my bed, and getting herself comfortable.

"I thought they didn't like us being around?" I asked, confused by the sudden hospitality. Shika simply shrugged, her focus fixed on the TV as she changed the channels as if a dinner invite from the team who hated our existence until an hour ago was the most natural thing.

With a glance at the clock that read quarter to seven, I settled beside her on the bed. Shika finally settled for a rom-com and placed the remote away.

After a while, Shika got up to head to her room to get ready. We were originally supposed to share a room but since she'd decided to stay with her boyfriend, I had the entire room to myself.

I got dressed in a sleek black strap dress that ended just below my knees. With a light coat of lip gloss, heels, and a quick fluff through my hair- I was ready.

I walked out, heading towards Shika's room. But just as I was about to knock, I heard... *that* sound. The unmistakable, unholy sound from behind the door. Heat rushed to my neck and ears.

With a deep breath to steady myself, I was about to knock again when another moan echoed through the air, louder this time. I shut my eyes in frustration and cursed under my breath.

In my haste to move away, I bumped into something—or rather someone. I would've fallen if it weren't for the firm hand that steadied me, a familiar warmth wrapping around my waist. I turned, my cheeks flushed, already guessing who the person was. And it was Shaurya, staring down at me, amusement dancing in his eyes.

And then, as if on cue, a loud thud and a string of curses from inside the room made me cringe harder. "Fuck!" Shika's voice carried through the door, sending me into an even deeper state of panic and embarrassment. Why, God?

"Woh...I...I..." I stuttered, pointing helplessly from the door to him as if that would explain the awkward situation I was stuck in. He stared at me for a moment and then, burst out laughing, the sound filling the empty corridor, rich and carefree. His amusement only added to my embarrassment, making me want to shrink into the background.

"Looks like they'll need more time. Do you mind joining me instead?" he asked, his laughter finally subsiding. I just nodded my head, my cheeks flushed with embarrassment. With a tilt of his chin, Shaurya gestured towards the elevator, slipping his hands into his pockets.

We rode down in silence, with me cursing myself for the embarrassing situation I landed myself into. I knew they were in a relationship but didn't know they were so...into it. I became conscious when Shaurya leaned in, his proximity making my breath hitch. His scent, a subtle mix of musk and something distinctly him filled the space between us.

"You look gorgeous in black," he whispered, his breath warm brushing against my ear. The words sent a shiver down my spine, and I couldn't stop the blush that spread across my cheeks. What's wrong with you, Ananya?

It wasn't the first time someone complimented me but there was something in his proximity, in the way he uttered those words as if he meant every syllable, that left me speechless.

Before I could stitch the words together and thank him, the elevator dinged. He straightened his posture and stepped out like nothing had happened. I stood there, rooted to the spot, my heart pounding.

"Are you coming?" His teasing voice pulled me from my thoughts, and I hurriedly followed him out of the elevator, trying to calm down.

We reached the large, private dining room set up for the team's dinner. The table was huge, meant to accommodate everyone. While I searched for my collegues, Shaurya gravitated towards his teammates.

"Where's Shika?" I asked Nithin, who was standing near the dining table, discreetly observing the waiters walking in and out of the door.

"She'll be here in five minutes," He replied. His tone was so nonchalant, as if they weren't just...well, doing what they were doing upstairs. With a roll of my eyes, I made my way towards the buffet, grabbing a glass of juice from the waiter on my way.

When I reached the table filled with multiple cusines, ranging from Indian to continental, to Italian, I was amazed by the presentation and the aroma of the food. Vikram, however, seemed to be giving the pasta some serious side-eye.

"Anything suspecious?" I asked, my brows furrowed. The atmosphere seemed fine. The pasta looked fine too—maybe a bit stingy on the sauce, but nothing major.

"Huh?" He turned to me finally noticing my presence. "It's nothing," he muttered with a shake of his head. He was clearly lost in thought. Deciding to ask him later, I steered my attention back to the room, scanning the movements of everyone around me.

15 officers from the secret forces had been assigned to this mission. Six of us were tasked with staying close to the team, while the rest handled external security. Though causing harm in a stadium seemed impossible, we are taking no chances. Every precaution is being taken to ensure the safety of the players, mainly the coach.

After a brief exchange with Vikram and Bhavin, I turned around to find Shaurya looking my way, engaged in a conversation with Akshith and Dhruv. When our eyes met, I smiled. He returned it with one of those smiles that seemed to linger, before turning back to his friends.

When it was time for dinner, we all settled into our designated chairs. Much to my dismay, I found myself between Rakshith and Shika. Nithin was next to her. The dinner was served and we started having our food with a few conversations here and there.

Shika and Nithin were in their own bubble, throwing those teasing glances and smirks at each other, making me sigh. Honestly, those two could learn a thing or two about being discreet. I was minding my own business, happily munching on my pasta until I heard a screeching sound as Shika shifted in her seat.

My eyes moved to her and then to the front only to clash with Shaurya's teasing glance. He raised a brow at me, a knowing half-smirk forming on his lips. I felt my cheeks heating up again as the incidents from earlier started to play in my mind.

As I was enjoying my dessert—a glorious brownie—my eyes drifted toward Shika and Nithin again. His hand was on her thigh, moving up. I choked on my food. The sudden coughing fit grabbed everyone's attention, and Nithin quickly pulled his hand back.

"Are you okay?" Rakshith asked, immediately handing me some water. His concern was genuine, but my mind was still spinning from what I had just seen. Tears welled up in my eyes from the force of my coughing. With a shaky breath, I wiped my face and shot the duo a death glare. Idiots should learn to be discreet if they're so desperate.

Nithin maintained a stoic face while Shika turned bright red, looking anywhere but at me.

Shaurya leaned over from across the table, his voice soft with concern. "Are you feeling better?"

I nodded, offering a small, reassuring smile, and he turned back to his food, though not before throwing a glance around the table and smirking knowingly. What does that even mean? Huffing, I turned my attention back to the brownie waiting for me.

After dinner, we all started heading back to our rooms. The elevator ride was crowded, with everyone on the third or fourth floors. As we reached our destination, I teased Shika in a hushed tone, "Either close your doors or your mouth, girl. It was so embarrassing to hear your unholy noises."

Her face flushed red with embarrassment, but honestly, they should have known better. What if I hadn't knocked and just walked in?

Shaurya's chuckle broke the silence. "Stop cursing them in your mind, Ms. Shergill. They already left."

"How did you know?" I asked, genuinely curious.

"Your face gave it all away," he replied smoothly, his hands slipping into his pockets.

As we walked towards our rooms, the air between us was light, though I was still feeling a little flushed from the evening's events. Shaurya suddenly slowed his pace, turning to me with a teasing glint in his eyes. What now? I was already embarrassed enough for the whole week.

"You know," he began, his smirk making my heart skip a beat, "you have a knack for getting caught up in the most... interesting situations."

I narrowed my eyes, half-amused, half-embarrassed. "What do you mean by that?" If only he wasn't my favorite player and crush!

"Well..." he shrugged nonchalantly, stepping a little closer. "Standing outside a couple's door, looking all flustered? If I didn't know better, I'd think you were trying to... eavesdrop."

My eyes widened in disbelief and I huffed, crossing my arms. "Excuse me! I wasn't eavesdropping. I just... happened to be there at the wrong time!" Who wants to eavesdrop on such unholy things? Not me.

Shaurya chuckled, clearly enjoying my annoyance. "Mmhmm, and just happened to hear some... interesting noises?"

My face turned a deeper shade of red as the sounds replayed in my mind. Eww!. "It's not like I planned it! I was going to knock, but... well, you heard them too!"

"I did," he admitted with a laugh. "But you looked so guilty like you got caught in the act."

"I was not guilty! Just... embarrassed," I muttered, trying to hide my smile behind the facade of annoyance. He just mockingly nodded his head as if he didn't believe me.

I glared at him, trying to keep my cool, but couldn't help the smile tugging on my lips when I saw him smiling at me. "If you weren't so distracting, maybe I wouldn't be in these situations," I shot back. I wonder if he even heard that.

"Me?" He feigned innocence, his eyes gleaming with amusement. He did hear that. "What did I do?"

I shook my head, knowing he was loving every second of this. "Nothing," I muttered, not looking into his eyes, too embarrassed to say anything further.

He leaned in slightly, lowering his voice. "Well, for what it's worth, you're cute when you're flustered." He exclaimed. Did he just call me cute?

Shaurya tilted his head, studying me for a moment before his smile softened. "Good night, Ms. Shergill," he said, his voice dropping to that warm, low tone that made my stomach flip. "I'll try not to be too distracting tomorrow."

These damn butterflies!

I should give a comeback. I shouldn't let him win this. I bit my lip, holding back a grin. "Good night, Mr. Singhania. Try not to break too many hearts."

With a wink, he turned and disappeared into his room, leaving me both exasperated and amused. Now what does that wink mean?

As I entered my room, I couldn't help but smile to myself, still feeling the warmth of his presence. I changed into something comfortable and collapsed onto the bed, pulling out my phone and book. I quickly texted the group, "Who's going to take care of the dishes tonight?"

"Dishes" is our code for monitoring the security cameras. Though we had officers handling the control room, the team leader insisted one of us stay on watch overnight—just in case the players got any bright ideas about sneaking out.

"Me," Vikram replied after a few seconds.

"Okay, call me if you need any help," I texted back, receiving a thumbs-up emoji in return.

With that settled, I set my phone aside and curled up with my book, ready to lose myself in another world. But my thoughts kept drifting back to Shaurya, his teasing smile, and the way he had made me feel less stressed in this whirlwind of events.

CHAPTER EIGHT

Ananya

The blaring of alarm broke my peaceful sleep, mercilessly pulling me away from the dream world. Stretching lazily, I shuffled over to the balcony and glanced at the park below. A few early birds were already jogging under the dim glow of streetlights. It was peaceful—calm enough to tempt me into staying wrapped in my blankets a little longer, but I resisted.

Instead, I pulled myself away from the view. Getting dressed in a simple tee and tracks, I tied my messy and slightly unruly hair into a low ponytail. Lacing up my joggers, I grabbed my keycard and stepped out of the room.

By the time I reached the park, the fresh morning air embraced me, cool and crisp against my skin. I popped my earbuds, letting the music fill my senses as I began my jog.

The sun had yet to make its grand entrance, leaving behind a cozy world, the dew on the leaves shimmering like tiny diamonds, while the birds soared gracefully in the still grey sky. It was a beautiful morning.

I was just settling into my second lap when I noticed a figure keeping pace beside me. I glanced sideways and it was Shaurya. The corners of my lips tugged into a smile. I turned off the music, and he followed.

"Good morning," I greeted, my voice soft but cheerful.

"Good morning, Ms. Shergill," he retorted with a smile, his voice rich with that signature charm of his.

"Do you jog daily?" he asked, after a few moments of comfortable silence.

"Yeah, it's kind of a requirement. Can't slack off when my job demands us to stay fit," I shrugged, trying to sound casual. And then, his hand accidentally brushed against mine, sending a shiver down my spine. Why does this man have that effect on me?

We jogged in sync, letting the stillness of the morning and the rhythmic pounding of our feet fill the quiet. I could feel his glances, but tried to ignore it, along with the butterflies fluttering in my stomach.

It was peaceful. Too peaceful. I should say or do something before I go mad.

Without much thought to it, I turned away and the first thing I noticed was a few men doing stretches on the other side of the park. "Do you work out?"

Getting no reply from him, I turned to him and he was already looking...no glaring at me. I blinked up at him, my eyebrows furrowing. Did I ask something wrong?

"I do. Do you want to see?" His tone was sharp and irritated, but there was something playful in the way he looked at me. My cheeks turned pink, my heart fluttering under his gaze. Ugh, why and how does he always manage to fluster me?

"Wh-what?" I stammered, feeling the heat rush to my cheeks.

"I figured you like watching workouts, considering the way you were staring over there," He pointed towards the men with his chin, his lips twitched in distaste. "I can give you a free show anytime you want,"

What. The. Hell.

I should have felt offended by his cheeky remark, but instead, my stomach flipped. His teasing words sparked a wave of embarrassment, but also, annoyingly, a strange excitement. Butterflies. Freaking butterflies.

"I just happened to look there by mistake. I—I don't have any such interests, thank you very much!" I huffed, attempting to sound irritated, but my voice came out more like a whine. God, why was I acting so flustered? And why is it he who always catches me in such embarrassing situations?

"If you say so, Ms. Shergill," he said with a smug grin, his eyes twinkling with amusement. "But if you ever develop that interest, you know where to find me."

He winked, sending a shiver down my spine. My mouth fell open in disbelief. This guy had no shame! And yet, why did I feel so shy all of a sudden? And how did his mood change suddenly from angry to playful? He is really unpredictable off the field too!

"Okay, now it's getting too much," I growled, pointing a finger at his chest as if to warn him off. He was towering over me, his sheer height making me feel small in comparison. I barely reached his shoulders! I bet I'd only reach his ears if I wore heels.

Wait. Why was I even thinking about that? Snap out of it, Anu!

Shaurya raised his hands in surrender, chuckling. "Alright, alright. I'm sorry. I was just teasing you."

I scowled, showing him I wasn't entirely convinced. But before I could say anything more, I noticed a group of girls nearby giggling and staring at him—practically drooling. Ugh, their eyes were practically eating him alive.

He followed my gaze, turning back to flash them a friendly wave. Instantly, their smiles brightened, and I rolled my eyes.

"Looks like your fan club is here," I muttered, a little more bitterly than I intended.

"I'm not in the mood to talk to girls right now," he said, turning back to me with a smirk. "Come on, let's go."

Wait, what? "For your information, I am a girl, Mr. Singhania," I huffed, crossing my arms.

He chuckled again, his eyes sparkling with mischief. "You're different, Ms. Shergill."

Different? What was that supposed to mean?

"How so?" I asked, following him as he resumed his jog, feeling a twinge of curiosity mixed with annoyance at his comment.

"You are my fan, but I have never seen you getting flustered or excited on seeing me like my other fans," he said, leaving me thoroughly embarrassed. It felt like a taunt more than an answer. "I started to doubt if you even like me in real," he added further.

I blinked, unsure if I should feel insulted or relieved. "Excuse me? I do like you as a player but I respect your privacy. About getting excited or flustered, I don't want to make it uncomfortable for either of us while we are at work," I clarified, trying to salvage my pride.

He stopped jogging and looked at me, a grin creeping onto his face. "So, you do like me? You like it when we cross paths?"

There was this sudden brightness in his eyes, and I regretted my words instantly. Why did he look so damn happy about that?

"Well, I—" I fumbled, feeling flustered. "I mean, you're a great cricketer and I like watching you play. You are a good company to be around too." I added the last part quickly.

His grin widened like he'd just won some invisible prize, and I turned away with burning cheeks. When did I become such a mess?

"Alright, alright, I'll take that, for now," the last part was just a whisper against my ear before he stepped aside as we reached the elevator. He let me enter the elevator and gave an acknowledging smile to the fans waving at him cheerily.

"You're impossible," I muttered under my breath, though a small smile tugged at my lips. I hated how easy it was for him to mess with my head while acting so good with everyone else. I like it though. It makes me feel special and giddy.

Inside the elevator, the quiet buzz of the hotel filled the space as we waited for our floor. Shaurya glanced at me with that teasing smile still on his face, but this time, I ignored him. No more letting him get under my skin today.

"So, what's your schedule today?" I asked, keeping the conversation neutral.

"Well, it's not just my schedule. You're part of the team now, remember?" he replied, cocking an eyebrow.

I smiled at that. "Fair enough. So what are we doing today then?"

"We've got net practice, and then our first match is tomorrow. You're sticking with us through all of it," he reminded me.

The elevator doors opened just as a few of his teammates entered the corridor, exchanging greetings. As we walked toward our rooms, Akshith stopped us with a pointed look. This man doesn't like me a bit. Good for me, I don't like him either.

"Shaurya, you went jogging with her?" Akshith's tone was incredulous, his eyes darting between us.

Before I could respond, Shaurya stepped in front of me, blocking my view. "We bumped into each other. He said. "And stop staring at her like that. You look like a creep," he said, deadpan.

Yuvaan, who was standing beside Akshith, burst out laughing, and soon Siraj joined him, chuckling a little while Akshith turned bright red.

"What's so funny?" Akshith hissed, glaring at his friend. His face now looked like a half-boiled omelette.

I couldn't help it. I giggled.

"And you," Akshith turned to me, narrowing his eyes. "Stop laughing like a dying hyena!"

That did it. "Excuse me? I might sound like a hyena, but you look like a starved hippo!" I shot back, folding my arms.

Akshith stepped forward, glaring at me. "Oh yeah? Get your eyes checked, miss. Girls out there are dying to get a glimpse of me!" He exclaimed in self-pride. It is true though. Am I going to agree with him? Never!

"Girls' taste is awful these days. What can we do about it?" I coolly stated making him grind his teeth in annoyance.

"You!" Akshith stepped forward with a murderous glare. I stood my ground staring back at him.

Before I could escalate the situation, Shaurya once again stepped in, forming a human wall between us. "Alright, enough. Both of you cut it out." I stared at Shaurya's back, wondering whose side he would be taking if I and Akshith keep fighting like this.

"Anu! Rakshith is calling you," Shika's voice pulled me from my thoughts. I turned to see her standing at the door to her room, a confused look on her face as she took in the scene before her—Yuvaan and Siraj laughing hysterically, while Akshith and I remained grumpy with Shaurya still standing in between us, trying to diffuse the tension.

"Bye," I said with a smile directed at Shaurya. He nodded, a small smile tugging at the corner of his lips. I then offered a quick smile to Yuvaan and Siraj, who reciprocated with a wave and grin.

"Stay away from us if possible!" Akshith yelled after me, but I just stuck my tongue out at him as a final, playful gesture. He shook his head in exasperation, while Shaurya and the others chuckled at my antics.

I walked towards Shika, who was still standing by the door, waiting for me. Once inside, we closed the door behind us, and I let out a deep breath, plopping myself down on the couch beside Bhavin. He was busy munching on a pack of Lays chips, and when I reached out to grab one, he snatched the whole pack away from me like it was something precious.

"Seriously, Bhavin?" I rolled my eyes at him, amused and irritated by his possessiveness over the snack.

"Not yet, but they're on it," Vikram said, his voice laced with frustration as he entered the room, speaking about the investigation. He turned to us once he cut the call, "We have to keep a close eye on these players until they catch someone. Our favorite all-rounder sneaked out last night to meet his girlfriend."

I could hear the anger in Vikram's tone, and I understood it, but at the same time, it wasn't completely Siddarth's fault. He probably didn't know about the situation and just wanted to meet his girl.

"We can't blame him for meeting his lover," I said gently, trying to reason. "But yes, we should be more careful going forward."

Nithin nodded in agreement, placing a calming hand on Vikram's shoulder. "We'll just have to tighten our watch and make sure nothing slips through the cracks," he added. Vikram gave a reluctant nod, accepting the advice as the tension in the room slowly began to ease.

We all sat down to discuss the events of the previous night. Apparently, Vikram had followed Siddarth after calling Nithin to stay in the control room, but there hadn't been any further developments.

"You both rest until afternoon," I suggested, turning to Nithin and Vikram. "The team is going to have net practice, and everyone will be there anyway. The rest of us can handle it for now."

I knew this mission wasn't something that would end quickly. It would take days, maybe even weeks, and we couldn't afford to have anyone burning out too early. That's why we'd established shifts in the first place, to keep an eye on the players without overworking ourselves.

"Alright," Vikram agreed. "Call us if you notice anything suspicious, and take Vipul with you."

Vipul was another officer assigned to the mission, acting as the assistant to the team's doctor. With the plan in place, we all got ready to leave for the net practice.

Later that afternoon, the team gathered for their session. From the sidelines, I kept my eye on them, watching for anything out of the ordinary. But despite my focus on the mission, I couldn't help but notice Shaurya—especially in that sleeveless jersey and shorts. He looked undeniably good, his muscles flexing as he worked through drills with ease.

Stop it, Anu! Focus on the task at hand!

Bhavin, meanwhile, was busy recording some videos of the practice for appearances' sake, so the team wouldn't get suspicious of our true purpose. We managed to keep everything under control, and once the practice was over, we grabbed lunch together outside the hotel before returning to debrief and review our findings.

CHAPTER NINE

Ananya

The night stretched out before me, but no matter how many times I tossed and turned, sleep remained elusive. It was one of those nights where rest seemed like a faraway luxury, testing me with its absence.

I moved to the balcony, leaving the warmth of the room behind. The chill of the night wrapped around me like a familiar friend, and I welcomed it. I sank into the chair, propping my legs up on the table, savoring the sensation of the cool breeze brushing against my skin. The balcony was shared, divided by a glass door separating mine from Shaurya's. It could only be opened when unlocked from both sides—something I discovered the previous night when I curiously tried and failed to open it.

The moon hung low in the sky, a delicate waxing crescent glowing softly as it peeked out from behind the drifting clouds, as though playing a quiet game of hide and seek with the stars. They glittered far beyond, forming shapes that seemed like secret messages in the night.

Suddenly, a faint rustling from Shaurya's side of the balcony reached my ears, alerting me. I whipped my head towards his side to find him dressed casually in a tee shirt and shorts. With his hands resting on the railing, the soft highlighting his sharp features, there was something magnetic about him. I quickly looked away, not wanting to intrude on his moment.

"Hey," his voice drifted over, low and warm. I glanced at him, smiling softly.

"Hi," I replied with a small wave of my hand.

"Mind if I join you? That is, if I'm not interrupting your time with Mr. Moon?" he teased, his playful tone making me giggle. I got up and went over to the glass door to unlock it. He did the same on his side, letting the barrier between us disappear.

"Couldn't sleep?" I asked as we settled into the chairs again, this time side by side. He drew his chair closer to mine, his gaze lifting to the moon with a thoughtful smile curving his lips.

"Not really. You?" Turning to me as he asked the question. I shook my head.

"Coffee?" I offered tentatively. He nodded his head and I got up to brew some coffee for both of us.

I handed over his mug of steaming hot coffee to him and settled back into my seat. We slipped into a comfortable silence, the kind that didn't need to be filled. We sipped our coffee slowly, the heat from the cups mingling with the coolness of the night air, while the wind whispered through the leaves.

Once done with our coffee, when I reached out to grab the empty cup from him, he insisted on washing it himself. We walked to the small kitchen, laughter echoing between us as we washed the cups together. It felt strange, a good kind of strange, doing such an ordinary thing in the midst of night like this, but it felt equally special.

As we returned to the balcony, this time choosing to sit on his side. I took in the view of his suite. It can be called a cozy little home, complete with a bedroom, a small kitchen, and a living room—a perfect retreat in the midst of everything.

"So, when did you start playing cricket?" I asked, curious to know more about him.

"Who wants to know?" He shot back, a hint of mischief in his eyes. "You, or the journalist inside you?"

"The journalist in me doesn't work overtime," I said instead of giving him a direct answer. He chuckled softly, nodding in amusement. His smile lit up his face in a way that made him seem younger, almost boyish—such a contrast to the fierce determination he showed on the field.

"I started playing when I was about 12, but didn't join an academy until I was 16," he confessed, his expression shifting as if he was looking back at a version of himself from long ago.

We kept talking, letting the conversation meander through memories, dreams, and little details that only seemed to surface in moments like these, where there are no expectations, no threats, and no judgements.

The hours slipped by unnoticed until we finally realized it was nearly two in the morning. With a reluctant goodnight, I headed back to my room, the darkness of the night wrapping around me like a blanket as sleep finally claimed me with a gentle embrace.

CHAPTER TEN

Shaurya

There's some magic in Ananya. She makes it so hard for me not to look at her—her presence, her voice, the way she smiles. It's like every little thing about her has wrapped itself around me.

At first, when I heard their team would be staying with us, I was more than annoyed. The media and paps have always been a headache with their greed for news and masala. But these people...they are different. They respect our privacy in a way I've never seen before.

They ask for permission before clicking any photos, steer clear of our personal matters, and don't carry mics or cameras into our space without consent. It's rare to see this kind of decency in their profession. Or was it because they are not professionals in the first place? They work for the government so they don't need any hot topic to get promotions, I guess.

And then, there's her. She grabs my attention effortlessly whenever she's nearby. I don't lose my focus on the field, but off the field, she had me hooked on her. I find myself waiting for her smile—the one she gives me when our eyes meet. It's almost like she breathes life into everything around me, making even the ordinary seem extraordinary.

These routine morning jogs with her make me feel like a teenager again, all excited and giddy to meet her. The way her cute little frown forms when I say something she doesn't like, the look of irritation in her eyes when she catches other girls glancing my way, and those adorable glares she gives—everything about her stirs something deep inside me.

Until recently, it was only cricket that had this effect on me. But now, she brings out that same fire. It makes me want to try every possible way, go to any lengths, just to see her smile.

Last night, after talking to Maa, I wandered to the balcony and there she was—sitting quietly, wrapped in the stillness of the night. I leaned against the railing, debating with myself whether to break the peacefulness or not. I could feel her gaze lingering on me for a moment before she turned her attention to the moon.

"Hey," I greeted, finally giving in to the urge.

Her smile when she turned to me was worth everything. We ended up talking for three hours straight, sharing stories about our families, memories, and so much more. It felt like the world had disappeared, leaving just the two of us in that little bubble.

Time flew by, until she yawned. We said goodnight to each other and moved to our respective rooms. I went to bed that night with a sense of contentment—a feeling like I had achieved something precious by spending those moments with her.

By the time I rushed to our usual meeting spot, she was already waiting for me. With an apologetic smile, I wished her morning and she brushed it off with a giggle. We ran side by side for an hour, and I couldn't help but notice how the breeze tousled her hair, sending loose strands brushing against my neck and arm. Her subtle fragrance filled the air around us, and every now and then, I'd catch her beautiful eyes peeking over at me.

Back in my room, I shook off the lingering daydream and headed for a much needed shower. I threw on a comfortable tee and knee-length shorts, grabbed my sunglasses, and stepped out. Just as I was about to leave, I spotted Akshith and Siraj huddled together, whispering to each other. I crept up behind them and smacked their heads lightly.

"What the hell, Shaurya?" Akshith grumbled, rubbing his head. I just shrugged, hands in my pockets.

"What are you two plotting outside my room?" I raised an eyebrow, watching them exchange glances.

"We're planning to get drunk today. You in?" Akshith finally admitted. I stared at them incredulously. "It's 7 a.m., saalo!" I exclaimed. I knew we didn't have any matches today, and we were heading to Kolkata tomorrow, but drinking at this hour was a bit much.

"Not now, Bhaiyya! We meant in the evening," Siraj clarified with those puppy-dog eyes. I rolled my eyes, knowing they'd be doing it regardless of my answer.

"Fine, but don't go overboard. We've got an early start tomorrow," I relented. They grinned mischievously and pulled me into a tight hug just as my eyes landed on Ananya.

She stood across the hall in front of her room, dressed in a royal blue frock that flowed just below her knees. Her hair cascaded down her shoulders in soft curls, and her makeup was subtle yet striking, with just a hint of eyeliner and a touch of lipstick. A delicate pendant adorned her neck, small golden hoops glinting from her ears. The dress hugged her curves perfectly, accentuating her every move. And her legs...they looked as smooth as silk, utterly flawless.

Gorgeous.

That was the only word that came to my mind as I watched her standing there. But it did not justify describing her beauty. No word could. Her smile was gentle, the kind that crept up slowly and settled in her eyes, making them shimmer with a warmth that wrapped around me like a comforting embrace. She was a vision—an angel sent straight from heaven to walk the earth. I couldn't tear my gaze away. It was like time had frozen, and in that fleeting moment, it was just two of us, as if the rest of the world didn't matter, didn't exist.

My heart skipped a beat when she noticed my staring, her cheeks turning the faintest shade of pink as our eyes met. She tucked a loose curl behind her ear, a small, shy gesture that only added to her charm. I was drawn to her, as though some invisible force was pulling me closer to her, urging me to say something—anything—to break the spell that had been cast between us.

But I couldn't find the right words, not when she looked like that. She was ethereal, and I was afraid that if I spoke, the magic would shatter and she would vanish like a dream at dawn. For a second, I just stood there, completely caught up in the sheer perfection of her presence, as if she were a beautiful illusion I never wanted to wake up from.

And then, she tilted her head slightly, her lips curling into a playful smirk as she raised an eyebrow at me. "Are you going to keep staring, or will you say something?" She teased, her voice as light and sweet as the morning breeze.

I blinked, snapping out of my trance, and found myself chuckling softly. "I'm just wondering whom you plan on killing today, looking like that," I replied, a playful glint in my words. "You are too dangerous to be left unguarded."

She laughed, a musical sound that seemed to echo in the hallway, filling the space between us with a kind of joy I hadn't realized I needed. "Maybe

I'm here to kill you with kindness," She shot back with a wink, making my heart flutter.

"I guess I am ready to surrender," I said, my voice dripping a little lower. The intensity of the moment caught up to me again, and I took a step closer, feeling that familiar desperation to be close to her return—the urge to just reach out and touch her, to brush my fingers along her cheek and feel her warmth seep into me.

But I held back, choosing to simply enjoy the magic of our playful exchange, knowing that if I get too close, I might just forget myself completely.

The bubble surrounding us shattered as Akshith stepped between us, his presence snapping us back from our little world. A surge of irritation coursed through me at his interruption. His eyes darted between us as if trying to piece together what he had just walked into.

"What are you doing here?" he asked, his voice carrying a hint of suspicion as his gaze settled on Ananya. Her expression scrunched in annoyance, her lips pouting ever so slightly.

Cute.

"That seems to be your favorite line. Doesn't it?" Ananya shot back, a spark of defiance in her tone.

"Answer the question," Akshith grumbled, his brows drawing together in irritation.

"I'm here to talk with Shaurya. Now, if you please excuse me." She dismissed him with a wave, then turned her attention back to me. The smile returned to her lips, soft yet hopeful. "Can we have one-on-one interviews with the players on your practice days, if you don't mind?" she asked, her eyes shimmering with anticipation.

I couldn't resist that look. "I'll ask them once, but it's a yes for mine," I replied, surrendering to her request.

"Mine too!" Siraj chimed in, practically bouncing with excitement. Her smile brightened at his words before she shifted her gaze back to Akshith, who was eyeing her with suspicion.

"Say please," he said, folding his arms across his chest.

"Please, my foot. I'll drag you to the interview myself if you don't show up," she retorted, her eyes narrowing. Siraj's laughter filled the air, while Akshith just stared at her, as if she'd grown two heads. These two had been at each other's throats since the day they met, bickering like Tom and Jerry.

"The audacity," Akshith scoffed, taking a step closer as if to challenge her. They didn't seem interested in ending their little banter, so I stepped in, gently pulling Akshith back and positioning myself between them.

"Now, that's enough, my warriors. Stop fighting over everything," I said with a playful firmness.

Akshith gave me a look that clearly said I had betrayed him, while Ananya's reaction was entirely different. Her cheeks flushed a delicate pink, and she dropped her gaze to the marble floor, nibbling on her lower lip.

What had made her blush so suddenly?

Oh. I called them my warriors. I called her mine.

The realization sent warmth rushing to my ears. When she glanced up, her eyes met mine, and just like that, the world faded away. It was only us, wrapped in a moment that felt endless.

"Let's go, Akshith Bhai," Siraj's voice came from a distance, as though we were miles away. He tugged Akshith by the arm, leading him away. I'd have to thank Siraj for that later.

"I... I'll go arrange for today's interview." Her voice was almost a whisper, her cheeks still dusted with that lovely pink. Without waiting for my response, she turned and hurried away, leaving me standing there, captivated by the sight of her retreating figure, a smile tugging at my lips.

CHAPTER ELEVEN

Shaurya

As I settled in the cool shade of the dugouts after an intense practice, letting the breeze wash over me while waiting for Ananya. My mind kept replaying last night when she came into my room in those cozy, adorable pajamas, her hair pulled into a loose bun with a few rebellious strands tumbling down. A smile tugged at my lips just thinking about it.

It's been 28 days since they joined us, and somewhere along the way, they became more than just "the new additions." They're part of our lives now. From our morning discussions to late-night parties, they are everywhere except for the internal team discussions and meetings. And Ananya, she has become a special and important part of my life.

She has slipped into my life like a dawn creeping in unnoticed until it colors everything. My life wasn't bland before her, but with her it became more fun, more colorful, more exciting and happening.

Our days start together, matching each other's pace on our morning jogs, and end under the stars in either of our rooms, sharing pieces of ourselves that feel too precious to say aloud in daylight.

Every day, she's here, a constant presence—cheering us on, capturing moments of the game with her camera, or even just scrolling through her phone in the stands, and it's comforting. Sometimes, she glances up, catches me watching her, and flashes that heart-stopping smile.

I still remember the day we moved to Kolkata. The hotel we stayed at, unlike the previous one, didn't have an attached balcony, and her room was on the floor above mine. I was on the 17th floor and she was on the 18th.

That night, I didn't sleep even a wink. It had become a habit to talk to her for an hour before going to bed. I just kept staring at the ceiling like a possessed man, trying to think of some excuse to meet her.

She already doesn't spend time with me on Saturdays. She spends all her Saturdays with her friends. "It's our ritual to have a movie marathon on Saturdays," is what she said when I asked her. Knowing I wouldn't see her gnawed at me in a way I hadn't expected.

I showed up early for our jog the next morning, thrilled when she arrived ten minutes earlier than usual. I couldn't hide my joy. I suggested extra laps just to steal more time together, and she agreed, perhaps sensing my unspoken longing.

That night, my resolve broke, and I made a beeline to her room. I could feel my heartbeats turning erratic as I stood in front of her room. I wonder if she could hear them from the other side. With sweat ticking down my temples, I rubbed my sweaty palms against my short pants, and I took a few deep breaths as I decided to go for it.

I knocked on the door, softly. The silence was eerie, as I waited for her to open the door. At that moment, I was excited to see her but equally scared of her reaction. But I couldn't care less, as I knocked, again. I felt like the situation was of life and death and she was my life.

It was, as if, I was short of breath and she was the oxygen I was desperate for. As the seconds stretched, an internal war broke out between my heart and brain. My brain urged me to go back, while my heart remained stubborn, wanting to meet her. To stop the internal war between my Heart and Brain, I started to count numbers.

The door creaked open when I was at 55, and I felt relief washing over me as she smiled at me.

"Can... Can I have your pod charger, please!" I blurted out the excuse I prepared. She gave me a long stare as if assessing me. I skimmed in my place, my face paling as she kept staring at me. "Come in, Mr. Singhania," She finally smiled, stepping away, making me sigh in relief.

"Let me grab it," She turned away and started searching for the charger while I took my time to admire her room.

The bed was nestled against the wall beneath a striking painting of a yellow taxi on a bustling street, but what held me captive was the view from her balcony. I drifted towards it, captivated by the way the city lights flickered against the night sky, but truthfully, all I wanted was to stay near her a little longer.

I noticed Ananya moving towards me with the charger and walked to the balcony, not looking back at her.

"Your room has the most beautiful view of the night sky, Ms. Shergill. I can only see the flyover from mine," I pouted a little to add dramatic effect. Anya

came and stood beside me, without saying anything.

From the corner of my eye, I noticed a beautiful smile forming on her lips. " It would be scandalous if someone sees you coming in, or going out of my room at odd hours. It can affect your career," She knew it.

"Do you enjoy spending time with me, Ananya?" I asked the question directly, without beating around the bush. She took a step ahead and held the railing, looking down.

"I don't want you to risk your reputation and career, Shaurya," Her voice was a mere whisper. If it was not for the quietness of the night, I would have missed it. I took a step and stood beside her, my hands on the railing.

"Answer my question truthfully, Ananya. What do you want? Don't think about my career, media, paps, and all that crap. What does Ananya want? Does she like to spend time with Shaurya or not?" I asked, placing my hand over hers on the railing. Her body went rigid for a moment before she relaxed, heaving a soft sigh.

"I do want to spend time with you, Shaurya," She admitted, her cheeks turning crimson. That admission felt like everything. For the first time, I realized how much I would risk just to stay by her side, how I would face any consequence, just to see her smile and hear her laughter.

"Don't worry about anything else, then. I'll take care of it. I'll not let anyone harm either your or my reputation." I promised. I knew it was risky. I knew the consequences if the news leaked out. But the time with her is worth every risk in the world. She is worth every humiliation and every inquiry I would face if something goes wrong. I will face everything for her and won't even let a scratch on her career or image.

Ananya, being extra cautious, turned off the balcony lights, making me chuckle at her. She pouted at me, narrowing her eyes and god! She looked damn cute while doing so.

"Can I get a coffee, please?" I made a pleading face for extra effect and she went away to make a coffee, her cheeks flushing pink but a soft smile adorning her lips.

She came back with two cups of coffee and took a seat beside me. I moved my chair closer to hers, making her narrow her eyes at me but she didn't say anything. In silence, we sipped our coffee as the gentle night breeze caressed us. Strands of her hair brushed against my arm, leaving her scent lingering, intoxicating, and calming all at once. We started talking about random things and our first cooking experience.

Her first time cooking was apparently a disaster as she added too much red chili powder to the curry, to get a good color. She confessed to not having much knowledge of cooking except for a few dishes to survive. That's not an issue, I can cook for her and teach her if she is interested in learning.

As we talked further, she folded her legs, on her chair, and explained animatedly about how her mother scolded her for making the disastrous dish and how she completed the red chili powder meant for an entire month in a single dish.

As the conversation flew further, I couldn't help but notice how her face shined under the moonlight. Her eyes lit up like the most precious diamonds, competing with the stars shining in the sky, her fingers running through her wavy locks, as she tucked them from time to time and those lips, those cherry lips were testing my control.

I just wanted to grab her face and attach my lips to hers and suck the hell out of them. But, I knew it was not the time and I still had a long way before kissing her. I wanted to hold her hand, intertwine our fingers, and was almost desperate to grab her hand but controlled myself fisting my hands on the arm rest.

Her feet kicked my knee as she laughed uncontrollably at some memory of hers and she stopped abruptly. She tried to pull her leg back but I held her feet and kept it on my thigh, squeezing it with a smile.

"Let it be," I assured her and squeezed her toes once more. She heaved a sigh and started speaking again, a tint of pink adorning her cheeks, and I listened to her playing with her toes and soles. We kept talking till midnight until she finally pushed me out of her room, reminding me of my early morning practice.

We grew more comfortable with each other over time and the night talk ritual continued even when we moved to other cities for our matches. Either she came to my room or I went to hers except for Saturdays, of course.

As the days passed, I couldn't help but imagine my life with her. I am not sure where life takes me or how my future is going to be. The only thing I am sure about is my feelings for her. It's way past infatuation or attraction. It's deeper than those.

I want to have those long calls with her, when I am away for matches, I want her to travel with me for my matches, not as an employee but as my wife, and my partner. I want to celebrate her every success, every interview, every promotion, and every moment we spend together.

I want to give her lots of gifts, I want to dedicate my milestones to her, along with my family and friends. I want her to be a part of our family, the one I was born into and the one cricket bestowed me with. I want to be a part of her family, her friend circle, and everything that is a part of her. I want to be aware of everything that is dear to her.

"Shaurya, the ball!" I heard Yuvaan yell from the ground and that broke my trance. I smiled to myself, shaking my head as I got up from my chair, walking to the ball, which was a few feet away from me. I grabbed the ball and threw it to Yuvaan, who caught it with ease.

"Were you dreaming again?" I felt a hand around my shoulder as Akshith pulled me to him. I looked at him with an annoyed look etched on my face.

"I was doing no such thing," I grumbled, pushing his hand away.

"Quit acting, Shaurya. It's clearly not your forte," He stated in a matter-of-fact tone as he made me sit on the chair and took a seat beside me.

"We all know about your growing feelings for Ananya. We could see that," He blankly stated, making my eyes widen in surprise.

"There's no need to be that shocked. Neither of you were sneaky enough to hide it. Every time you come face to face, both your faces brighten up like a bulb, and that goofy smile, how can anyone miss that?" I heaved a sigh. So, they are only guessing it based on our interactions. Our little late-night dates are still a secret.

"Though I hate to admit it, she is a very nice person and she is the best for you," He squeezed my hand with an appreciative nod.

"What are you both discussing so seriously?" Yuvaan joined us, pulling a chair for himself.

"Shaurya's budding love story," Akshith bet me in replying and I could feel my cheeks heating up at his comment.

"Oh! But Shaurya, I am really happy for you man! Ananya is such a sweet soul to be around," He exclaimed, making my cheeks heat up more. They should at least give me a warning before uttering such sweet words.

"Did you propose to her yet?" Yuvaan suddenly turned serious and Akshith too sat straight, eager to know about our story. I shook my head, making them both sigh in disappointment.

"Are you waiting for any Muharat, Captain?" Akshith mocked, making me glare at him but my glare, like always, did not affect him.

"Then?" Yuvaan pressed, impatiently.

"What...what if she rejects? Even our friendship would end," I replied meekly.

"What?" Both of them yelled, getting up, and pressing their temples, dramatically.

"Have you lost it, Shaurya? We all can see how much she is into you and you, you can't see it, you stupid?" Yuvaan exclaimed dramatically.

"Um...guys, hello?" We all whipped our heads towards Ananya who was looking at us like we were all aliens from another galaxy. She fidgeted with her fingers, looking between me, Yuvaan, and Akshith, before finally settling her gaze on me.

"Siraaj said you were looking for me. Should I come back again?" She asked doubtfully and I shook my head hysterically in no.

"No, it's fine, Anu. We were just discussing our captain's new phobia," Yuvaan said. I nodded agreeing with him but stopped abruptly when I realized what he said. What? From when do I have a phobia?

"What? Is it something serious?" Her brows creased in concern as she took a step towards me.

"Nothing to worry about, Miss. Monkey. He's just suffering from confessophobia," Akshith replied, casually resting his hand over Ananya's head, making her step away with a scowl.

"Confesso what? Does that even exist?" She narrowed her eyes at Akshith, her finger pointed to his face.

"They are just sprouting nonsense, Ananya. Let's go from here." I grabbed her hand and walked away, not giving her a chance to ask anything further. I could hear both of those idiots laugh behind us but didn't stop to look back. I would have made them shut up, but taking Ananya away from those idiots is more important right now. I will see them later.

"What was cockroach saying back there?" Ananya asked, finally, after we reached the food court. Only ours and her team, along with a few ground staff, were present in the stadium as today was just practice day, and for some weird reason, the stadiums are not allowing spectators from the last month like they normally do. It's good in a way, I can spend more time with Ananya.

"You know him. He was just pulling my leg," She made an 'O' with her lips at my reply and I changed the topic, asking her about the interview with our coach. Thankfully, she started describing how it went, making me relax a little. I will kill that Akshith.

"Shaurya, the coach is calling you," Dhruv called out from the entrance and I gave a smile to Ananya who was pouting at Dhruv with puppy eyes. She is really a cutiepie when she is off-duty.

"Let's meet in the evening?" I raised a brow at her and she nodded, the pout still intact on her lips. How I wish to kiss those lips!

"Bye," She mumbled lowly, making me chuckle at her unwillingness to part ways. I quickly pecked her forehead and practically ran away from there before she could yell at me for doing that.

Only when I reached the entrance did I turn back to look at her and she was smiling to herself, her cheeks coated in pink, and her hand caressing the place I just kissed. Maybe they were right, maybe she too feels the same as me.

CHAPTER TWELVE

As promised to Ananya, Shaurya discussed with his team and confirmed the one-on-one interviews as per her wish. For the team, the interviews were another chance to laugh, connect, and, maybe, offer glimpses of their unspoken bond with the "new additions," they affectionately call Ananya and her team.

Shaurya's own excitement was unmistakable; he was eager to see what Ananya had prepared for him. But, of course, Ananya's friends couldn't miss a chance to tease the duo. So, Rakshith chose to lead the interviews, starting with bowlers, leaving Shaurya to wait his turn until he was the last.

"Saving the best for the last," In Vikram's words.

Akshith and Yuvaan along with Siraj and others had already given their interviews, sharing moments from their initial days as players and their bonding with their teammates.

Siraj's words brimmed with respect for Shaurya when questions were about the captain, while Akshith and Yuvaan took the opportunity to reveal every embarrassing story, making Ananya's cheeks flush with laughter and curiosity. The growing affection between her and Shaurya wasn't lost on the team—they saw it, felt it, but all chose to act blissfully ignorant, waiting for the two to figure it out themselves.

Ananya's interview with Akshith was by far the most chaotic, each trying not to lose their cool as playful insults and daring glances were exchanged. At one point, Akshith boldly declared he was the "most important part of Shaurya's life," and would remain so "even when they grow old." just to instigate Ananya and attain a reaction from her.

Though Ananya was annoyed by the way Akshith was trying to irritate her, she appreciated their bond. But that didn't stop her from making another cheeky remark to rile him up.

Finally, it's time for Shaurya's interview.

The room had been set up with soft, warm lighting, casting a golden glow on the dark mahogany furniture which consisted of two flush single-seater couches and a coffee table in the middle. There was a subtle aroma of coffee lingering in the air, adding a comforting touch to the setup.

Ananya adjusted her notes, her fingers tapping against the pages as she glanced at her watch, waiting. She'd chosen a lovely emerald-green dress that hugged her silhouette perfectly, the color complementing her deep brown eyes, which were now fixed on the door.

Just as she tucked a stray strand of hair behind her ear, the door swung open, and Shaurya walked in. He was effortlessly handsome, dressed in a casual, yet tailored, light-blue shirt with sleeves rolled up, revealing his strong forearms, and charcoal gray trousers.

His charm was undeniable, with that usual confidence in his eyes and strides. His eyes softened, an amused smile forming on his lips as he noticed her staring a bit too long.

"Good evening, Ananya," he said, settling into the chair opposite to her, his tone laced with gentle teasing and amusement.

"I hope you are ready for all my truths," he added further, his smile widening.

Ananya chuckled, feigning confidence, "Only if you're prepared to share them, Shaurya. I promise to keep it fun and only slightly invasive." Her eyes sparkled, hinting at a playful challenge.

They started with the basics, but as the questions flowed, so did the layers of Shaurya's cricketing life.

"Shaurya, your career skyrocketed after that unforgettable match two years ago," she began, leaning forward slightly, "Whad did that moment mean to you?"

He took a thoughtful pause, his gaze unfocused as he recalled the moments. "You know it was one of those moments where everything else fades except for the goal in your mind. There's a crowd, the noise, the cameras...but for me, it's like a silence settles. That silence helps me find my focus. It's my team, the game, and the thrill of every ball, every run."

Ananya found herself captivated, not just by his words, but by the quiet intensity in his voice, his passion for the sport. "So, your fans..." she started, grinning. "They say you are one of the most down-to-earth players out there, despite the fame and volcanic eruptions you display on the field. How do you keep it that way?"

They shared a laugh at her choice of words regarding his aggressive nature on the field. He shrugged, smiling softly. "It's simple. Cricket is my passion and when you are doing something you are passionate about, your emotions are high. My family and friends are my roots. I am still the same guy to them – no matter how many stadiums chant my name. And they make sure I stay so with everyone around."

She tilted her head, a smile on her lips. "Talking about friends, is there someone you can always lean on, someone who's your go-to?"

For the first time, Shaurya hesitated, a flicker of warmth crossing his face. "Akshith and Yuvaan are always there. But I feel like I found another person to lean on too," he admitted, looking directly into her eyes, his voice full of sincerity, "someone who always makes things better...beautiful."

Ananya felt a blush rise to her cheeks, and, with a quick recovery, she cleared her throat and moved to her next question, her voice a bit unsteady.

"And...cricket. You must have some strong opinions about how the game has evolved over the years. Any thoughts on the difference between the old-school and modern approach?"

Shaurya's eyes twinkled, a smile curling onto his lips as he leaned back in his chair. "The game has definitely changed, technology, strategies, even the audience's expectations from players and teams as a whole. I respect the legends because they shaped what we play now. But there's something in this generation's hunger...we're always striving, adapting. I think that's what makes it exciting."

The conversation effortlessly steered to lighter topics, with Ananya asking cheeky questions about his pre and post match rituals, favorite moments on the field, and how he maintains his focus in pressure situations. Shaurya animatedly explained everything to her, the smile never leaving his face as he spoke. Ananya even slipped a few playful jabs in the middle, making him laugh in that relaxed way only she could bring out.

Ananya leaned forward, her voice laced with a spark of mischief, "So, Shaurya...where do you see yourself in, let's say...the next five years?"

Shaurya raised an eyebrow, his amusement clear as daylight. "Five years, huh?" he murmured, letting his eyes linger on her face as he answered," I see myself playing a lot of cricket, of course. But maybe...with someone by my side to celebrate each win, or, you know, keep me grounded after every loss."

Ananya could feel her heart race at his words and the intense stare he pointed at her. She let out a nervous laugh, quickly looking down at her notes in a futile attempt to hide her blush. But she couldn't resist but steal a glance at him from the corner of her eyes. "Well, I'm sure that someone would be...very lucky."

Shaurya didn't miss a beat. "I'd say we'd be lucky together, Miss. Ananya."

Ananya's pulse quickened at the subtle suggestion in his words. She glanced down, trying to hide her smile, but it was impossible to resist the shy smile gracing her lips as she looked at his neatly polished shoes, fidgeting her fingers.

Trying to stay focused, she cleared her throat and leaned back. "Alright, Shaurya, tell us about your early days in the team, especially with Akshith and Yuvaan. I've heard you three were quite the mischievous trio. Can you share any such incident with us?" She scooted to the edge of her seat, bubbling with curiosity.

Shaurya settled deeper into his chair, chuckling softly, as if recalling the memories from the past. His eyes met Ananya's with a playful glint, and she couldn't help but smile back, waiting for him to talk.

"We were just a bunch of ambitious rookies, fresh out of junior cricket, ready to take on the world with, with only a little knowledge on how things worked."

He leaned forward, waiting for her reaction. "Please continue. I am excited to know what kind of mischief you three did back then,"

"Well, it was our very first tournament together," he started, a bit of nostalgia lining his voice. "We had just joined the team and our coach warned us about the strict diets and fitness regimes. Now Akshith, as you probably know, has a sweet tooth like no other."

Ananya laughed with a nod of her head. "He stole my share of dessert yesterday." She complained. Shaurya laughed at her words.

"Don't worry, I'll treat youto a dessert after this interview," he promised. Ananya's eyes lit up in excitement.

"Deal. Now tell me what did Akshith do back then?" Her curiosity was palpable as she eagerly waited for Shaurya to continue with his tale.

Sbaurya grinned, leaning forward, caught up in the memory. "One evening, we'd all slipped out to 'explore local culture', as he put it, which actually meant sneaking out to grab gulab jamuns. We weren't exactly being stealthy, and before we knew it, our coach was hot on our trail. Akshith panicked and, in his brilliance, decided to stuff his pockets with gulab jamuns so he wouldn't have to leave them behind. Yuvaan and I were just trying to hold our laughter as we sprinted back to the hotel."

Ananya burst out laughing, tears forming in her eyes as she clutched her stomach. "Akshith doesn't look so...dumb?" She managed to breathe out between her giggles.

"Trust me, Akshith's brain stops functioning in panic situations."

Ananya covered her mouth, stifling her giggles, her eyes bright with amusement. "And the coach didn't catch on?"

"He did," Shaurya laughed. "But he just shook his head, muttering something about 'hopeless rookies.' We all thought we'd be benched for life, but I think he actually found it funny or maybe stupid. Akshith didn't hear the end of it for weeks. Yuvaan and I, in fact, the whole team made sure to remind him every time we saw the gulab jamun."

Ananya shook her head, a mischievous smile dancing on her face as she declared, "I will make sure to tease him the next time I see gulab jamun."

"So, can we assume you three were the troublemakers of the team?" she asked further.

"Something like that," Shaurya replied, a gleam of mischief in his eyes. "Yuvaan was always the quiet one, though. Thoughtful, observant...but you wouldn't believe the pranks he'd pull on us. Before my very first big match, he managed to swap my shoes with two left feet. I was rushing to put them on and couldn't understand why they felt so wrong. When I realized what happened, he was already laughing from outside the door like a lunatic."

Ananya's laugh rang through the room, making Shaurya pause to take in her joy. For a moment, he seemed almost transfixed, lost, as he stared at her like she was the answer to all his prayers.

"Those sound like the best of times," Ananya said, catching her breath. "It's rare to have friends who feel like family."

Shaurya's expression softened." They are my family," he said, his voice filled with conviction. "Through every struggle, every high and low. I wouldn't have made it here without them."

Ananya let his words settle, feeling the warmth and gratitude in them, and then—almost shyly—she dared to ask, "Do you ever think about what the future holds for all of you? I mean, after cricket, once life settles down..."

Shaurya's gaze turned thoughtful, and he smiled, more to himself. "We talk about it sometimes. Akshith jokes that he's going to retire in a little hill station, open a bakery, and live on sweets. Yuvaan wants to coach young kids, give back to the sport that's given him so much." He hesitated, his voice dropping a little. "And as for me... I haven't thought much past today. But maybe one day... I'd like to have someone by my side, someone who's there not just for the wins, but for the quiet moments too."

Ananya felt the blush raise to her cheeks as Shaurya's eyes remained fixed on her. Clearing her throat softly, she asked, "Someone to share every little thing with, huh? Sounds like you're a bit of a romantic, Shaurya."

He laughed, leaning back and giving her a half-smile. "We all need someone by our side," he said, his voice low. "And with the right person, everything seems easier," he added, a small, suggestive smile playing on his lips.

Ananaya's heart skipped a beat at his words. Trying to brush it off, she moved to another question in an attempt to steer the conversation towards the game, though her voice trembled slightly. "So, tell me, how do you feel playing against other teams, especially those known for their aggressive game? Any rivalries to share?"

Shaurya's eyes lit up with a playful glint, his lips stretching into a knowing smirk. His words were affecting her and he knew it. But he decided to play along. For now. "It's all professional, of course...but I'd be lying if I said there wasn't a thrill going head-to-head with the best. There's a team from Australia we've played against for years. Yuvaan and I joke about it every time—how they get so fierce, as if they're the only ones allowed to win."

Ananya chuckled, picturing it. "And you? You don't feel the need to get back at them?"

"Let's just say I make sure the game speaks for itself," he replied with a wink. "I let them chase me on the field."

His gaze lingered on her face, tracing the delicate curves with his eyes. Trying to keep her cool, Ananya gave a small smile. "Well, Shaurya, it sounds like your future and your present are pretty well planned. Here's hoping you find that 'someone special' to share it all with."

For a moment, he was silent, his eyes fixed on her as if searching for something. Then, he spoke, his voice soft and filled with confidence." Maybe I already have."

The words hung between them, carrying a promise yet to be spoken, an intimacy that filled the space with an electric warmth. In that golden lit room, they both realized, the interview had turned into something far deeper than either had expected.

They just sat there, lost in each other, while the others silently slipped away, leaving them alone. Shaurya's eyes scanned the room before finally finding their way back to Ananya, who sat there looking at him as if mesmerized.

"Ananya," he called out softly, reaching out for her hand. Ananya blinked slowly, coming back to her senses. She looked at Shaurya as though trying to gauge his feelings through his eyes.

"I think we are done here," she finally managed to let the words out, standing up quickly and accidentally knocking her phone from the table. Shaurya's reflexes kicked in and he caught it before it hit the floor.

"Here," he muttered in a low, husky voice, extending her phone back to her. With slightly shaky hands, Ananya reached for her phone, only for Shaurya to clasp her hand, the phone trapped between their intertwined fingers.

"Wh-what are you doing, Mr. Singhania?" she asked, her voice barely a whisper as she tried to pull her hand back. Shaurya stepped closer, closing the distance between them.

"What is this, Ananya?" He exclaimed, feigning disbelief. "Back to Mr. Singhania once you are done with your interview?" he teased, tucking a loose strand of hair behind her ear. His fingers lingered, grazing her skin in a way that made her eyes flutter closed, her lips parting as she felt the warmth of his touch.

"Call me Shaurya," he whispered, caressing the back of her palm. Ananya was too caught up in the moment to respond, her body reacting instinctively. Sensing her silence, Shaurya pressed his thumb gently against her neck, drawing a soft gasp from her lips.

"Wh-what?" she breathed, her heart racing wildly.

"Call me Shaurya, Ananya," he coaxed. The closeness was unlike anything they'd shared before as if every unspoken feeling was in this moment. Over the past months, they had exchanged glances, teased each other and shared brief moments, but this—this was on an entirely different level.

Sure, they spent almost every night of the past month, in either of their balconies talking, even when they moved to other cities, but they never took that step to let out their feelings for each other and always kept things as hidden as they could, from each other.

"Shaurya.." she whispered finally, her eyes shut, fingers curling into his shirt, trying to ground herself as she felt his breath near her neck. She clung to him, the name slipping from her lips as her heart pounded in sync with the closeness between them.

Just when Shaurya was about to give in and wrap her in his arms, the quiet atmosphere was interrupted by the sound of footsteps outside the door, reminding them of the team and their duties.

Shaurya chuckled softly as Annaya took a back step, startled by the interruption. Shaurya's eyes never left hers, "Well," he murmured, afraid the sound would break the moment. "I guess we'd better get back to being professionals." The longing in his voice was unmistakable.

"For now," he added further.

Annaya nodded, biting her lip to hide the smile tugging at the corners of her mouth. "Right," she replied softly, gathering her scattered notes.

Shaurya turned to leave, but paused, leaning close enough that she could feel his warmth. "Ananya...I'll be waiting. To meet you again, this time just as Ananya, in our little space," The sincerity in his voice made her heart flutter, and before she could even respond, he turned, offering her one last lingering smile before stepping out.

She watched him leave, her heart pounding, a quiet sense of joy and excitement settling within her. Whatever lay ahead—on the field or off it—she knew, deep down, that this was only the beginning. Their beginning.

CHAPTER THIRTEEN

Two weeks after Shaurya's interview

"Did you get any clue?" Shika asked tensely.

Vikram's fingers flew over the keys of his laptop, the glow of the screen reflecting his intense focus. The room was silent except for the faint hum of the air conditioner and the soft click-clack of keys. Around him, the team sprawled across the bed and couches, their postures betraying a mix of exhaustion and anticipation. They were waiting—praying—for any lead from the phone seized earlier that morning from the mysterious attacker.

It had been a chaotic start to the day.

Ananya had been on her routine jog with Shaurya. The early morning breeze carried the faint aroma of freshly brewed coffee from a nearby café, mingling with the earthy scent of dew-kissed grass. The rising sun bathed everything in a soft, golden hue, making the moment feel almost surreal.

"You are getting slow, Shaurya," she teased, a playful smirk lighting up her face as she glanced sideways at him.

Shaurya raised an eyebrow, his lips curving into a slow, deliberate grin. "Slow? I am pacing myself. Didn't want to embarrass you by leaving you behind."

"Embarrass me?" Her laughter bubbled out, a sound so light it seemed to dissolve the crispness of the morning air. "You wish. Someone has to carry the team spirit while you're busy admiring the scenery."

His eyes flicked to her, lingering just a moment too long. "Trust me, the scenery is worth admiring."

Ananya's step faltered briefly, her pulse hitching at the quiet weight in his words. She tried to mask it off with a roll of her eyes. "Spare me the poetry, Shaurya. Focus on keeping up."

Shaurya let out a low chuckle, his tone warm but laced with something she couldn't quite place. "Keep talking, Ananya. I love it when you're competitive."

Her gaze narrowed, the teasing glint returning. "Competitive? It's not my fault you can't keep up." She picked up her pace, challenging him.

For a few strides, he matched her, their breaths mingling in the cool air. Then, with a burst of speed, he pulled ahead, glancing over his shoulder with a grin. "Still think I can't keep up?"

"Oh, it's on," she shot back, quickening her pace again. For a brief, breathless moment, they were neck and neck, their movements perfectly synchronized, their shared laughter a melody against the backdrop of the waking city.

But then Shaurya slowed, letting her win. "There. Happy now?" he asked, his voice quieter, his gaze softer as he watched her.

Ananya smirked, though her heartbeat betrayed her composure. "Happy to prove my point. Don't let it bruise your ego too much."

His smile faltered just slightly, replaced by an intensity that made her chest tighten. "You've got a way of keeping me on my toes, Ananya. I'll give you that."

Her breath caught at the unspoken layers in his tone. "Someone has to," she replied lightly, but the words felt heavier between them.

For a moment, the silence stretched, charged with an unspoken pull neither of them could name but both could feel.

Then, Ananya's gaze shifted, catching sight of a man standing at a distance. His posture was too stiff, his attempt to blend in too forced.

Her instincts kicked in. She forced herself to relax, not wanting to alert Shaurya. "I need water," she said abruptly, brushing off the sudden tension in her voice.

Shaurya frowned, his brows knitting in concern. "Now? We're barely halfway through."

"I'll catch up," she assured him, keeping her tone airy as she gestured toward a nearby stall.

He hesitated, his gaze searching hers as though trying to read something she wasn't saying. "Alright," he said finally, though his reluctance was clear. "Don't take too long. The track isn't as fun without my competition."

She managed a small smile. "Try not to miss me too much," she quipped, but the moment his back was turned, her focus shifted, her expression hardening.

Her steps carried her toward the man, her senses on high alert. The teasing warmth of the moment faded, replaced by the cold precision she relied on when danger lurked nearby.

Once she was out of his line of sight, her demeanor shifted. Her every move was precise, like a predator stalking its prey. She closed the distance between herself and the man, careful not to draw any unwanted attention.

When she was just a step behind him, the man tensed, as though sensing her presence. He spun around, his fist slicing through the air toward her face.

But Ananya was faster. She dodged, her instincts honed from years of training kicking in. With a swift, calculated motion, she delivered a hard blow to his stomach. The attacker stumbled back, clutching his midsection, but before he could cry out, she clamped a hand over his mouth. Her grip was firm, unrelenting, as she maneuvered him out of sight.

Once he was unconscious, she quickly dialed Nithin. Minutes later, he and Bhavin appeared, expertly hauling the man into Bhavin's room without raising suspicion while Ananya jogged back to Shaurya to avoid suspicion.

Inside the room, the air was thick with tension. The attacker was securely tied to a chair with belts, his head lolling forward as they splashed cold water on his face to wake him.

Rakshith wasted no time. His voice was ice-cold, his questions sharp and relentless. But the man remained silent, his jaw set in defiance. Hours passed, the interrogation escalating, yet he refused to break. The team's frustration grew palpable, but they masked it behind a professional calm.

After an exhaustive search, they retrieved a phone and a few odd items from his pockets: pens, coins, and a suspicious stash of sleeping pills.

Vikram immediately set to work. He powered up his laptop, his sharp gaze scanning the attacker's phone for anything—messages, call logs, hidden apps—that could provide a lead. The team watched in silence, their breaths collectively held as the minutes dragged on.

Finally, Vikram groaned, running a hand through his hair. "There's literally nothing here. He must have wiped it clean."

"Can you restore it?" Ananya's voice broke the silence, laced with hope.

The group looked at Vikram, their expressions mirroring her desperation.

"I'll try," he muttered, his fingers once again dancing over the keys. His jaw tightened, and the furrow in his brow deepened as he delved into the phone's encrypted files.

Meanwhile, Rakshith glanced at the clock, realizing he hadn't left the room all morning.

"What's the status of the team?" he asked, his tone clipped. "Anyone have matches lined up?"

Shika was the first to reply. "No matches for the next two days. A few of them are planning a trek."

"Shaurya and his friends are heading out to explore the city," Ananya added, her voice betraying a trace of worry.

"The coach and some others are off to play golf," Bhavin said, leaning back against the wall.

Ananya frowned. "We should stop them." Her voice was soft but resolute.

"That's easier said than done," Nithin sighed. "If everyone scatters, it'll be impossible to secure them. Not with the kind of threats we're dealing with."

Ananya bit her lip, her mind racing. After a moment, she straightened. "I have a plan."

The team turned to her, their eyes expectant.

She explained her idea in detail, her tone steady yet urgent. When she finished, a hush fell over the room. Slowly, one by one, they nodded. It wasn't a perfect solution, but they wanted to try it out.

With time running out, they sprang into action, each person determined to play their part.

The group was gathered in the recreational lounge of the hotel after breakfast. Sunlight streamed in through the glass walls, reflecting off the shiny floor and highlighting the playful banter echoing through the spacious room. Akshith, ever the charmer, lounged on the edge of a pool table, spinning a cue stick between his fingers, while Ananya stood with her arms folded near the foosball table, her sharp gaze fixed on him.

Shaurya sat on a nearby couch, leaning back casually, his watchful eyes bouncing between the two as a small smile played on his lips. Yuvaan occupied the beanbag next to Shaurya, sipping on a smoothie, while Bhavin and Nithin flanked Akshith like his hype squad.

"So, let me get this straight," Ananya began, her tone dripping with mock incredulity. "You think you're better than me because you've got a national team jersey?"

Akshith smirked, clearly enjoying her irritation. "I'm not saying that outright, but if the shoe fits..."

"The shoe doesn't fit," Ananya interrupted, stepping forward. "It's oversized and filled with delusions. Just because you swing a bat around doesn't mean you're better at everything."

"Swing a bat around?" Akshith echoed, feigning offense. "That's rich coming from someone whose job is to sit behind screens or ask questions to people, my dear devil!"

Nithin snickered. "She's got a point, Akshith. Strategy's her thing, and it takes more brains than swinging a bat."

Akshith rolled his eyes, retorting, "Oh, come on! Cricket is a game of strategy too! You think just anyone can pull off a last-over chase or set up a perfect field placement?"

"I'm not denying that," Ananya countered, her voice steady but challenging. "But I'd like to see you apply that supposed strategy in something off the pitch as you think you are Mr. 'I am perfect at everything'."

"Like what?" Akshith raised a brow.

"A quiz, maybe?" Yuvaan piped up, his grin mischievous. "Test his general knowledge. I'd love to see him fumble over capitals and presidents."

Akshith waved the suggestion off. "Too boring. I need something that requires real skill."

"Like badminton," Shaurya interjected smoothly, finally breaking his silence. He leaned forward, his tone calm but teasing. "It's fast, it's strategic, and it's not cricket—so you two can settle this fairly. Unless, of course, Akshith is too scared to take on Ananya in a sport outside his comfort zone."

Ananya's lips twitched, trying to suppress a victorious grin as she turned to Akshith. "Well? Scared?"

"Scared?" Akshith scoffed, his pride clearly at stake now. "Please. If anyone should be scared, it's you."

"Then prove it," Ananya said, her eyes gleaming. "Your team versus mine. Badminton. Unless you want to keep hiding behind that cricket bat of yours."

Bhavin nudged Akshith with a smirk. "Sounds like she's calling you out, man. Are you going to take that?"

Nithin chimed in, adding fuel to the fire. "C'mon, Akshith. You've been bragging all morning. Time to back it up."

Akshith straightened, his competitive streak kicking in. "Fine. Let's do it. But don't cry when we wipe the court with you."

Ananya chuckled, shaking her head. "You'd better bring your A-game, Akshith. I don't like playing with amateurs."

Yuvaan laughed outright, high-fiving Shaurya. "This is going to be legendary!"

Shaurya's eyes twinkled with quiet admiration as he watched Ananya hold her ground, her confidence lighting up the room. Leaning toward her, he murmured just loud enough for her to hear, "I am rooting for you, Ananya. I wish you win this,"

She glanced at him, her expression softening for a fraction of a second before she quipped, "Thank you, Shaurya. I will be waiting to see you there,"

The hotel's indoor badminton court had been hastily set up for the match, the polished wooden floors gleaming under the bright lights. Everyone except Vikram and Rakshith had gathered in the spacious area, their faces lit with excitement and anticipation. The sound of the shuttlecock whizzing through the air mixed with the occasional smack of the rackets.

Vikram and Rakshith were determined to get some information out of either the device they seized or from the man tied in the room while the rest of the team remained on high alert in the badminton court, searching for any threats.

Akshith had pleaded and argued for what seemed like an eternity, trying to convince his teammates to cancel their outdoor plans. He even went as far as claiming it would be "an insult to his talent" if they didn't show up to support him. His charm and persistence wore down their resistance, and soon enough, his team was gathered and ready for battle.

Yuvaan smirked as he watched Akshith jump around, full of energy. "Can't believe we're actually doing this. But it's fun to see you squirm, Akshith."

"You know I never lose," Akshith replied, grinning, his ego larger than life. "And don't get too cocky, you'll be in for a surprise." He added, looking at Ananya and Bhavin.

Ananya stood with Bhavin on the opposite side, checking her racket and eyeing Akshith with that quiet confidence that sent a thrill down Shaurya's spine. He leaned against the wall, arms crossed, a half-smile playing on his lips as he observed the tension building up.

As the teams prepared to face off, Akshith raised an eyebrow at Ananya. His voice was dripping with sarcasm. "You sure you're ready for this, Ananya? You should be on the mic, asking interview questions or something. Leave the sports to people who can actually play."

Ananya's lips quirked into a sly smile. "Don't worry, Akshith, I'm more than capable of handling a simple game. Maybe you should go easy on me; I wouldn't want you crying after losing."

"Crying?" Akshith scoffed, glancing at Yuvaan, "I'm worried for Bhavin here. He'll have to face two people, as you won't be helping him anyhow. I'm really sorry for him."

Bhavin raised an eyebrow and let out a low chuckle. "Oh, she's going to make you regret saying that."

Ananya could feel the competitive fire in the air, but she was already tuned into something else. She had been playing badminton since childhood, trained by none other than her father, a former world badminton champion. His stern lessons, mixed with moments of quiet joy between them, had shaped her skill. Little did Akshith know, she wasn't just some 'amateur'—she was a force to be reckoned with.

"Let's see if you can back up all that talk," Ananya said calmly, stepping up to the court with a poised confidence that had Shaurya raising an eyebrow.

The match began with a flurry of quick, fast-paced action. The shuttlecock zipped from one side to the other, with Akshith and Yuvaan taking the early lead. Bhavin's powerful smashes and Ananya's swift, strategic movements were still managing to keep up, but Akshith was relentless, his competitive streak shining through. He was clearly enjoying every moment of teasing Ananya.

"You sure you want to be here, Ananya?" Akshith called out, sending a particularly fast shuttle toward her. "You're looking a little out of your depth."

But the second the shuttlecock came her way, Ananya's reflexes kicked in. She didn't just return it—she slammed it back with an intensity that made everyone freeze for a split second.

Akshith's jaw nearly dropped. "What the—"

Ananya's eyes sparkled with the thrill of the game. "Keep up, Akshith." She smirked, sending the shuttle back over his head, where Yuvaan scrambled to reach it, failing to keep it in play.

Shaurya, watching from the sidelines, felt a sudden surge of admiration. He had always known Ananya was talented, but seeing her in action—her focus, her strength, and her effortless mastery of the game—left him speechless. His heart skipped a beat as she moved, graceful and powerful, her every shot landing with precision.

The match became more intense with every rally, and the spectators were absolutely captivated. Yuvaan could barely hide his disbelief at how easily Ananya moved across the court, her coordination flawless as she effortlessly placed each shot where Akshith couldn't reach. Bhavin, who had been playing mostly defensively, started to take more chances, trying to match Ananya's energy.

"This isn't just luck anymore," Yuvaan admitted, clearly in awe. "She's... incredible."

Shaurya stood there, his gaze fixed on Ananya as she returned yet another hard smash with cool confidence, leaving Akshith stunned at the speed of her movements. His heart seemed to tighten with an overwhelming admiration. Something was mesmerizing about the way she played, her concentration so sharp, her every move sending ripples of intensity across the court.

Akshith, now clearly rattled, tried to keep his cool. "Okay, okay. She's good. But we're not done yet."

Ananya shot him a playful grin. "Ready to surrender yet?"

"Not in your dreams," Akshith growled, but even he couldn't hide the trace of respect in his voice now.

As the match continued, Shaurya couldn't help but smile. He wasn't just mesmerized by Ananya's skills—he was proud. And he was more than happy to be the one standing by her side, watching her shine.

As the rally continued, Ananya's presence on the court became undeniable. The match had shifted in her favor, and Akshith was growing more and more frustrated with every point he lost. His team was beginning to lose their cocky edge, their smiles turning into uncertain glances as Ananya skillfully placed her shots, pushing them to their limits.

Bhavin, still trying to hold his own beside Ananya, shot her a quick grin. "You're amazing. Didn't expect this kind of fire from you after the long break."

Ananya smirked, her focus never wavering. "Maybe all the practice over years,"

"Yeah, that's the Ananya I know!" Bhavin laughed, his voice teasing but filled with admiration. "It's like watching a pro in action!"

Ananya's movements were fluid, her body perfectly in tune with the rhythm of the game. Her reflexes were lightning-fast, and her strategy was flawless. Akshith was struggling to keep up, his competitive nature pushing him to take bigger risks, but it wasn't enough.

"Come on, Akshith Bhai! Show us what you're really made of!" Siraj shouted, laughing as Akshith lunged for a shuttle that barely missed his reach.

But Akshith wasn't one to back down easily. He gritted his teeth and took a deep breath, then threw himself into the next rally with renewed determination. This time, he managed to outplay Bhavin, sending the shuttle flying toward Ananya.

Shaurya leaned in slightly, his eyes narrowing as he studied Ananya's body language. He could see the precise moment when Ananya's eyes flickered to the shuttle. She was ready, and for a second, the entire court seemed to hold its breath.

With a fluid movement, Ananya jumped and executed a near-perfect smash. The shuttle whizzed past Akshith, who barely had time to react before it landed, just out of reach.

The sound of it hitting the floor echoed through the court, and for a split second, everything was still.

Akshith stood frozen, his racket in mid-air, as the realization hit him—he had just been outplayed. His mouth parted in disbelief. "What the hell? How—?"

Ananya turned to him, a playful glint in her eyes, her lips curving into a grin. "That's what happens when you underestimate me."

Yuvaan burst into laughter beside her. "I told you she was going to kick your butt, Akshith. Looks like you've met your match!"

Shaurya watched from the sidelines, his admiration for Ananya only growing with each passing moment. He wasn't just amazed by her skill but by her poise—her ability to stay so calm under pressure, to carry herself with such grace. As she moved effortlessly around the court, her focus never wavering, he found himself more drawn to her than ever before.

When the match paused for a short break, Shaurya couldn't help himself. He made his way over to her side, his eyes never leaving her as she wiped the sweat from her brow with a towel.

"You're incredible, Ananya," he said, his voice soft yet sincere. "I don't think I've ever seen someone play like that."

Ananya met his gaze, her eyes filled with a mix of excitement and concentration. "Thanks, Shaurya. But we're not done yet. Don't make me arrogant with your praises," she teased, giving him a playful wink.

Shaurya grinned, leaning against the side of the court. "I wasn't praising you. Just... stating facts."

Yuvaan, standing next to him, nudged him with a grin. "You've been watching her like that the whole match. Should I be worried, bro?"

Shaurya shot him a side glance. "Focus on your own game, Yuvaan. We don't want you to end up like Akshith here, do we?"

Yuvaan laughed but turned back to the court with a renewed focus, sensing that the final rounds were about to get even more intense.

Meanwhile, Akshith was trying to shake off the shock of being so thoroughly outplayed. "Alright, alright, Ananya, I see you," he muttered, trying to regain his confidence. "But this isn't over yet."

Ananya's smile only widened, and she bent slightly to ready herself. "It's never over until it's over, Akshith. So, let's see what you've got left."

The game resumed, the tension rising with each powerful stroke. Bhavin, despite his impressive skills, found himself increasingly outmatched by Ananya's precision and agility. Yuvaan, though still full of his usual bravado, was beginning to see the undeniable truth: this match was Ananya's to win.

Shaurya couldn't tear his eyes away as Ananya executed another powerful shot, sending the shuttlecock hurtling over Akshith's head with a perfect arc. He was struck, once again, by the way her body moved—graceful, yet undeniably strong. It wasn't just her athleticism that mesmerized him. It was her spirit, her drive, her unyielding confidence.

Shaurya had always admired strength, but what he admired most in Ananya was her ability to shine in her own right, without any hesitation or second thoughts.

As the final point neared, Ananya looked over at Shaurya, catching his gaze. A small, secret smile tugged at her lips, and Shaurya felt a sudden flutter in his chest. At that moment, it wasn't just the badminton match that mattered—it was the connection, the unspoken understanding between them that felt even stronger than before.

As the game came to a close and the shuttle landed decisively, Akshith wiped the sweat from his brow, his lips twitching in frustration. His competitive spirit, usually unshakable, was clearly bruised. He looked at Ananya, still catching her breath, and raised an eyebrow with a playful smirk.

"So, tell me, Ananya," Akshith began, his voice dripping with mock suspicion, "were you hiding something? By any chance, were you a pro player? Did you just make me lose on purpose?"

Ananya's eyes sparkled with amusement as she wiped her forehead with a towel, playing along. "Oh, I'm just naturally gifted," she teased, a mischievous grin curving her lips. "Guess I just have it, you know?"

Akshith shook his head, still not entirely convinced. "Seriously, Ananya. I'm starting to think you've been hiding your true skills from us all this time. There's no way you're that good by accident."

Just as he spoke, Bhavin, who had been quietly observing the banter, couldn't resist chiming in. "Oh, you have no idea, Akshith." His voice was full of pride. "Ananya isn't just some random player—she's the daughter of one of the world's top badminton players back then."

Ananya's eyes flickered with a slight blush, but she didn't deny it. Akshith looked at her in disbelief. "Wait, what? You're the daughter of—?"

"Yup," Bhavin interrupted, grinning. "Her dad's a legend in the badminton world. She's got those genes. All that skill? It's in her blood."

Akshith's jaw dropped as he looked from Bhavin to Ananya, who simply shrugged with a sheepish smile. "Guess I've been playing with the wrong team all along."

"Yeah," Ananya chuckled, glancing at him playfully, "you might want to rethink your strategy next time."

"Unbelievable," Akshith muttered, shaking his head in awe. "I should've known there was more to you than just that microphone."

"I told you not to underestimate me," Ananya quipped with a wink.

As the group shared a laugh, Shaurya took a few steps closer to Ananya, his gaze softening as he looked at her. His usual teasing nature was gone, replaced with something more sincere. His eyes held admiration and something deeper—an undeniable fondness that he couldn't quite hide.

"You were incredible out there," he said, his voice quiet yet full of admiration. His words lingered between them, charged with an emotion that felt different from the usual camaraderie.

Ananya felt her heart flutter at the genuine warmth in his words. She looked up at him, smiling shyly. "Thanks, Shaurya," she said softly. "It felt good to play again."

Shaurya, unable to hide his grin, leaned in just a little closer. "You know," he began, his voice lower now, "I have to say, watching you play... I'm kind of glad I'm on your side."

Ananya's heart skipped a beat, her smile widening at his teasing yet endearing tone. "Oh, so now you're not worried about losing, huh?"

He chuckled, his gaze not leaving hers. "I never was. I'd rather lose with you on my side than win with anyone else."

There was a brief, sweet silence between them, the kind that felt full of unspoken promises. Ananya's cheeks flushed slightly, but she didn't look away. Shaurya was close enough now that she could almost feel the warmth of his presence, his words hanging in the air, wrapped in something deeper.

"So, what happens now?" Ananya asked, her voice quiet but with a playful edge as if the playful banter had shifted into something more personal.

Shaurya grinned, his eyes sparkling with a mix of warmth and mischief. "Now?" He took a step back, winking at her. "Now we celebrate. But just so you know, Ananya, you owe me a match. Just us,"

She raised an eyebrow, a glint of challenge in her eyes. "You sure about that? I don't think you're ready for a match with me."

"You'd be surprised. I am waiting to have a match with you," Shaurya replied, his voice teasing but filled with that same earnestness that had been there all along.

As they shared a moment of quiet laughter, their bond seemed to strengthen, their connection becoming more tangible with every word and glance. The tension of the game had faded, replaced by a sweet, lingering energy that felt like the beginning of something more.

CHAPTER FOURTEEN

After the electrifying badminton match that had the players laughing and joking about their performances, the mood shifted as they retired to their suites. Outside the players' rooms, the officers subtly blended into the hotel staff, their keen eyes scanning every movement, every shadow, ensuring the safety of their charges.

Meanwhile, in a dimly lit, soundproof room on the hotel's lower floor, the air reeked of sweat and fear. A man sat bound to a steel chair, his face battered, his breathing ragged. Dried blood caked the corner of his mouth, and his eyes darted around the room, pleading for mercy he would never receive.

The door creaked open, and Bhavin entered, his gaze sharp as he quickly scanned the surroundings before locking it behind him. He turned to the team huddled near the prisoner. "Did he spill anything?" he asked, his voice low and cold.

Rakshith stepped forward, his silhouette imposing under the dim, flickering light. "Not yet," he replied, his tone calm but laced with a quiet menace. Rolling his sleeves up, he approached the prisoner with slow, deliberate steps. "But he will," he added, his confidence chilling.

Ananya stood to the side, her arms crossed, her expression a perfect mask of professionalism, though her mind raced with the stakes of their mission. Her sharp eyes turned to Vikram, who was pacing near a laptop. "Any leads from the phone?" she asked, a slight edge of urgency in her tone.

"Nothing solid," Vikram said, cracking his knuckles in frustration. "Clean as if someone scrubbed it professionally."

The room fell into a tense silence, broken only by the whirring of the ceiling fan and the prisoner's labored breathing. Then, Rakshith struck. The prisoner's scream tore through the air as Rakshith applied precise pressure to his dislocated shoulder, sending a fresh wave of pain coursing through his body. "We're done playing games," Rakshith hissed, leaning in close. "Talk, or I'll make sure you never use that arm again."

The man's cries grew desperate, but the officers remained stone-faced, their resolve unshaken.

Ananya leaned against the wall, her gaze unwavering. "He's close to breaking," she muttered to Bhavin, who nodded grimly. The room was a pressure cooker, and the timer was about to hit zero.

"I... I'll say!" The man's voice cracked, his resolve shattered after hours of relentless torture. His body sagged against the chair, every muscle trembling from exhaustion and pain.

Rakshith crouched in front of him, his fingers digging mercilessly into the man's hair as he yanked his head up. The man whimpered, tears streaking his bruised face. "Bark," Rakshith ordered coldly, his expression a mask of steel.

"They... They're planning to kidnap the coach today," the man stammered, his voice raw from screaming. "They forced the chef to help them!" His words tumbled out in a desperate rush as he winced at the sharp pull on his scalp.

For a moment, the room was deathly quiet, the team exchanging tense glances as they processed the revelation. The only sound was the man's ragged breathing and the faint buzz of the fluorescent light above them.

"How is the chef supposed to help them?" Rakshith's voice broke the silence, sharp and unyielding. His gaze bore into the prisoner, demanding answers.

The man hesitated, his lips trembling as he glanced between the officers. That brief moment of silence was enough to ignite Bhavin's simmering frustration. Without warning, Bhavin stepped forward and delivered a resounding slap across the man's face. The force sent the chair screeching back a few inches, the sound jarring in the enclosed space.

"We don't have all day to entertain your games," Bhavin snapped, his voice like the crack of a whip. He leaned in, his glare piercing and unrelenting. "Now bark. Or you won't like what comes next."

The man's resolve crumbled further, his body visibly shaking. "He... He's going to add something to the food," he blurted out, tears streaming down his cheeks. "Something meant for the players... tonight's dinner!"

His voice broke into pleas, begging for release, but his words were drowned out by the officers' focused determination. The team exchanged grim nods before stepping out of the room, their boots echoing ominously against the tiled floor.

Ananya paused by the door, her hand lingering on the lock. She glanced back at the prisoner, her gaze icy. "You've earned yourself a longer stay," she said flatly before turning the key with a decisive click. The sound of the lock engaging was final, a reminder that his fate was no longer in his own hands.

Outside, the team huddled together, their expressions grim but resolute. "We need to find that chef now," Ananya said, her voice sharp with urgency. "And we need to secure the players before this gets out of hand."

The officers reconvened in Ananya's room, the air thick with urgency. Ananya's hands moved swiftly over her phone as she dialed Mr. Kulkarni, their superior. The rest of the team gathered around her, their faces set with grim determination.

After briefing Mr. Kulkarni on the situation, Ananya turned to her team. "We're going to need full cooperation from the hotel staff. No delays, no excuses," she said firmly. Her words carried the weight of command, and everyone nodded in agreement.

The hotel manager's resistance was expected but short-lived. A single warning from Vikram had him relenting, his tone shifting from outrage to begrudging compliance. The team wasted no time assembling the chefs in one of the hotel's meeting rooms.

Inside the room, a dozen chefs stood in uneasy silence, their starched uniforms now feeling like straight jackets under the officers' watchful eyes. Ananya and Vikram stood at the head of the room, their expressions impenetrable.

"We'll speak to you all one by one," Ananya announced, her voice calm yet authoritative. "Please cooperate fully. The safety of lives depends on it."

The officers began their interrogations. One by one, the chefs were called into an adjoining room. Outside, the rest waited, their nervous glances betraying their unease. Meanwhile, police teams had been dispatched to check on the families of the chefs, a crucial step in unraveling the kidnappers' leverage.

Finally, it was Mr. Ahuja's turn. The man in his 50s shuffled into the room, his demeanor nervous despite his attempts at bravado. He sat down, his hands fidgeting as Vikram leaned forward, his gaze unyielding.

"Mr. Ahuja, what are you planning to add to tonight's dinner for the players?" Vikram asked bluntly. His tone was sharp, slicing through the chef's attempt at composure.

"What will I add? I don't know what you're talking about," Mr. Ahuja replied, his voice defensive, though a slight tremor betrayed his fear.

Ananya stepped closer, her presence steady and grounding. "Mr. Ahuja," she began, her voice softer yet no less firm. "We know you've been threatened. We're here to help. But we need you to trust us and tell us the truth."

The chef's eyes darted nervously, sweat beading at his temples. "I... I don't know what you mean," he stammered, but the slight quiver in his tone didn't escape their notice.

"Anchal is your daughter, isn't she?" Vikram's question landed like a thunderclap. Mr. Ahuja froze, his face draining of color.

He nodded slowly, his lips trembling as his facade began to crumble. "Y-yes," he whispered, his voice barely audible.

Vikram didn't pause. "We know she's been kidnapped. We also know they've threatened you to tamper with the players' food."

At those words, the man broke. He clutched his head in his hands, his shoulders shaking as sobs racked his body. "They'll kill my Gudiya if I don't do as they say," he cried, the anguish in his voice cutting through even the hardened resolve of the officers.

Ananya knelt beside him, her hand resting gently on his shoulder. "We'll get her back," she promised, her voice steady and resolute. "But we need you to work with us. Trust us to protect her."

Tears streamed down Mr. Ahuja's face as he nodded, the image of his battered daughter flashing in his mind. The kidnappers had sent him a video—a cruel display of her suffering to ensure his compliance.

"They told me to mix something in their food... some kind of sedative," he confessed, his voice trembling.

"Good. That's all we need for now," Ananya said, handing him a glass of water. "You'll go back to your station and act normal. Don't let on that anything is wrong. We'll take care of the rest."

Vikram added sternly, "And don't breathe a word of this to anyone. Not a soul."

Once the interrogation was complete, Mr. Ahuja was escorted back to the kitchen, his steps heavier but steadier now, bolstered by the officers' assurances.

As the chefs were dismissed, the team regrouped, their expressions a mix of determination and empathy. "We've got a lead," Ananya said, her eyes meeting Vikram's. "Now let's make sure it counts."

The stakes had never been higher, but they were ready. The clock was ticking, and failure was not an option.

"Shika, keep a close watch on Mr. Ahuja. Monitor his every move and anyone who interacts with him," Rakshith commanded, his tone sharp and unwavering. Shika nodded briskly, her focus immediately shifting to the task at hand as she left the room.

"Nithin, the surveillance room is yours. I want eyes on every corridor, every entrance, and every exit. No blind spots," he continued, turning to Nithin.

"Understood," Nithin replied, determination flickering in his eyes. He headed straight for the surveillance room, his mind already mapping out the camera angles to prioritize.

"Ananya, coordinate with the local police. Get a discreet team assigned to handle Anchal's matter. We don't want to tip anyone off," Vikram instructed, his voice steady yet urgent.

Ananya nodded, pulling out her phone with swift efficiency. Within moments, she was on the line, issuing orders to ensure Anchal's rescue operation was underway without compromising the larger mission.

Rakshith's gaze swept over his team, his jaw tightening. "Today is the day. We either stop them here, or we risk losing the coach—and who knows what else."

"Can't we shift Mr. Mishra somewhere safe before the kidnappers arrive?" Bhavin asked, his tone genuinely curious.

"That's risky. If they are planning to take him today, they must be keeping a watch on the hotel right now. One wrong move and they will wreak havoc. If the situation seems to go out of hands, we will shift him to the guest house. Make arrangements for that too," Rakshith explained, his jaw ticking in determination.

"Failure isn't an option." Bhavin said, his voice firm, his words aligning with the resolve in the room.

" Let's hope we don't need to blow our cover today," Ananya added.

The four of them regrouped in Rakshith's suite, the walls now covered with a map of the hotel, blueprints, and surveillance screenshots. Each of them scanned the plans meticulously, their sharp minds identifying weak spots and potential vulnerabilities.

"Hidden exits here and here," Ananya pointed at the map, her finger tapping on service doors that led to the back alley.

"They'll likely use one of these if things go south," Bhavin added, marking escape routes that fed into the city's busiest areas.

"They'll need a quick getaway. Have the local police secure these routes without being too conspicuous," Rakshith said, glancing at Vikram.

"Already on it," Vikram replied, sending out a series of encrypted messages.

The local police mobilized swiftly under their instructions. Bus stations, railway terminals, and the airport came under discreet surveillance. Checkpoints were quietly established on all major roads leading out of the city. Officers in plain clothes blended seamlessly with civilians, their eyes scanning for any suspicious activity.

Meanwhile, back at the hotel, Ananya's phone buzzed with updates from the team handling Anchal's case. "They've located her," she announced, her voice steady but tinged with relief.

"Condition?" Vikram asked immediately.

"Stable, but she's still being held. The kidnappers are staying put for now, likely waiting for confirmation of the coach's capture before making their move," Ananya replied, her brows furrowed.

"Good. Tell them to maintain surveillance but hold off on the rescue until we secure the coach. We need to coordinate both operations perfectly," Rakshith instructed.

The team worked like clockwork, refining their strategy with precision. They knew the terrorists would be watching for any misstep, any indication that their plans had been discovered.

As the clock ticked closer to dinner service, tension filled the air. Rakshith stood by the window, his gaze fixed on the bustling city below. "They think they have the upper hand," he murmured, a determined glint in his eyes.

"But they don't know who they're up against," Ananya finished, her voice filled with quiet confidence.

The stage was set, the pieces in place. All they had to do now was wait—and strike when the moment was right.

"They shouldn't leave this hotel today," Vikram said firmly, his voice carrying a sharp edge of resolve. The others nodded in agreement, their faces shadowed with determination.

As the evening deepened and the sky turned an inky black, the hotel's atmosphere seemed untouched by the tension simmering beneath. The players, blissfully unaware of the lurking danger, mingled in the dining hall, their laughter and chatter blending with the soft clinking of cutlery. Guests wandered through the lobby, some heading to the lounge, while others enjoyed the live music echoing gently through the corridors.

In the heart of the action, the kitchen staff bustled about, appearing busy but keeping a sharp ear out for any unusual commands. The officers stationed throughout the hotel adopted an air of nonchalance, masking their vigilance with casual body language and polite smiles.

The real work began soon after the players vacated their rooms for dinner. Moving with precision, the officers quietly entered each suite, conducting a meticulous sweep. Every nook, every corner, every piece of furniture was examined for hidden devices or signs of tampering. Rakshith's sharp gaze lingered on a suspiciously misplaced pillow before discarding it as harmless.

Bhavin kept watch outside the corridors, alert for any unexpected movement. His hand hovered near his concealed weapon, ready to act at the faintest hint of trouble.

Ananya worked methodically, her mind ticking through a mental checklist as she ensured the rooms were free from danger. The gravity of the situation weighed heavily on her, but she pushed it aside to focus on the task.

"Clear," she whispered into her communicator as she slipped out of a room, closing the door softly behind her.

Each officer completed their sweep in silence, their footsteps light against the carpeted floors. By the time the players returned to their suites after dinner, there was no trace of the intrusion.

The officers regrouped discreetly in a designated spot, exchanging brief nods as they confirmed that everything was in order. From the outside, they seemed to blend seamlessly into the bustling activity of the hotel, but beneath their calm exteriors, they were ready to pounce at the first sign of a threat.

The night was far from over, and as they joined the crowd, their resolve only deepened. This wasn't just another operation—it was a fight to ensure that no harm came to those under their protection.

"Shaurya," Ananya called softly, her voice hesitant but firm as she spotted him strolling casually in the lobby, his eyes fixed on his phone.

"Hmm?" Shaurya looked up, raising an eyebrow as a playful grin curved his lips. His relaxed demeanor momentarily eased the tension in her chest.

"We won't be able to meet tonight," she informed him, her teeth catching her lower lip as she braced for his reaction. Her heart sank a little at the thought of disappointing him, but she couldn't risk him wandering out of his room during the operation.

"Why is that?" he asked, folding his arms over his chest. The slight furrow of his brow and the way his lips pressed into a thin line betrayed his displeasure.

"Shika isn't feeling well," she explained, her voice faltering slightly as she tried to make it sound natural. "So I'll need to take care of her tonight."

Shaurya stared at her for a moment, his intense gaze making her shift uncomfortably. Then, with a resigned sigh, he nodded. "Alright. But," he added, his expression softening into a mischievous smirk, "you better make up for it."

Ananya couldn't help but chuckle, relief washing over her at his understanding. "I will," she promised, her voice light but sincere.

"Good." With that, Shaurya reached out and pinched her cheek playfully, the unexpected gesture sending a warm flush across her face. His laughter rang softly as he turned toward the elevator, leaving her standing there, cheeks tinted and lips curved in an involuntary smile.

She watched him until he stepped into the elevator, his casual wave disappearing as the doors slid shut. The moment he was gone, her smile faded, replaced by the weight of responsibility that pressed heavily on her shoulders.

Straightening her posture, Ananya inhaled deeply, willing the calm Shaurya's presence brought her to linger a little longer. But reality crept in fast, and she steeled herself, her mind returning to the mission ahead. There was no room for distraction tonight, no matter how much she longed for just a little more time with him.

As the night wore on, a thick tension hung in the air. The hotel, once bustling with laughter and activity, now felt eerily still. The only sounds that echoed through the dark hallways were the distant footsteps of late-night guests and the hum of the security systems—until, without warning, it all went dark. The lights blinked off one by one, plunging the entire building into a suffocating silence. The generators sputtered, and soon the hum of electricity ceased entirely.

Ananya's breath caught in her throat as the sudden blackout enveloped the hotel. It wasn't just the lights that went out—it was everything. The cameras monitoring every inch of the building flickered and died, leaving the team blind in the darkness. In a fraction of a second, the entire world felt like it had gone to sleep, but not for the team.

In the deafening silence, Bhavin's voice came through their Bluetooth, steady and focused. "I guess they're here."

Ananya's pulse quickened as she exchanged a glance with Vikram. His lips were pressed together in a thin line, his eyes scanning the pitch-black hallway with a sharp focus. The mission had officially entered its most dangerous phase.

"Stay focused," Rakshith's voice came through the comms, low but urgent. "We've got to act fast."

The sound of footsteps echoing through the halls was deafening as the attackers, now emboldened by the darkness, moved through the hotel, unaware of the traps set in place by the officers. The team's coordination was flawless, a well-oiled machine that had been working towards this moment for days.

In a split second, the officers leaped into action. Bhavin, with a quick hand movement, signaled the others, and within moments, the first two kidnappers were taken down. Their bodies hit the ground with muffled thuds as the team expertly dragged them into a nearby utility closet, their movements swift and silent. The power may have gone out, but the team's training never did.

Despite the two attackers being neutralized, the challenge had just begun. As the hotel's power outage threw the building into disarray, the guests—unaware of the situation—began to spill out of their rooms, curiously and unknowingly stepping into the path of danger. The once-quiet hallways soon began to fill with the soft murmur of confused voices. The last thing the team needed was civilians getting caught in the crossfire.

"Ananya, Vikram," Rakshith's voice cut through the chaos, "Go and check on the coach. Stay with him. Get him out of here. The attackers are more in number and we can't risk losing Mr. Mishra," His tone was clipped, and professional, and Ananya didn't hesitate. She shot Vikram a nod, and together, they moved swiftly into the shadows, their footsteps muffled by the plush carpeting beneath them.

The hotel's dim emergency lights barely illuminated the corridor as they approached the coach's suite. Ananya's heart beat faster with each step. They couldn't afford any mistakes tonight—not after everything that had been set into motion. The stakes were too high. The plan had to succeed.

Ananya paused at the door, her hand hovering just above the handle as she signaled for Vikram to check the area first. He nodded and, with the speed of a shadow, moved down the hallway, disappearing into the darkness. Ananya remained still, every muscle in her body tense, her senses heightened. She could hear the faint sounds of people moving in their rooms, unaware of the chaos happening just beyond their door.

"All clear," Vikram whispered through the Bluetooth, his voice like a ghost in the night. Ananya exhaled softly, relieved but not yet comfortable. There was still so much that could go wrong.

Ananya's mind raced. Their mission had gone from covert operation to imminent danger in a heartbeat. They had to get the coach to safety before the kidnappers realized what was happening. And the coach—he had no idea what was going on. He was just a celebrity, unaware of the deadly game unfolding around him. The officers were about to break the news to him, but once they did, there would be no turning back.

Without a word, Ananya turned the handle and slipped into the coach's suite. The room was dark, save for the emergency lights flickering on the edges of the furniture. The coach sat at his desk, oblivious to the impending danger as he flipped through papers. He hadn't noticed the team's arrival. Ananya's heartbeat quickened as she scanned the room, every inch of it, searching for any signs of movement, any indication that the kidnappers had gotten to him first.

"Coach," Vikram spoke up, his voice steady but low enough to not draw attention.

The coach jumped, startled by the unexpected voices, but quickly relaxed when he saw who it was. "What's going on? Why is the power out? And why are you two in my room?"

Ananya stepped into the room, her voice calm but firm. "Coach, I need you to listen carefully. What I'm about to tell you isn't easy, but you must understand. You're in danger, and we're here to protect you."

The coach blinked, clearly confused. "Danger? What are you talking about? I thought you were reporters, working on the documentary about the players."

Vikram, standing slightly to the side, stepped forward. "We are reporters, but we're also part of a special team. Our job isn't just to document your life—it's to ensure your safety. We've been assigned to protect you because there's a threat against your life tonight."

The words hit the coach like a sledgehammer. He blinked, his mind struggling to process what he was hearing. His hands trembled slightly as he set down the papers.

"Threat? What are you talking about?" His voice wavered slightly, the hint of panic seeping through.

Ananya approached him, her tone steady but filled with urgency. "There's a group of men here who plan to kidnap you. We don't have much time. We need to get you out of here, Coach, and we need to move quickly."

The room seemed to tilt around the coach as the truth began to settle in. He stared at Ananya and Vikram, disbelief etched across his face. "Kidnappers?" he repeated, his voice hoarse. "But why me? What do they want?"

Vikram exchanged a glance with Ananya before stepping forward, his eyes narrowing slightly. "We'll explain everything later. Come with us for now."

The coach's jaw tightened as he processed the information, his mind racing. He hadn't signed up for anything like this. He had been told it was just a documentary—an opportunity to show the world the behind-the-scenes life of a cricketer. The idea that he was now the target of a kidnapping plot seemed almost unreal.

"I don't understand," he murmured, running a hand through his hair. "This isn't supposed to be happening. This is all... so much."

Ananya's gaze softened for a moment before she steeled herself again. "We understand that this is overwhelming, sir. But there's no time to explain everything right now. We need to move. If we don't get you out of here now, it'll be too late. You'll be right in the middle of their plans."

Vikram stepped in, his voice firm but comforting. "We have a plan, but we need your cooperation. There are police officers outside, and they're going to help guide us through the safest route. All you have to do is stay close to us, and don't make a sound. You won't be in any danger as long as you follow our instructions."

The coach looked at both of them, his face pale but his eyes steady. "I trust you both. Just... tell me what to do."

Ananya gave a tight nod and moved toward the door, signaling for Vikram to follow her. They couldn't afford to waste another second. "Good. We're getting you out of here. Stick to us, and don't look back."

The trio moved quickly but quietly down the hallway, the weight of their task hanging heavy in the air. Every creak of the floorboards underfoot seemed magnified in the silence. Ananya's senses were heightened, and her body was trained to anticipate every possible threat. The stakes had never been higher.

Outside, the hotel had descended into chaos. The blackout had thrown everyone into disarray, and people were beginning to spill out of their rooms, unsure of what was happening but curious nonetheless. The attackers were scattered through the building, and the officers were working hard to keep the situation under control.

Bhavin's voice crackled in Ananya's earpiece. "We've neutralized two of the attackers, but we still have more to deal with. Stay sharp, and keep moving. We'll cover you."

Ananya's heart raced. The coach was too important to risk. She had to keep him focused, keep him moving. She reached for his arm and guided him swiftly through the hallway, her eyes scanning every shadow, every corner. Vikram was on high alert, flanking them as they navigated the maze-like corridors.

It was as though the walls themselves were closing in. But despite the danger, Ananya's training kicked in. She knew exactly what to do, and more importantly, she knew how to keep the coach calm.

They reached the stairwell, the final checkpoint before they could reach the designated exit. Ananya glanced at Vikram, and then at the coach. "We're almost there, Coach. Just a little further. Stay close, and don't make a sound. We'll be out of here in no time."

Just then, a door at the end of the hallway creaked open. Ananya's heart stopped. She froze, her eyes locking on the figure that had just stepped into the hallway—one of the kidnappers.

The man was tall, dressed in black, and his eyes were scanning the darkness, clearly looking for anyone out of place.

Ananya's hand instinctively went to her stun gun, her fingers tightening around it.

The coach's eyes widened in fear as he noticed the man too, but before he could make a sound, Ananya grabbed his arm, pulling him behind a corner.

Vikram's hand shot out, signaling for silence. They needed to be quick.

The attacker stepped closer, and Ananya's pulse raced as she counted the seconds. It was too close. They had no choice but to move.

"On my count," she whispered. "One, two..."

"Three."

The moment Ananya gave the signal, she sprang into action. She grabbed the coach's arm and yanked him swiftly around the corner. The move was calculated, and precise—there was no time to hesitate. The kidnapper was only a few steps away, and every breath they took seemed to echo in the tension-filled hallway.

Vikram was right behind them, his hand already on the stun gun at his belt, ready to incapacitate the enemy if necessary. But Ananya's mind was working quickly—there had to be a way out without alerting anyone else.

She pushed the coach against the wall, her body positioned between him and the kidnapper. Her breath was shallow, her heart pounding in her ears, but her focus was sharp. She listened intently, waiting for the sound of the attacker's footsteps to draw nearer, waiting for the perfect moment.

The kidnapper was just two feet away now. He stopped, sensing something was off. He paused, his head tilted slightly, scanning the hall. Ananya held her breath, praying he wouldn't hear the rapid thumping of her heart.

But Vikram was ready. He moved in behind the kidnapper, and in a fluid motion, he reached out, wrapping his arm around the man's neck. The kidnapper let out a startled gasp, but it was too late. Vikram applied pressure, locking the man in a chokehold that sent him to the ground in a matter of seconds.

Ananya's pulse raced as she gave Vikram a quick nod. "Nice work. Let's move."

The coach looked at them, wide-eyed, his face pale with fear. "What was that? Who was he?"

Ananya didn't stop to answer him. "Not now, Coach. We need to get you out of here—right now."

They moved swiftly through the hotel, silent and steady, sticking to the shadows, avoiding any other potential threats. Ananya kept glancing behind them, her mind scanning the surroundings, looking for any sign of movement. They couldn't afford to be ambushed, not now when they were so close to the exit.

They made their way to the rear service entrance of the hotel. The door was slightly ajar, a signal from the backup team that the way was clear. Ananya gestured for the coach to follow her, and they moved quickly through the darkened back hallways, passing the deserted kitchen and storage areas. The smell of cold food and cleaning supplies filled the air, but there was no time to notice the details.

The sound of shuffling footsteps echoed faintly from the front of the building, and Ananya's heart skipped a beat. The attackers were moving, and they were closing in fast. It was a race now—a race to get to the secure vehicle parked outside and away from the hotel before the kidnappers figured out what had just happened.

They reached the service entrance, and Vikram held the door open for them. Ananya led the coach out into the cool night air. The city was dark, the streetlights casting long, dim shadows along the deserted road.

Ananya's pulse quickened. They were so close. They had to make sure the coach got to the van before the kidnappers could close in on them.

The coach, though startled, kept up with their pace. "Are you sure?" he asked, his voice laced with disbelief.

Ananya didn't have time to reassure him. "No time for doubts. Move!"

They reached the kitchen's back exit, where the rear service door was already open, ready for them to slip out undetected. Shika appeared from the shadows, her stance poised and calm, her gun ready, just in case.

"Coach," she said quietly, "Go to the van. Nithin's already got the route mapped out. Police are waiting for you. We'll keep you safe."

Nithin, his voice clear over the comms, spoke directly to Shika. "I've got eyes on the van. It's clear, but hurry. They're getting closer."

The coach hesitated, his fear still evident, but something in Shika's unwavering confidence seemed to calm him. He nodded, trusting her words. "Alright. I'll go with you."

The team watched as the coach made his way toward the van, the sound of his footsteps echoing in the now-empty corridor. Ananya and Vikram remained on high alert, their eyes scanning the space around them.

"Shika, Nithin, you two keep moving. Don't let the coach out of sight," Rakshith commanded through Bluetooth, his voice a low rumble of authority.

"On it," Shika replied, her eyes locked on the coach as he disappeared into the darkness, making his way to safety.

But their work wasn't done. Ananya, Vikram, Shika, and Nithin had to return to the hotel. The attackers were still inside, and they needed to take them down before they could make another move.

The team split up again. Ananya and Vikram went one direction while Shika and Nithin took another. The hotel's corridors were still eerily quiet, but they could feel the tension creeping up on them like an impending storm.

Shika and Nithin moved swiftly, their eyes darting around as they reached the stairwell. The attackers had begun searching the floors, creeping into rooms. A muffled shout came from one of the hallways—an attacker had just found a cricketer. The hunt had begun.

"Shika, Nithin, get to the fourth floor. I'll go up to the fifth," Vikram's voice echoed in their ears, calm but laced with urgency.

"Roger that," Shika said. "Keep an eye out, Nithin. We don't want any surprises."

They reached the fourth floor, and before Shika could move further, a figure appeared at the end of the hall. The attacker's eyes locked on them. Shika was ready. She swiftly ducked behind a pillar, motioning for Nithin to stay low.

Nithin crouched, eyes never leaving the attacker. His fingers gripped his stun gun tightly. Shika stayed silent, holding her breath, waiting for the perfect moment to strike.

The attacker came closer, oblivious to the trap set for him. He took one more step forward, and with a fluid motion, Shika emerged from the shadows. In one smooth movement, she knocked the stun gun from his hand and brought him down in a single, swift motion.

Nithin moved to secure the attacker, tying him up before he could recover.

"That's another one down," Shika said, exhaling slowly as she surveyed the surroundings. "We're almost done here. Keep moving."

The night had descended into chaos. The power had been cut, the emergency lights flickered weakly, and every shadow in the hotel seemed to hold a hidden threat. The tension was palpable, and the officers had become one with the darkness, blending in, ready to strike. There was no more room for mistakes.

The team was in position: Rakshith, Bhavin, Ananya, Shika, Nithin, and Vikram. Six highly trained individuals who had come together to face a common enemy. The mastermind of the kidnapping plot was still in play, but they were closing in on him. Every moment counted.

Ananya's breath was steady, her hand tight around the stun gun. She moved with purpose, her mind focused, her thoughts sharp. There was no hesitation in her now. The mission wasn't just about rescuing the coach anymore. It was about stopping a far-reaching criminal network that had infiltrated every part of the city.

"Vikram, Bhavin, you two take the east corridor. We'll handle the west," Rakshith's voice crackled through their earpieces, the command sharp and clear.

Ananya, Shika, and Nithin had already positioned themselves in the west wing of the hotel. The hallway was eerily silent, the only sound the soft thud of their footsteps. As they rounded the corner, the sound of a door creaking open caught their attention. It was the coach's suite.

"That's our cue," Ananya whispered, signaling for the others to fall in line.

Shika and Nithin followed closely behind her as they approached the door. Ananya glanced at Nithin, who gave her a quick nod. They had done this countless times before—no room for mistakes.

But as they neared the door, it suddenly slammed shut. Panic surged through Ananya's chest, but she fought it back, her mind racing. The mastermind had to be in there.

"Stay alert," she whispered to the team, motioning for them to move back into the shadows.

In the blink of an eye, the door opened again, and a figure stepped out. Tall, cloaked in black, with a sinister aura. The man. The mastermind.

Ananya's grip on her stun gun tightened. This was it.

"I see you've found me," the man's voice was smooth, filled with confidence. He didn't even flinch when he saw them.

"I'm not here to chat," Ananya shot back, her tone icy. "You're coming with us."

Before she could move, the man snapped his fingers. Two of his henchmen appeared, each armed and ready for a fight. The atmosphere shifted instantly, the air thick with the tension of a coming battle.

"Take them out," the mastermind commanded.

Without warning, the henchmen opened fire. Bullets whizzed past Ananya, who dove behind a pillar for cover. Shika and Nithin followed her instinctively, their bodies reacting faster than their minds.

"We need backup!" Shika's voice rang through the comms.

"On it," Rakshith's voice came through immediately. "Stay put, we'll be there in seconds."

The sounds of chaos erupted in the hallway, but Ananya remained focused. Her heart pounded, but she wasn't afraid. She'd been trained for moments like this.

The henchmen charged, guns blazing, but they hadn't expected Ananya's team to be so prepared. As the attackers advanced, Rakshith and Bhavin emerged from the opposite side, moving with the precision of a well-oiled machine. Bhavin took out one of the henchmen with a stun gun before the man even had a chance to react. Rakshith, with his signature calm and lethal demeanor, took down the other with a well-aimed shot, leaving the mastermind alone.

"You're surrounded," Ananya said, stepping forward with authority, her eyes locked on the mastermind.

The man, undeterred, pulled out a knife, a cruel grin curling on his lips. He swung it toward Ananya in a swift, calculated motion. But she was ready. She ducked under the blade, using her agility to get in close. With a swift motion, she jabbed the stun gun into his side, sending a surge of electricity coursing through his body.

The mastermind collapsed to the floor, twitching, unconscious.

"Nice work," Vikram's voice came through, his presence now behind them.

But there was no time to celebrate. The hotel was still swarming with attackers, and Ananya knew they couldn't rest until every last one was dealt with.

"Rakshith, what's the status?" she asked, already moving toward the next task.

"All clear on this side. We'll clear out the rest of the hotel," Rakshith responded, his voice calm but full of determination.

"Shika, Nithin, take the west wing. I'll cover the east with Vikram," Bhavin commanded, stepping toward the central lobby.

Ananya nodded, giving Shika a brief, reassuring look. They had come this far together, and they would finish it together.

They moved quickly, checking rooms and hallways, taking down any remaining attackers. The hotel that had once been filled with music, laughter, and celebration was now eerily quiet. The only sounds left were the occasional thud as an attacker fell, taken down by one of the officers.

With the last of the attackers incapacitated and the hotel secured, the team reconvened in the lobby. Their eyes met—tired but victorious. They had done it.

"Mission complete," Rakshith said, the smallest of smiles tugging at the corner of his lips.

Ananya couldn't help but exhale in relief. The adrenaline had drained from her body, leaving her feeling light-headed, but she was proud. They had protected the coach, taken down the kidnappers, and dismantled a dangerous network.

The subdued attackers were swiftly dragged into the staff quarters, a secluded area dimly lit and shadowed by years of neglect—a perfect spot for holding their captives without drawing attention. The officers had chosen this location deliberately, knowing the chaos of the operation required a fallback space for contingencies. The attackers' faces were covered with cloths, muffling their curses and groans. Their hands and legs were tightly bound, leaving no room for escape.

Ananya's sharp gaze swept over the scene, her mind already racing with the next steps. "We have to keep them restrained," she resolved, her voice steady despite the adrenaline coursing through her veins. "We can't afford any mistakes now."

Rakshith and Bhavin exchanged nods before taking positions by the door, weapons ready, their senses heightened. Shika and Nithin began inspecting the subdued men for concealed weapons or clues about their motives. Meanwhile, Vikram crouched near the attackers, scanning their expressions for any sign of defiance or fear.

Ananya stepped away from the group and raised the encrypted communication device to her lips. The familiar static of the secure line crackled before Mr. Kulkarni's composed voice came through.

"Sir, the operation is a success," Ananya reported, her tone clipped but professional. "The coach has been safely escorted to the van. The attackers are in our custody."

There was a pause on the other end before Kulkarni replied, his voice carrying the weight of authority. "Good work, Ananya. Now listen carefully. Ensure the handover to the local police is executed without drawing attention. The secrecy of this operation is paramount. We need to stay invisible. Your team remains on high alert until we extract a confession from these men. Is that clear?"

"Understood, sir," Ananya said, her resolve firm as she disconnected.

She turned back to her team, her expression grim. "Kulkarni sir wants us to stay alert until we get confessions from these guys. No one drops their guard."

"What's the plan for the handover?" Vikram asked, his voice low but urgent.

"We'll use the service elevator to move them out," Rakshith explained. "Shika, Nithin, and Bhavin will cover the route to the loading dock. Ananya and Vikram, you're with me. We'll oversee the transfer."

The team nodded in unison, their trust in each other unshaken.

As the minutes ticked by, the officers executed their plan with precision. Shika led the way, her keen eyes scanning for any movement in the hotel's dimly lit back corridors. Nithin and Bhavin followed closely, dragging the attackers behind them, their movements calculated to avoid creating any noise that might draw attention.

Rakshith and Vikram brought up the rear, their senses attuned to every creak and shadow. Ananya walked alongside them, her mind a mix of calculated focus and unyielding determination.

The loading dock was eerily quiet, the only sounds coming from the distant hum of traffic outside. A nondescript van waited in the shadows, its engine idling softly. Two plainclothes officers from the local police stood by, their faces obscured by caps pulled low.

"Transfer them quickly," Vikram instructed. "And remember, this never happened. No records, no slips."

The local officers nodded, understanding the gravity of his words. One by one, the subdued attackers were loaded into the van. The process was seamless, the shadows and silence acting as their allies.

As the van pulled away, Ananya exhaled a breath she didn't realize she was holding. Her team regrouped in the staff quarters, their energy drained but their vigilance unbroken.

"Handover is done," Rakshith said, breaking the silence. "What's next?"

Ananya tapped her communication device, reopening the line to Kulkarni. "Sir, the attackers have been handed over to the local police. The transfer was executed without incident. We're holding position at the hotel."

Kulkarni's voice came through, calm but layered with caution. "Good. But until we get concrete information from their interrogation, consider yourselves still on the clock. Stay in position and blend in. If there is any sign of trouble, you alert me immediately."

"Yes, sir," Ananya replied before disconnecting.

She turned to her team, her expression softening slightly. "He wants us to stay put until the attackers talk. That means we're still in the game. Everyone, keep your covers tight and stay vigilant."

Shika leaned against the wall, her face betraying her fatigue. "What about the cricket team? They'll start asking questions soon."

"We'll handle it," Ananya said, her tone resolute. "Right now, let's make sure no one suspects a thing. We have to clean every mark, no one should suspect a thing."

The team dispersed, their movements fluid and purposeful.

Inside the hotel, the power had been restored, casting warm light over the lobby and corridors as guests began to relax and return to their routines. The tension that had gripped the air earlier started to dissipate, replaced by the hum of normalcy. However, for the officers, their mission was far from over.

Rakshith, with his usual commanding presence, stepped forward to address the staff. His demeanor was calm yet firm, exuding the kind of authority that ensured compliance without inciting panic.

"Listen carefully," he said to the hotel manager, whose face was pale and drawn from the night's chaotic events. "Announce to the guests that there was a minor electrical fault that caused the outage. Assure them that everything has been resolved. No unnecessary details."

The manager, still visibly shaken, stammered, "O-of course, sir. I'll handle it immediately." Without waiting for further instructions, he hurried off toward the reception desk to make the announcement.

Rakshith glanced at Vikram, who was already coordinating with the rest of the team. "Vikram, oversee the cleanup. I'll make sure the guests don't start poking around."

"On it," Vikram replied, his sharp gaze sweeping over the now-lit hallways.

Shika and Nithin were stationed in the security control room, their eyes glued to the surveillance screens. They worked with precision, erasing every piece of incriminating footage from the night's attack.

"Focus on the key areas," Shika instructed, her fingers deftly navigating through the footage logs. "We can't afford any gaps in the timeline. Replace anything that looks suspicious with neutral footage."

"Already ahead of you," Nithin muttered, his attention fixed on the screen. He isolated and deleted sequences showing the attackers entering the hotel and the brief but intense skirmish that followed.

After a few minutes of tense silence, Nithin leaned back in his chair, exhaling a deep breath. "All clear here. I've looped the backup feed to show nothing out of the ordinary."

Shika double-checked the footage, her sharp eyes scanning for any missed details. Satisfied, she nodded. "Good work. Let's keep it that way. Make sure the live feed is functional again—we don't want anyone questioning why the cameras are offline."

Meanwhile, Ananya worked alongside Bhavin in erasing any physical traces of the attack. They moved through the hallways and lobby, replacing broken furniture, patching up scuff marks, and meticulously wiping away the faint bloodstains left behind.

"Careful with that," Bhavin murmured as they lifted a shattered side table into a supply closet. "We can't leave even a scratch for someone to notice."

"Don't worry," Ananya replied, her tone steady despite the exhaustion etched across her face. "Every detail counts. We'll make this place look as pristine as it did this morning."

In the dining area, Rakshith blended effortlessly among the guests, his sharp eyes taking note of any signs of suspicion. The players were gathered at a table, chatting casually about the blackout. Shaurya, however, kept glancing toward the entrance, his brows furrowed slightly.

Ananya entered moments later, her expression composed, though her heart raced as she felt Shaurya's gaze land on her. Ignoring his questioning look, she walked over to Rakshith.

"Everything's almost done," she whispered. "The staff is cooperative, and the manager has made the announcement. No one suspects a thing."

"Good," Rakshith replied, his voice low and firm. "But keep an eye on the guests. If anyone starts asking too many questions, we redirect them."

"Ananya," Shaurya walked to her, his face morphed with worry.

"Shaurya, are you alright?" She asked, worry laced in her tone as she checked him for any traces of injuries.

"Ananya," Vikram called out, his tone laced with urgency.

"Shaurya, I'll be back," She didn't give him a chance to argue as she made her way towards Vikram, leaving Shaurya worried and confused.

As the officers regrouped in Vikram's room to review their work, Vikram took the lead. "Let's recap. Shika, Nithin, what's the status on the surveillance footage?"

"Completely clean," Shika replied confidently. "We've erased every second of incriminating footage and replaced it with neutral feeds. The cameras are live again."

"Good. Ananya, Bhavin, how's the cleanup?"

"Done," Bhavin said. "The bloodstains are gone, and the broken furniture is stashed away. It's like nothing ever happened."

"Then we stick to Kulkarni sir's orders," Vikram said, his voice sharp with focus. "We maintain our cover and stay alert until those attackers confess. No one relaxes until we're officially cleared."

As the team dispersed, each officer resumed their respective roles, their movements calculated to avoid drawing attention. The hotel had returned to its usual state of luxury and calm, but for the officers, the night's events had etched themselves deeply into their minds.

Ananya and Vikram lingered in the room, reviewing their encrypted communication devices for updates from Kulkarni.

"Do you think they'll talk?" Ananya asked softly, her voice betraying a hint of fatigue.

"They will," Vikram replied with quiet certainty. "People like them always do when the right pressure is applied. Until then, we wait."

"And what if someone on the team starts connecting the dots?"

Vikram's gaze met hers, his expression unreadable. "Then we make sure they don't. It's what we signed up for, Ananya. No one can know who we really are."

Ananya nodded, her resolve hardening once more. Together, they stepped out into the hotel's brightly lit corridors, their expressions calm and their movements unremarkable. To the world, they were just reporters who were here to cover the lives of cricketers. But beneath the surface, the team's vigilance remained unbroken, every action a testament to their unyielding dedication to the mission.

The dining hall buzzed with chatter as the players unwound after a tense day. The blackout was a hot topic, with theories ranging from faulty wiring to overused generators. Amid the noise, Shaurya sat silently, his usually calm demeanor replaced by visible unease. His eyes darted toward the entrance every few seconds, searching for a familiar face.

He wasn't paying attention to his friends' banter as worry gnawed at him. Where was Ananya? She had been by his side earlier, a calming presence amid the chaos, and now she was nowhere to be seen. Every minute that passed only heightened his anxiety.

When the doors finally swung open and Ananya walked in, relief flooded through him. He rose from his seat almost instinctively, his steps quickening as he approached her. The sight of her safe and sound steadied his racing heart, though the tension in his eyes lingered.

"You disappeared," he said softly, his voice laced with concern rather than accusation. "Where were you?"

Ananya paused, caught off guard by the depth of emotion in his tone. She plastered on a smile, aiming for nonchalance. "Just helping Vikram with the medicines we ordered for Shika. Sorry to keep you waiting,"

Shaurya's gaze didn't waver. He studied her carefully—the faint sheen of sweat on her forehead, the slight tremor in her hands. She looked fine on the surface, but something about her posture told him otherwise.

"You've been running around all day," he said gently, stepping closer. "You don't have to take everything on yourself, you know."

Her smile faltered for a split second before she regained her composure. "Someone has to," she quipped lightly, hoping to ease his worry.

Shaurya wasn't convinced. "Ananya," he began, his voice barely above a whisper, "you don't always have to be the one holding things together. You can let someone else step in."

Her heart ached at the concern in his words, but she couldn't afford to let her guard down—not now. "I'm fine, Shaurya. Really."

He sighed, running a hand through his hair. "You say that, but you look like you're about to collapse. Have you even eaten?"

"I'll grab something soon," she assured him, trying to sidestep his scrutiny.

"Now," he insisted, guiding her toward an empty table. His usual playfulness was replaced by a quiet determination. "Sit. I'll get you a plate."

Before she could protest, Shaurya was already at the buffet, piling food onto a plate. Ananya watched him, a mix of guilt and gratitude swirling in her chest. She hadn't expected him to notice her absence so keenly, let alone care so much.

When he returned, he placed the plate in front of her and sat down, his eyes never leaving hers. "Eat," he urged softly.

Ananya picked up her fork, feeling oddly comforted by his presence. "Thank you," she murmured, her voice barely audible.

"Don't thank me," he replied, his tone gentler now. "Just... don't scare me like that again. I didn't know where you were, and with everything going on...and then you again ran away..."

He trailed off, the words unsaid hanging heavily in the air. Ananya swallowed hard, the weight of her secret pressing down on her. She wanted to tell him, to explain everything, but she couldn't. Not yet.

"I'm sorry," she said finally, her voice tinged with sincerity.

Shaurya reached across the table, his hand brushing hers for a fleeting moment. "Just take care of yourself too, okay? You're not alone, Ananya. Remember that."

Her chest tightened at his words, and for a moment, she allowed herself to bask in the warmth of his concern. She nodded, forcing down the lump in her throat. "I will," she promised, though she wasn't sure if it was a lie or the truth.

As the players' laughter and chatter filled the room once more, Shaurya stayed by her side, his silent support a balm to her restless soul. Though she couldn't reveal the truth to him, his presence reminded her of the strength she carried—not just for herself, but for the mission she couldn't afford to fail.

In the dimly lit safe house on the outskirts of the city, the coach sat in a plain chair, his hands gripping the edges of the seat as if the firmness of the wood could ground him. His face was pale, beads of sweat clinging to his forehead despite the cool air from the overhead fan. The events of the day had unraveled his normally composed demeanor.

The soft creak of the door announced Rakshith and Bhavin's entrance. They stepped in, their presence calm yet commanding. Rakshith was the first to speak, his voice steady and soothing.

"Mr. Mishra, I understand this has been a long and difficult day," he began, pulling up a chair to sit across from the visibly shaken man. "But you're safe now. We've made sure no harm will come to you."

The coach looked up, his eyes clouded with lingering fear and confusion. "Safe? Is that what you call this? I was almost—" His voice broke, and he leaned back, exhaling shakily. "I still don't even know who you really are. You're not reporters, are you?"

Bhavin, standing by the doorway with his arms crossed, softened his stance and stepped forward. "No, we're not. We're operatives working for the government. Our job is to protect you and ensure no harm comes your way."

The coach's brows furrowed. "If you're protecting me, then why all this secrecy? Why not let the authorities handle it?"

Rakshith exchanged a brief glance with Bhavin before responding. "Because secrecy is the only thing keeping you and the rest of the team safe right now. If the attackers or their allies find out we've intervened, they'll try again, and we can't allow that to happen."

The coach's hands loosened their grip on the chair. His fear was giving way to reason, though a sliver of doubt lingered. "And you expect me to just trust you? After all this?"

Bhavin crouched beside him, his voice dropping to a sincere tone. "We understand how hard this must be for you. But trust us when we say we've done this before. We've dealt with worse, and every single time, we've succeeded in keeping those under our watch safe."

Rakshith leaned forward, his eyes steady and resolute. "Coach, tomorrow's match is crucial, not just for the team but for maintaining the illusion that everything is fine. If you don't show up, it'll raise questions—questions that could lead back to this incident. We need you to be there, to act as if nothing happened."

The coach's lips tightened. "You're asking me to walk into a stadium full of people, with who knows what kind of threats still out there. Do you have any idea what that feels like?"

Bhavin's hand rested lightly on the coach's shoulder. "We do. That's why we're promising you—on our lives—that nothing will happen to you. We'll be there, watching every corner, covering every angle. No harm will reach you, Coach. That's a guarantee."

There was a long pause as the coach weighed their words. Finally, he exhaled deeply, the tension in his shoulders easing just a fraction. "Fine," he said, his voice barely above a whisper. "I'll be there. But only because you're asking me to."

Rakshith stood, his tone laced with quiet determination. "Thank you. We won't let you down. For now, get some rest. You're safe here, and the police are monitoring the perimeter. We'll regroup early in the morning."

As the two officers prepared to leave, the coach called after them, his voice tinged with lingering apprehension. "What happens if... if they try something again tomorrow?"

Rakshith turned, his expression a mixture of assurance and unyielding resolve. "Then we'll stop them before they get close. That's our job, Coach. Trust us to do it."

With that, Rakshith and Bhavin exited the room, closing the door softly behind them. Outside, Bhavin glanced at Rakshith, his voice low. "Think he'll hold up tomorrow?"

"He has to," Rakshith replied, his tone firm. "And so do we."

The safe house fell quiet once more, the faint sound of crickets filling the night air. Inside, the coach sat alone, his thoughts a tumult of fear and hope. But for the first time since the ordeal began, he felt a small measure of security, a fragile belief that maybe, just maybe, these people could deliver on their promise.

The morning sun glared down on the stadium as it began to fill with excited spectators. Flags fluttered in the breeze, and chants of fans echoed throughout the massive arena, creating a charged atmosphere. The smell of freshly watered grass mingled with the aroma of snacks from concession stands, making the air electric with anticipation.Banners with players' names, particularly Shaurya's, fluttered in the breeze. The arena was alive, yet beneath this celebratory facade, tension simmered.

In the dressing room, the cricket team huddled around their coach, whose normally steady hands now gripped the edge of the whiteboard tightly. His face was pale, but he forced a determined expression as he reviewed the strategies for the day.

"Focus on the basics," the coach said, his voice firm but slightly strained. "Stick to the game plan we've practiced. Openers, build a steady foundation. Bowlers, keep it tight and don't let them dominate."

The players nodded, their adrenaline surging for the match ahead, completely unaware of the storm raging in their coach's mind. He felt the weight of the previous night's events pressing down on him, yet he pushed it aside. For the sake of his team and the audience, he needed to act as if everything was normal.

Shaurya addressed his team with his usual captain's charisma, though his sharp eyes occasionally darted toward the "reporters" or to a particular reporter stationed nearby.

Shaurya adjusted his gloves, turning to Akshith. "All-rounders are key today. If we falter anywhere, it'll be up to you."

Akshith gave a confident nod. "Got it, captain."

Yuvaan, standing nearby, was fidgeting with his bat. "Let's give them a show they'll remember."

Siraj smirked. "And keep the opposition's batsmen scrambling with my bowling."

The officers, stationed strategically around the players under the guise of filming, communicated in coded phrases. Ananya adjusted her camera lens, capturing Shaurya's pre-match pep talk while discreetly observing the staff moving around the locker room.

Vikram, holding a microphone for "interviews," casually remarked, "The focus today should be on close-ups of the action," subtly signaling his vigilance over every corner of the players' area.

Rakshith hovered near the entrance to the locker room, pretending to supervise equipment logistics while keeping a sharp eye out for any suspicious movements. Bhavin handled the tech setup for the fake documentary, his earpiece buzzing softly with updates from Shika and Nithin, who were stationed near the control room and perimeter respectively.

"Area clear so far," Shika whispered.

"Nothing unusual here," Nithin added.

The toss was won by Shaurya, who elected to bat first, a decision that immediately electrified the crowd. The openers—Shaurya and Yuvaan—walked out to the middle amidst roaring cheers.

The first over was a cautious start, with Shaurya defending skillfully against the opposition's lead pacer. On the fifth delivery, however, Shaurya stepped out and sent the ball soaring over mid-wicket for a stunning six, igniting the crowd.

"Classic Shaurya! That's why he's the captain," the commentator exclaimed.

Yuvaan, at the other end, complemented Shaurya's aggressive strokes with measured precision. Their partnership built steadily, frustrating the bowlers as boundaries began flowing. Akshith joined the fray after Yuvaan's dismissal and immediately made an impact with his powerful lofted drives and quick singles.

The opposition fought back with disciplined bowling, and a few wickets fell in quick succession. By the end of the innings, the team posted a competitive total of 175 runs, thanks largely to a fiery 65 from Shaurya and a crucial 30-run cameo by Akshith.

Despite the thrill of the game, the officers remained vigilant. Ananya caught sight of a man in the crowd acting suspiciously, his hand constantly reaching for his phone and glancing around nervously. As the players retreated to the dugout for a brief break, the officers intensified their focus.

"Possible suspect in Stand C, near the aisle," she whispered into her comms.

"Noted. I'll send someone," Shika replied.

Shika approached the man casually, pretending to be a vendor offering snacks. As she got closer, she noticed a bulge in his jacket pocket. Her heart raced, but she kept her demeanor calm, handing him a packet of chips with a bright smile while discreetly snapping a photo of him to send to the team.

The officers moved swiftly yet inconspicuously, their actions seamlessly blending into the activities of the media crew. Meanwhile, Vikram hovered near the players, ensuring no one got too close to them.

The second innings began with Siraj charging in for the first over. His fiery pace left the opposition batsmen scrambling, with the ball missing the stumps by mere inches several times. The crowd roared with every near-miss, the tension palpable.

By the third over, Siraj struck, shattering the stumps with a perfect yorker. The stadium erupted as he celebrated with his trademark fist pump.

Shaurya's sharp captaincy came into play as he rotated his bowlers strategically. Akshith's all-round skills shone brightly when he took two key wickets in his spell, breaking the opposition's middle-order backbone.

The fielding was sharp, with Yuvaan diving to stop crucial boundaries and Siraj taking a stunning catch at the deep mid-wicket boundary, silencing the opposition fans.

Meanwhile, Bhavin intercepted a man loitering near the players' entrance with a suspicious bag. "Excuse me, sir, can I help you?" he asked, his tone polite but firm.

The man stammered, clutching the bag tighter. Bhavin's sharp eyes caught the beads of sweat forming on his forehead despite the pleasant weather. "I'm just waiting for someone," the man said, avoiding eye contact.

"Mind if I check your bag? Standard security protocol," Bhavin said, motioning to a nearby guard to assist.

The man hesitated but relented under Bhavin's unwavering gaze. The bag contained nothing more than fan merchandise, but the man's demeanor was enough to keep him under watch for the rest of the match.

The match came down to the final over, with the opposition needing 15 runs to win. Shaurya handed the ball to Akshith, whose nerves of steel were evident in his measured run-up.

The first ball was a dot, followed by a wicket on the second—a crucial breakthrough that left the crowd roaring. The next delivery went for a six, reigniting tension, but Akshith kept his cool, delivering two consecutive dot balls.

The final ball required the batsman to hit a six to tie the game. Akshith delivered a clever slower ball that the batsman mistimed, sending it high into the air. Shaurya positioned himself under it and caught it cleanly, sealing the win.

The crowd erupted, chants of Shaurya's and Akshith's name filling the air. The players celebrated on the field, lifting Akshith on their shoulders for his stellar final over.

The officers, however, remained on alert even amidst the celebration. Vikram gestured subtly to Rakshith, signaling that their mission was still ongoing.

The coach, standing with the players, finally allowed himself a relieved smile. For now, the threat had been contained, and the team had triumphed. But as the officers regrouped post-match, their focus was unwavering.

"The match may be over, but we're not done," Rakshith reminded them firmly.

As the crowd dispersed, the officers stayed behind, ensuring every loose end was tied up. For the players, it was a day of glory. For the officers, it was just another mission accomplished—quietly and in the shadows.

CHAPTER SIXTEEN

Ananya

It's been 56 hours since we handed over those attackers to the local police, and not a single one of them has opened their mouths. It's frustrating. Yesterday, Rakshith had requested permission from Kulkarni sir to handle the interrogation ourselves, but we were met with a firm refusal. "Focus on your duty. Let the police do their job," he said, and that was that.

The weight of the situation pressed down on us all, anger simmering beneath the surface, but we had no choice but to stay put and follow orders. We knew the stakes were high, but we were helpless, waiting for any breakthrough. The only solace came from the coach, who agreed to keep our identities concealed. He's still visibly shaken from the ordeal, but he's doing a good job of masking it. We all know he's terrified, but he hides it well—perhaps too well.

In the meantime, with no matches scheduled for the next four days, some of the players were eager to visit their families. They hadn't seen them in ages, and we understood that. But we also knew it was a risky move. With the tension still thick in the air, we couldn't afford to let them slip out of our watchful eyes.

We approached them gently, explaining that we needed them to stay back for a few more details to be covered. A simple request, nothing more. But their response was immediate. They were annoyed—frustrated even—and refused to cooperate at first. They couldn't understand why they couldn't just take a few days off to see their families. What harm would it do?

I could see the resentment building, their eyes narrowing as if we were imposing some unnecessary restriction on them. But we couldn't back down. The safety of everyone here—of the team—was more important than anything. We tried to keep it polite, explaining our reasoning, but they weren't having it.

Eventually, Kulkarni sir had to make a call to the BCCI president. After that, we had no choice but to insist further, and it wasn't until the coach stepped in, urging them to stay, that they agreed. But the mood shifted. There was an undeniable coldness in the air. We could see the change in their expressions. They weren't as warm, not as welcoming as before.

I couldn't blame them, though. I knew they felt restricted and perhaps even betrayed, but we were doing what we had to do to protect them. As much as it irked them, we were not about to let any threat slip through.

And yet, despite all the tension, we held our ground, knowing that it was only temporary. We won't be seeing them regularly after the threat dissipates.

"Damn bro, he's practically digging holes into your skull," Shika muttered, eyes darting behind me. I casually turned around, and sure enough, one of them was staring at me like he could burn a hole right through my head.

I shook my head and turned back to my breakfast, trying not to let the tension bother me.

"He's stabbing me with his eyes," I deadpanned, not missing a beat.

"Don't worry, Anu. I'll protect you," Bhavin chimed in, the ever-charismatic joker, suddenly appearing behind me. He wrapped his arms around my neck in what was supposed to be a protective gesture but felt more like a bear hug from a playful giant.

Vikram raised an eyebrow, casting a quick glance between Bhavin and me, but said nothing.

"Ouch! He's stabbing my ass now!" Bhavin exclaimed dramatically, as if struck by an invisible sword. With a swift movement, he pulled me backward, trapping me between the chair and his hands, practically choking me in the process.

Rakshith and Vikram both shot him a weird look, then playfully hit his arms, setting me free from his vice-like grip.

"Assholes!" Bhavin cursed under his breath, though the smile on his face gave away that he wasn't actually upset. He slumped back into his seat, pouting dramatically at Rakshith and Vikram.

I couldn't hold back my laughter anymore. I burst into laughter, and soon, Shika and Nithin joined in. The sound of our collective laughter filled the room, lightening the mood as the tension from earlier seemed to dissipate for the moment.

We continued our breakfast, teasing each other, the banter flowing effortlessly between us. It was moments like these that reminded me how much I treasured having them around—despite all the chaos that always seemed to follow us.

"Ananya, why aren't you ready yet?" Yuvaan's voice snapped my attention away from the breakfast table.

Yuvaan and Siraj had promised to teach me some cricket after the badminton match, but after the recent tension, I figured they might distance themselves just like their team members had.

"Well, I thought you wouldn't be interested in teaching me anymore after that," I said sheepishly, smoothing out my top, trying to hide my nervousness.

"Nonsense! We're friends, Anu," Yuvaan insisted, his grin widening. "Come on, go get ready. Shaurya is also getting ready."

The last part came with a playful wiggle of his eyebrows, and my cheeks instantly flushed. I quickly tucked a stray strand of hair behind my ear, trying to act unfazed, but my heart was definitely racing a little faster.

"Oye madam, take your phone at least!" Bhavin called out just as I stood up, his voice teasing but warm.

I closed my eyes in embarrassment, praying I didn't turn as red as I felt.

"She would forget everything after hearing Shaurya's name," Shika piped up with a smirk, and that made my cheeks burn even more.

I shot her a glare but couldn't hold back the small laugh that escaped, my face still burning with all the teasing. Snatching my phone from Bhavin, I hurried toward the elevator, trying my best to ignore the teasing from all directions.

I was glad to get away from them before they could say anything else, but deep down, I couldn't deny the fluttering feeling in my stomach every time Shaurya's name came up.

I quickly slipped into a pair of jeans and a casual top, brushing through my hair with one hand. A little moisturizer and sunscreen later, I sprayed my favorite fragrance, the one that always made me feel confident yet calm. With one last glance at myself in the mirror, I locked the door behind me and stepped out.

As soon as I reached the lobby, I found Shaurya, Yuvaan, Siraj, and Akshith already waiting for me. My heart skipped a beat at the sight of Shaurya, who looked effortlessly handsome, his posture relaxed but his eyes alert.

I quickly called Shika and asked her to contact me if anything unusual happened, before bidding a quick farewell to the boys. As I joined the others in the lobby, my gaze met Shaurya's, and he smiled softly, a quiet, reassuring smile that made my heart flutter in ways I couldn't explain. I returned his smile, a little shy, but the warmth of his gaze sent a thousand butterflies fluttering inside me.

"If you're done talking with your eyes, let's go?" Akshith's teasing voice broke through the moment, and I instantly felt my cheeks warm. Shaurya cleared his throat, his smile tightening into a small, sheepish grin as he looked away. I, on the other hand, couldn't help but stare down at the carpet, suddenly finding the pattern on the floor more interesting than ever.

The air between Shaurya and me shifted, filled with an unspoken connection, and I tried to focus on anything other than the effect he had on me. I was sure the others noticed, and that's the reason for their teasing but none of us confessed it—yet.

"Why is he coming again?" I shot a disgusted look at Akshith, who rolled his eyes dramatically at me. We were settled into the car, with Shaurya behind the wheel and me beside him. The others were squeezed into the back seat, Akshith sitting in the middle.

"He wanted to tag along," Yuvaan shrugged, glancing at Akshith with a raised eyebrow.

"I wanted to make sure you don't cast any magic on my friends, you witch," Akshith declared, narrowing his eyes at me with exaggerated suspicion.

"You..." I grabbed a handful of his hair, tugging it just enough to make his knee slam into the middle console. I smirked, enjoying his dramatic reaction.

"Ouch! You—" He quickly slapped my bicep and leaned back in his seat, muttering, "Monkey."

"I heard that, cockroach!" I shot him a sharp glare, unable to hold back my grin.

"It was meant to be heard, monkey!" Akshith replied smugly, clearly enjoying our banter.

I was about to throw another retort his way when Siraj, who was getting visibly tired of the back-and-forth, intervened. "Can you both stop fighting like kids?" he asked exasperatedly, like he'd been dealing with this nonsense for years.

"She started it!" Akshith pointed an accusing finger at me.

"And you kept it going!" I pointed back at him, standing my ground.

Before we could continue, Shaurya reached over, gently taking my hand in his, turning me to front. His touch was soothing, his fingers caressing my knuckles in a way that completely melted any frustration I had. "Leave it, Ananya," he said softly, and the warmth in his voice made me feel like a puddle of mush.

I nodded, fully intent on ignoring Akshith's antics, but not before sticking my tongue out at him.

"Shaurya, did you see that?" Akshith complained with an exaggerated pout.

"Akshith, you're not a kid, behave!" Shaurya and Yuvaan hissed simultaneously, making me burst out laughing.

"She isn't either. And you two are my best friends, idiots. Not hers!" Akshith deadpanned, folding his arms like a little brat.

Shaurya just shook his head, a small smile tugging at his lips as he watched his friend's drama unfold. "I swear, you two," he muttered with fond exasperation.

I was about to tease him some more, but then Shaurya gave me a soft look, his voice dropping into a playful warning. "No more masti, Ananya."

I nodded like a good girl, playfully saluting him, and turned my attention to the passing buildings, the city blurring by as we continued the ride in comfortable silence.

Once inside the stadium, the boys scattered to collect their kits and get ready. I stood off to the side, quietly observing them, a little out of place but still eager to be part of it all. The sound of their laughter and light banter filled the air, and I couldn't help but smile at their camaraderie.

"Do you want to bat or bowl?" Shaurya quirked a brow at me, a playful glint in his eyes. I had bowled a few times with Vansh and his team—just for fun, never seriously—but I'd never actually picked up a bat before.

"I'll bowl," I replied with a shrug, trying to sound confident even though the nerves were swirling in my stomach. I couldn't back out now, could I?

Shaurya nodded, a small smile tugging at his lips, and reached into his bag, pulling out a box of cricket balls. "White ball it is," he muttered, checking each one before tossing one at me. I caught it effortlessly, the cool, smooth surface of the ball fitting perfectly into my palm. His appreciative nod sent a warm rush of pride through me.

I grinned back at him, feeling a little bolder now. "Not bad," I thought, feeling the adrenaline of the moment kick in.

"What did she decide?" Yuvaan called out, the boys a little ways off, already getting into position.

Shaurya gestured to me, pointing to his own bowling action and giving me a thumbs-up. Yuvaan smiled back, clearly glad with my choice.

But of course, Akshith had to be Akshith. He cocked a brow at me, his trademark smirk forming. I could practically hear him about to say something cocky.

"Here we go," I muttered to myself, bracing for whatever teasing was about to come.

Akshith raised an eyebrow, an amused smirk tugging at his lips. "So, Ananya," he started, leaning casually on his bat, "do you even know the formats of cricket? Or are you just here to look pretty?"

The other boys paused, waiting for my response. I could feel the heat creeping up my neck, but I wasn't going to back down. I'd had enough of his teasing. I shot him a pointed look, crossing my arms, my eyes narrowing slightly.

"Of course, I know the formats," I said coolly, stepping toward him. "Cricket has three main formats—Test cricket, One Day Internationals, and T20s. Tests are played over five days with two innings per team, ODIs are 50 overs per side, and T20s are 20 overs. I know that Akshith, even the kids do."

The boys smiled at me with a nod, but Akshith didn't back off just yet. His smirk only deepened. "Alright, alright, smarty-pants. What about the balls? Do you even know the difference between them?"

I couldn't help but smirk back. Oh, this was fun.

"Akshith," I said, walking over to the box of cricket balls that Shaurya had pulled out earlier, picking up each one in turn and holding them up for the group to see. "Here we have the red ball, the white ball, and the pink ball. Red balls are used in Test cricket because they offer more durability and are easier to see in daylight. The white ball is used in ODIs and T20s because it's more visible under artificial lights, but it wears out faster. And the pink ball?" I raised my eyebrows as I continued, "It's mainly used in Day-Night Tests, offering a balance between visibility and durability."

I paused, giving them a moment to absorb that. The boys stood silent, clearly impressed.

I wasn't done yet, though.

"For each format, the balls are chosen based on the pitch conditions, the weather, and the type of game being played. The red ball's seam stays prominent for longer, allowing spinners to get more grip. The white ball, though, is great for swing bowlers—particularly in the early overs, but it tends to get dirty quickly, which is why it's best suited for limited overs cricket." I glanced over at Akshith, who was now looking at me, speechless. "There, now you know. That's why the ball is chosen for the format."

The boys were absolutely stunned, exchanging looks with one another.

"Wow," Yuvaan murmured, eyes wide. "Didn't expect that level of detail, Ananya."

"I'm impressed," Siraj added, nodding with a grin.

"Well, I told you I know my stuff," I said, tossing my hair back with a little flair, my smile triumphant.

Akshith raised his hands in mock surrender. "Okay, okay, Ms. Monkey. I know you must have read some PDFs before coming here. But let's see if you can handle the actual game," he said, still grinning but with a new respect in his eyes.

I turned back to the field, ready to start the bowling. "Sure, shall we get to the real fun?"

The boys scattered to take their positions, and Shaurya came up beside me, offering a mischievous smile. "You ready, Ms. Cricket Expert?" he teased, his voice low and inviting.

I grinned at him, feeling my heart race. "You bet I am," I said, eyeing him with a playful challenge.

I took my stance and rolled the ball toward him with a smooth, confident delivery. Shaurya's eyes sparkled as he readied his bat, timing it just right as he hit the ball back toward me with a playful flourish.

"Nice one," he said, winking at me, clearly enjoying the moment more than just a regular cricket match.

I leaned forward, pretending to think. "That was just a warm-up, Shaurya. Let's see if you can handle a real delivery." I winked back at him.

He chuckled, adjusting his stance. "I'll be ready for you, Ananya."

The ball left my hand again, faster this time, and Shaurya reacted with expert precision, sending the ball flying.

The moment felt electric, charged with something more than just the game. As we played, I could feel the playful teasing between us, the chemistry simmering beneath the surface with every glance and every challenge.

"You really know your stuff," Shaurya said again, his voice hushed as he watched me closely.

"Just trying to keep up," I replied, unable to hide the smile tugging at my lips.

"Okay, I've bowled. Now I want to try batting," I said, feeling a sudden rush of excitement to try something new.

Shaurya raised an eyebrow, clearly concerned. "Are you sure you want to bat? It's not as easy as it looks."

I grinned, trying to sound confident. "Of course, I can handle it."

Akshith, of course, had to add his two cents. "You only know the theory, Ananya. You sure you can handle it in practice?" His tone was mockingly sweet, like he was daring me to prove him wrong.

I huffed, annoyed, and shot a glare his way. "I know enough to hit a ball, thank you." I glanced at Shaurya, hoping he wouldn't let Akshith's teasing get under my skin.

Shaurya hesitated for a moment before standing up and grabbing a bat from the kit. "Alright, but let's get you ready properly. You need to wear pads."

I froze. "Pads? I don't even know how to tie them."

Shaurya's eyes softened with concern. "I'll help you, no worries."

Akshith, ever the troublemaker, grinned. "Of course. All theory, no practice," he teased, leaning on his bat with a smug smile. "Let's see if you can even tie them."

I huffed, rolling my eyes. "I know how to bat, Akshith. It's just... the safety stuff is tricky."

Shaurya chuckled softly, stepping closer. "Alright, let me help you out here." He kneeled in front of me, and the moment his hands touched the pads, I felt a rush of warmth flood my chest. His fingers brushed against mine as he tied the straps, his movements so careful, and my heart fluttered despite my best efforts to stay calm.

"You're doing this very slowly," Akshith teased from behind us. "Maybe you should just read the manual."

I shot him a playful glare, then turned back to Shaurya, who was still in the middle of securing the pads. "Is this how you tie everything, Shaurya?" I asked, trying to keep my tone light, but my heart was racing as he adjusted the last strap.

He glanced up, a small, teasing smile tugging at his lips. "Only when I'm dealing with something precious."

I swallowed hard, my breath catching. "You're all set," he said softly, standing up and looking me over. "Now, let's get you to bat."

I grabbed the bat with newfound determination, but as I stood there, I felt the weight of the stick, and my nerves crept up. When the ball came flying at me, I swung early, missing it completely.

Shaurya chuckled lightly. "Not bad for your first try, but try to focus on the ball this time."

I nodded, mentally preparing myself, but the nerves kept crawling in. I swung again—way too soon. The bat swished through the air, but I missed again.

Akshith burst out laughing from the sidelines. "See? Told you! All theory, no practical skills!"

I turned to him, my hands on my hips, annoyed. "Shut up, Akshith. I'm getting there."

Shaurya, noticing my frustration, stepped closer, his eyes softening with that signature calm. "Ananya, relax. It's all about timing," he said, his voice warm and steady.

He stepped behind me, positioning himself so that his body was almost pressed against mine. "Hold the bat like this," he said, placing his hands gently over mine. His breath was warm against my ear as he guided me through the motions, his body aligning with mine. My pulse quickened, but I focused on his instructions.

"Now, just wait until the ball comes closer and follow through smoothly," he instructed, his lips almost brushing my ear.

"Now, just follow through when the ball comes," he instructed, his voice a gentle whisper in my ear.

I nodded, trying to calm my breath, but the proximity was making my skin tingle. Shaurya shifted slightly, his hands guiding mine as I prepared to face the next ball.

I swung again, but this time I was a little more in sync. Still, the bat swung just after the ball passed.

"Close," he murmured, moving even closer. "Let's try again."

His hands gently guided mine again, this time pulling me closer into him, his body pressed lightly against my back. "Focus on the ball, not me," he teased with a smile, his breath sending shivers down my spine.

I shot him a playful glance over my shoulder, my lips curling into a teasing smile. "I'm trying. But it's kind of hard when you're this close," I said, my voice teasing yet breathless.

Shaurya chuckled, his chest vibrating against my back. "You'll get used to it," he whispered, leaning his head closer to mine. "Now focus."

As the ball came, I swung with more confidence this time, following through just as he had shown me. This time, I connected with the ball, sending it flying toward the mid-on.

The boys cheered, and I couldn't help but laugh, turning to Shaurya with a grin. "I did it!"

He smiled down at me, his eyes soft and proud. "Told you. You just needed a little guidance." His voice was so warm, but there was a teasing glint in his eyes that sent a shiver down my spine.

Akshith, unable to resist, piped up, "Yeah, right. Let's see if she can do that again."

I grinned and nodded. "Sure, let's see if you can stop me, Akshith."

I turned to face Shaurya again, ready for another attempt. But this time, I decided to make things more interesting. I gave him a playful wink, swinging the bat just before he could say anything, missing it entirely.

"Oops," I said, feigning surprise. "Looks like I still need some help."

Shaurya's eyes narrowed in mock seriousness. "You're impossible, Ananya." He stepped in closer again, his chest brushing against my back, his hands gently guiding mine once more. "But I'll make sure you get this right."

I could feel his heart beating slightly faster through his shirt, and I knew that the tension between us was far from just about cricket.

"You ready?" he whispered, his breath so close I could feel it on my skin.

I nodded, trying to hold back the smile that was threatening to break out. This time, as the ball came flying, I swung in perfect sync with his guidance, connecting with the ball and sending it flying farther than before.

"Well done," Shaurya murmured, his voice thick with something more than praise.

I turned to face him, my smile soft but playful. "Thanks, I couldn't have done it without you," I said, leaning in just slightly, feeling the heat between us.

"You're doing really well," Shaurya said, his voice almost too soft, like he didn't want anyone else to hear it. His eyes were focused on me with such intensity that I almost forgot where I was.

"Thanks," I said, trying to keep my voice steady, even though the butterflies in my stomach were doing their own chaotic dance. "I think I've got the basics down now."

He nodded slowly, his lips twitching like he was holding back a smile. "You're a natural, Ananya."

I couldn't help but feel a little proud. But then I glanced around, remembering where we were, and a mischievous thought crossed my mind.

"You know," I said, turning to face him with a grin, "I think it's time I show off a little more. How about a challenge?"

"A challenge?" Shaurya raised an eyebrow, clearly intrigued. The boys heard me and immediately perked up.

"What kind of challenge?" Akshith asked, narrowing his eyes like he thought he knew where this was going.

"Simple," I said, batting my lashes dramatically. "If you can help me hit a six for the next ball, I will give you a treat. How does that sound?"

Shaurya chuckled, the sound low and rich. "I would love to have you treat me, Ananya. But you do know that a six isn't as easy as it sounds."

"Let's see about that." I took a deep breath and lined myself up. I could feel Shaurya standing just behind me, his presence like an electric charge in the air.

"Ready?" he asked, his voice suddenly serious, though his lips betrayed a small smile.

I nodded, eyes locked on the ball. The others fell silent, sensing the shift in the air. The field seemed to narrow as I focused entirely on the ball that Yuvaan had just bowled.

Shaurya's hand rested on my shoulder, just the slightest pressure, like he was there for me but also... watching me. And then he slid it down, holding my hands that were gripping the bat. The pressure of it made me want to prove him right, but also something more. It was like he was rooting for me, and that made everything sharper. I pulled the bat back, preparing to swing, knowing this was my moment.

"Here goes nothing," I muttered under my breath.

With a swift, precise movement, he swung the bat, our bodies following through with the momentum. The ball shot off the bat and flew high into the air, sailing toward the boundary. For a moment, time seemed to slow down, and then—wham—the ball cleared the fence. I had done it.

The boys erupted in cheers, but all I could focus on was Shaurya's expression. He was staring at me, eyes wide with disbelief... or maybe admiration. I wasn't sure.

"You—" He stopped himself, blinking a few times. "That was... incredible."

"See?" I smirked, walking over to him and swatting his arm lightly. "I told you, you could help me do it."

"Yeah, yeah," he laughed, running a hand through his hair. "You really outdid yourself, Ananya. Maybe I should start calling you 'The Pro' now."

"Oh please," I teased, "we both know who the pro is around here."

"You," he said, stepping a little closer, lowering his voice so only I could hear. "But not just because of that shot. You've got a lot of other skills I'd love to see." His words hung in the air, sending a shiver down my spine.

I raised an eyebrow, a playful smile tugging at the corners of my mouth. "I'm glad to know you're impressed, Shaurya."

"You've definitely got my attention," he replied, his eyes never leaving mine, that mischievous glint still dancing in them.

Akshith groaned from behind us, "Could you two not make it so obvious? Some of us are trying to play here. Or should we just let you two have your moment?"

Shaurya chuckled softly, but his eyes never left mine. "You're just jealous you can't hit it as far. But yeah, let's get back to some actual cricket. " He gave me one last look, that familiar glint in his eye, as though we were both still caught in the same shared secret.

"Next time, I want to see you hit a six too, Shaurya, but without me in your arms" I teased, walking back to my position.

Shaurya chuckled, shaking his head. "Oh, you'll see that for sure. But I love this six more than all the others."

Heat rose to my cheeks hearing him. I glanced over my shoulder, catching him still watching me with that smile that made my heart skip a beat.

I stood at some distance, watching them play, but my eyes remained fixated on Shaurya following his every move. I smiled and leaned back slightly, allowing myself to enjoy the moment. Shaurya and I, surrounded by our friends, but still somehow lost in our own little bubble. It felt natural, comfortable, and something I wasn't sure I ever wanted to leave.

CHAPTER SEVENTEEN

Ananya

It's been ten days since the attack. After days of uncertainty, the attackers finally gave up our needed information. Four days of silent tension, but it was worth it. The teams moved swiftly, arresting everyone involved, including the informers.

Two days ago, Kulkarni sir told us the case had been officially closed. Still, he asked us to stay for another month, maintaining the same appearance we'd kept up until now—keeping up the facade so the cricketers and the public wouldn't suspect anything.

Right now, I am sitting in Shika's room. I've got a book in my hands, but I can't focus. How can I? When all I could see was the woman's face? I could feel the anger bubble inside me along with the frustration.

"I saw her yesterday." My voice trembled, barely above a whisper. The confession slipped from my lips like a forbidden truth, the truth that cut through our hearts deeper than any wounds we got on missions. As the words left me, I regretted uttering them. But it was already late.

Shika's head snapped toward me, her eyes wide with disbelief. "What? When?"

I swallowed hard, trying to push back the rush of memories that came crashing in. "During the match. When I saw her, everything came rushing back—her betrayal, the fight between Rakshith and Vikram, their separation, Vikram's suicide attempt... Bhavin's anger... everything. She was the one who broke us, Shika. She broke us all."

My throat tightened as I relived it all, the way she had shattered something that we are trying to repair, even after years. She was the reason behind the cracks that ran through our gang, through Rakshith and Vikram's brotherhood. Vikram and Rakshith—two souls bound together since school—had been torn apart by her lies.

I tried to steady my breath, but the ache in my chest only grew heavier. "She separated them. Vikram was so blinded by her that he didn't even see it coming. And when she left...leaving him torn and broken, he was too ashamed to return to Rakshith, too ashamed to come back to us." The words felt like a dagger through my heart. We were supposed to be a team, a family. And he hesitated to come to us.

Shika's voice broke through the fog of my pain, filled with empathy and understanding. "Everything will be fine, Anu. They are talking again, right? They'll be back to begin best friends soon."

I wanted to believe her. But a small voice inside me whispered doubt. How could things ever be the same again when those men are not ready to confront each other? The hurt was too deep, too raw. I wanted to fix it, to put everything the way it was, but it was not mine to fix. It was theirs. Vikram and Rakshith's. Only they can fix their broken friendship.

Shika seemed to notice the conflict I was going through. Sensing my need for distraction, she began talking about random things, filling the air with chatter. Slowly, I allowed myself to be swept in her words, her voice grounding me, even if just for a little while. I welcomed the relief of not having to think about it at the moment.

We moved to the hotel's restaurant for lunch. Vikram and the others joined us, and the moment we sat down, they wasted no time teasing me about the recent segment with the cricketers.

"Looks like you finally found your fictional man in the reality, Anu. Your hero Shaurya, he swept you off your feet," Vikram winked, nudging me playfully.

"Shut up, Vikky. He was just helping me," I muttered, but my cheeks flushed anyway. It had been the talk of the day. We were shooting some practice shots, and the ball had come flying toward me, speeding with a force that would have knocked me out cold if it hit. Before I even had time to react, Shaurya leaped forward, his hand gripping my arm and pulling me to safety in one swift motion.

As I think of it now, I could still feel the heat of his body so close to mine, his heat hammering beneath my palm, the way his eyes locked onto me, filled with concern and something deeper, for that brief, heart-stopping moment before everyone gathered around us.

After ensuring both of us were safe, it became a topic of discussion between both the teams, everyone laughing and chatting about it like it was the most interesting thing that had happened in a while. Shaurya's friends, his team, were just as relentless, joking about his "heroic save," and now my friends seemed to join the club.

"You owe him your life, Anu!" Rakshith grinned. "What's the deal? Did he sweep you off your feet and to a romantic duet after that?"

"You guys are too much," I groaned, burying my hands in embarrassment.

Shaurya, who was seated at the far end table, caught my eye from across the room, and the corner of his lips twitched into that smirk I'd come to recognize all too well. My heart skipped a beat as our gazes locked, and for a moment, everything around me seemed to blur. His friends nudged him, and he just leaned back, acting cool, as if the teasing didn't faze him.

"Ananya! Tell us the truth," Bhavin pulled my attention back to the table. "Don't you really feel the chemistry between you two? Everyone around you can sense it," he leaned closer, curiosity dancing in his eyes as he awaited my answer.

My cheeks burned even more. How could I explain the rush I'd feel whenever Shaurya comes near to me? The way his presence both unsettles and comforts me at once? It is like something flickers in the air between us every time our gazes lock, something unspoken but very real.

"You guys are delusional," I said, trying to brush it off. But I couldn't shake the feeling that Shaurya's protective gesture had meant something more than just a reflex to him. I felt it.

"Hey, guys!" Akshith's cheerful voice broke through our little teasing session, and we all turned to face him. But the sight of the woman standing beside Chirag made my stomach churn, the anger bubbling inside me. I glanced over at Vikram, whose expression had gone completely blank, as if his mind had shut down.

Suddenly, it felt like the air had gotten thicker, charged with an awkward tension. The playful banter around the table faded away, and all I could focus on was the way the woman stood beside Chirag with a smug expression, her presence like a dark cloud looming over us. It was like a sudden jolt of reality, reminding me of the things we had all tried to ignore.

I whipped my head back to Vikram. His eyes were trained ahead, a blank mask over his face, but I could feel the storm brewing beneath that facade. I couldn't tell if it was anger or hurt that I felt for him, but the weight of it pressed heavily on my heart.

"You are a real idiot, Akshith," I muttered under my breath, leaning in close enough to his ear to make sure only he could hear me. My voice was laced with frustration and something else, a sense of helplessness that I couldn't shake off.

Akshith looked at me, dumbfounded, like he hadn't noticed the shift in the atmosphere. "What?" he asked, completely unaware of how things were unraveling before him.

I exchanged worried glances with my team. They all looked just as uncomfortable, caught between not knowing how to react and trying to respect what was unfolding in front of us. It was a tight spot. The tension was suffocating.

"I'm done with my lunch," Vikram said abruptly, his voice flat, void of any emotion. His words hit like a slap, and before any of us could respond, he stood up and started walking away from the table.

"Vikram," I called out, my voice tight with concern, but it fell on deaf ears. He didn't even look back, his pace unwavering, as if he had already checked out of the situation entirely.

I looked helplessly at Rakshith, who exchanged a knowing look with me, before quickly getting to his feet. Bhavin followed him without a word, both of them silently choosing to support Vikram, to follow him into whatever place he was retreating to. The unspoken bond between them, forged through years of friendship, was the only thing that seemed to be anchoring them to reality right now.

"Hey, Ananya. Nice to see you again," the woman cooed in a sickly sweet tone, and I swear, the sound of it made my blood boil. The words twisted in the air, a mockery of politeness that only added fuel to the fire building inside me. I could feel my hands balling into fists, my body tense with the overwhelming urge to snap her neck and rid the world of her.

"You both know each other?" Yuvaan asked, his voice full of curiosity.

I didn't even spare him a glance. My eyes were locked on the woman, the one who made my insides churn with disgust. "What the hell is she doing with you guys?" I demanded, the words tumbling out sharper than I intended. I didn't care if I sounded rude; the anger was too raw, too real.

The men around me looked taken aback by my tone, their faces frozen in confusion as they tried to process my outburst. But I didn't care. I wasn't going to hide what I felt. My glare never left her, pure venom in my eyes, and her smirk made my blood run hotter. It was as if she knew exactly what buttons to push.

Can I just kill this woman? The thought flitted through my mind like a dark cloud.

"Um...she...we met her after the match yesterday," Akshith stammered, his nervous energy evident as he shifted on his feet. He looked uncomfortable, but I wasn't about to let that make me feel sorry for him. He had brought this mess into our lives.

I shot the woman one last disgusted look, my stomach churning at the thought of seeing her again, before I turned on my heel and stomped off. Each step I took was filled with irritation, my mind spiraling.

Was seeing her at the match not enough of a punishment? Hadn't it been enough to make her disappear from my life? But no. They had to bring her here.

I made a beeline for my room, slamming the door shut behind me with a force I didn't even realize I had. I needed space, needed to breathe without the suffocating presence of that woman and all the turmoil she stirred. But just as I was about to turn away from the door, a knock made me freeze.

I hesitated for a moment, a wave of frustration hitting me. When I opened the door, Shaurya stood there, concern etched deeply on his face, his eyes searching mine like he could read the storm brewing inside me.

"Can I come in?" he asked, his voice low but steady.

I didn't respond immediately, just stood there, staring at him. Then, I stepped aside with a small nod, silently inviting him in. He entered, his presence filling the space, and I felt a flicker of comfort in the chaos swirling around me.

"What happened, Ananya? You seem stressed," Shaurya's voice was soft, but it had that urgency I could never ignore. He reached for my hands, pulling them gently into his, his touch grounding me.

I didn't answer at first, my throat tight, my thoughts all jumbled. Without saying a word, I wrapped my arms around his torso, pressing my cheek against his chest, the familiar beat of his heart thudding in my ear like a lifeline. I closed my eyes, trying to block out the noise in my mind, trying to find peace in this moment.

Shaurya, ever patient, began to caress my hair, his fingers threading through the strands with a tenderness that made me melt into him. I sighed deeply, letting the softness of his touch wash over me.

"I'm here," he murmured, his voice a soft whisper as his hand continued its soothing path through my hair. It was enough to make the raw edges of my frustration dull, like the world outside didn't matter as long as he was here, holding me.

And for a moment, just a moment, everything felt okay again.

"That woman with you, she is Vikram's ex." The words slipped from my mouth like venom, each syllable thick with disdain. The very thought of her made my skin crawl, and saying her name aloud twisted something deep inside me.

Shaurya's expression shifted, his brow furrowing as he processed my words. His gaze softened as he nodded slowly, a quiet understanding settling in.

"Bad breakup?" he asked cautiously, as though treading lightly on fragile ground.

I felt the bitterness rise in my throat, the sting of those painful memories threatening to suffocate me. "He caught her cheating," I spat out, my voice tight with repressed anger.

Shaurya didn't respond immediately. His silence spoke volumes—he understood the weight of what I was saying. Instead of saying anything more, he simply pulled me closer, his arms wrapping around me like a shield. His hands moved gently over my hair, soothing me in a way only he could, as though his touch was the only thing that could calm the storm within me.

We stayed like that for a while, the silence between us comfortable, yet heavy. The world outside seemed to fade as Shaurya's presence enveloped me, offering a temporary escape from the chaos that had been raging in my heart.

Finally, Shaurya gently pulled away, guiding us both to the couch. His arms never left me, though, still wrapped around me as we sank into the cushions. I rested my head on his shoulder, grateful for his quiet strength, the way he just was when everything felt out of control.

In that moment, all I could think was how lucky I was to have him here, to have someone who understood without needing to say a word.

"Shaurya?" I called out, craning my neck to look at him, my voice teasing as it slipped through the quiet room.

"Hmm?" he hummed, his eyes meeting mine with that familiar warmth.

"Are you by any chance taking advantage of me?" I wiggled my eyebrows mischievously, pointing to his hands still wrapped comfortably around my waist.

A grin tugged at the corner of his lips, and his eyes sparkled with amusement. "What if I am? You have a problem with that?" He raised an eyebrow, his gaze locking onto mine with a mischievous glint.

I felt a smile tug at my own lips, my heart fluttering as I shook my head. "Not really," I confessed, letting my head drop back onto his chest, my voice soft and content.

A low laugh rumbled through his chest, vibrating against me in the best way. It made butterflies dance in my stomach, and for a moment, everything felt lighter, and warmer, as if the world outside didn't exist at all.

He pressed a gentle kiss to my hair, his hold around me tightening, as though making sure I was safe, sound, and right where I belonged.

CHAPTER EIGHTEEN

Ananya

Though our mission was successfully completed, Kulkarni sir's orders to stay back for a few more days felt like a borrowed time—time I wasn't ready to let go of. But like every beautiful thing, it is also going to end. The thought of not being able to be a part of the team after these two days loomed over me like a heavy cloud.

Am I ready to leave? To step away from the chaos and laughter of Akshith's endless teasing, the camaraderie of teaming up with Yuvaan to prank others, and most importantly...Shaurya?

A pang shot through me.

No more watching the team practice with such intensity it felt like an art form. No more evenings filled with lighthearted banter, singing, dancing, and endless cups of coffee. No more late-night talks with the team where they shower their raw, vulnerable sides. No more Shaurya's carefree laugh echoing around me, or the way his face lit up with boyish pride after pulling off a brilliant catch or when the team scores.

And those smaller, quieter moments with him—would I lose those too?

I wouldn't sit beside him anymore, watching the stars as if they were telling secrets only we could hear. There'd be no more shared sunrises on our morning jogs, his teasing remarks making me laugh even when I was too breathless to respond. I wouldn't get to steal those fleeting glances at him, memorizing every detail of his face—the way his jaw clenched when he was focused, the warmth of his smile when he wasn't.

My breath hitched at the thought. In just two days, I would have to say goodbye to him. To the team. To everything we built in these three months.

When had this happened to me? When had *he* become the center of my thoughts, my memories, my heart? A slow ache spread through me, and I realized my cheeks were wet. Tears.

What's wrong with me? Why am I crying?

Every mission before this one brought pride and accomplishment, a sense of closure. But this time? It feels like I am losing despite being successful. It feels like I am being torn away from something I am not ready to give up.

Someone I am not ready to give up.

Why does leaving feel so unreasonable? Why does it feel like walking away from him would mean leaving behind a piece of myself?

I've spent months—years, even—with people, worked alongside them, and shared laughter and success, but never felt this... this unbearable weight in my chest at the thought of leaving them behind. Why is it so different with him? How did he become so important to me in just a few days?

Why does the mere thought of parting from him make me feel suffocated?

A soft knock on the door broke my spiraling thoughts. I hastily wiped the tears from my cheeks and opened the door, only to be greeted by *him*.

Shaurya stood there, leaning casually against the doorframe, his hands folded across his chest. His shades perched atop his head, slightly tousling his hair. And that smile—oh, that smile—so carefree and childlike, it tugged at something deep within me.

I felt my heart skip a beat. How could a person manage to look this adorable and irresistibly attractive at the same time?

For a fleeting moment, I couldn't decide whether I wanted to pinch his cheeks like a doting grandmother or kiss him senselessly until all coherent thoughts vanished.

Am I even sane any more? My mind is a mess.

The warmth of his presence filled the air, chasing away the sadness that had clung to me moments ago. Yet, beneath the warmth, the ache remained—because I knew I wouldn't have this for much longer.

"Are you okay? Why are your eyes red? Do you have a fever?" he bombarded me with questions, his voice laced with concern as he leaned closer. Before I could find words to respond, his hand reached up, the back of his palm brushing against my forehead. The tenderness of the gesture sent a fresh wave of tears welling up in my eyes.

Why is this man so caring? So effortlessly kind? It's aching my heart to be at the receiving end of his kindness and care when I know it's going to end within hours.

His hand moved from my forehead to cup my cheek, his eyes scanning mine as if searching for an answer I was too overwhelmed to give. He finally heaved a sigh, while I stood frozen, tongue-tied, and utterly consumed by the emotions surging through me.

"What happened, Ananya? Did someone say something to you? Why were you crying?" he asked, his hands gently gripping my shoulders.

I barely registered his words; my world stopped at the sound of my name on his lips. *Ananya.* Though it was normal for him to use my name, it wasn't the same. No, this was different. Intimate. Beautiful. Hearing him say my name like that set my heart racing and sent butterflies soaring in my stomach.

"Ananya?" he said again, his voice softer this time as he gave my shoulders a gentle shake.

Every part of me wanted to collapse into his arms, to hold onto him as though he was my anchor in the storm. But I forced myself to stay grounded, even as my heart screamed otherwise.

"I am fine, Shaurya," I managed, my voice barely above a whisper. "It's just...shampoo got into my eyes." The lie felt bitter on my tongue, and I swallowed hard against the lump in my throat.

His eyes narrowed slightly, unconvinced. "Do you want me to get you some eye drops or contact a doctor?" he asked, his voice still gentle, laced with concern.

I could feel the tears gathering in my eyes. Before I could answer, his hand reached up again, his thumb brushing against my cheek to wipe away a stray tear. His touch was warm, grounding me in a way nothing else could. Then, without a word, he leaned in and pressed a soft, reassuring kiss to my forehead.

The world seemed to be still.

That kiss—it wasn't rushed or fleeting. It lingered, filled with so much care, so much unspoken affection, that I felt myself melting into the moment. His lips stayed against my forehead for what felt like an eternity, and I closed my eyes, savoring the purity of it.

When he finally pulled back, his hand slid down to entwine with mine, his thumb brushing over my knuckles, grounding me.

"Will you come out with us? We're planning to visit a nearby market," he asked, a flicker of doubt in his tone, with a hint of hope shimmering in his eyes.

For a second, I hesitated, the weight of our impending goodbye pressing heavily on my heart. But if I only have two days left with him, I want to gather memories to hold onto when he's gone.

"Okay," I replied meekly, my voice barely audible. "But I have to change," I added after a pause.

He nodded and, slowly, almost reluctantly, released my hand. As the warmth of his touch faded, my gaze dropped to my now-empty hand. For a fleeting moment, I simply stood there, staring at it, wishing I could somehow hold onto him longer.

When I stepped out a few minutes later, dressed and ready, he was still there, waiting patiently by the door.

"Shall we?" he asked, his voice carrying a playful edge as he extended his hand toward me.

Without hesitation, I slipped my hand into his in a heartbeat. His fingers immediately clasped mine, and the broad smile that lit up his face was enough to bring a small, involuntary smile to my lips.

We walked to the elevator together, his grip on my hand firm. As the elevator doors closed, I felt a sudden pang of self-consciousness when a few people joined us midway. I tried to pull my hand out of his grip, not wanting to draw unnecessary attention to him.

But he tightened his grip, his fingers pressing against mine as if silently urging me not to let go.

I looked up at him. My breath hitched when I noticed the determined glint in his eyes. He didn't need to say anything; his hold spoke volumes. Taking a hesitant step closer, I allowed our arms to brush slightly, a quiet acknowledgment of the bond we were silently building.

From the corner of my eye, I caught the faintest hint of a smile tugging at his lips, one that sent my heart racing faster than I cared to admit.

In that crowded elevator, the world outside faded away, leaving just the two of us suspended in a fragile moment of connection.

We stepped out of the elevator onto the basement, and Shaurya's friends were already waiting, casually leaning against sleek bikes with their helmets in hand. My eyes flitted to the vehicles, a silent question lingering in my mind.

"Yes," Shaurya said, his tone laced with amusement as if he could read my thoughts. "We are going on bikes."

I didn't bother asking how they managed to arrange the bikes; by now, I know their ability to make things happen in record time.

"Here," he said, holding out a helmet. I silently grabbed the helmet and we walked to the bike—a Kawasaki Versys 1000, its sleek black frame gleaming under the streetlights. It looked gorgeous, but the man beside me looked even more so.

He wore his helmet, and I found myself inexplicably mesmerized by the simple act. The way his hands moved with ease, the casual tilt of his head—it was all so effortlessly attractive. My heart skipped a beat, and I couldn't stop the unbidden thought that flashed through my mind. Since when did something as mundane as putting on a helmet become this...alluring?

"Come, hop on," Shaurya's voice cut through my daze, and I quickly climbed on behind him, trying to hide the blush that had started creeping up my neck due to my little distraction.

The engine roared to life, the vibrations humming through me as the bike surged forward. I jerked forward at the sudden movement, my chest brushing against his back.

"Hold me," he said over the sound of the engine. His voice was calm, yet there was a subtle playfulness in it.

I hesitated a little, my hands hovering just above his jacket, not sure if I could trust his playful instruction. When I caught his amused smile in the bike's side mirror, my cheeks flamed, and I quickly fisted my hands over the back of his jacket.

"Good," he murmured just loud enough for me to hear, and I felt the adrenaline surge through my veins as the engine purred.

The ride was a mix of thrilling speed and quiet moments, the world around us blurring into streaks of light and sound. The wind whipped against my face, but all I could focus on was the warmth radiating from Shaurya, steady and comforting.

After about forty-five minutes, we arrived at a bustling marketplace. I marveled at the vibrant colors, the hum of chatter, and the aroma of street food wafting through the air.

But then, reality hit me like a freight train—Shaurya and his friends weren't just any group of people; they were celebrities. The kind of people who drew crowds in seconds.

I glanced around nervously, imagining the frenzy that could erupt if people recognized them. It seemed to be a disaster in the making.

"People are going to recognize you," I whispered into his ear once he parked the bike. I could smell his cinnamon fragrance, and it was addicting. I love the closeness between us, even when I know it won't last longer.

"They won't," he replied in two words, his confidence leaving me amused and worried at the same time. He gestured for me to get down, and I did as asked, my mind spiraled with the thoughts of everything that could go wrong if people recognized them. I took a step back to give him space to dismount.

He reached into his pocket, pulled out a surgical mask, and slid it on with a nonchalance that I couldn't help but roll my eyes. "Really? That's your master disguise?"

"It works," he shot back, offended, his voice muffled slightly behind the mask. Adding a pair of goggles and a cap, he gave himself a quick once-over in the bike's mirror.

"You three look like thieves now," I teased, watching Yuvaan and Akshith do the same. I giggled at the sight of them. With their masks, jackets, and shades, they looked more like a group of misfit spies than cricketers. "Give you guys a knife or something, and you'll look like professional assassins."

Yuvaan placed a hand on his chest, feigning hurt. "Excuse me, we're trendsetters, not criminals."

"Trendsetters of thieves?" I quipped, earning a disapproving head shake from Akshith and a soft chuckle from Shaurya.

"Careful, Ms. Shergill," Shaurya whispered, stepping closer, his voice low enough to send shivers down my spine. "If we really were thieves, you'd be the first thing I'd steal."

I stood rooted in my place, my cheeks flushing pink.

"I guess we would make great spies if we can get some guns," Akshith chimed, breaking the fog of my thoughts, his three fingers folded, and pointed at us like it was a gun.

Shaurya chucked at his comment, the sound muffled by the mask but still warm and teasing. "Professional spy, huh? Maybe we should add that to our skill set," he said, sliding his hand into his jacket pockets with a mock air of mystery.

I giggled, unable to help myself. The way they all played along with my silly remark only made them more endearing.

"You'd be worst spies," I teased, folding my arms. "Your strong cinnamon fragrance would give you away before you could even take a step closer to your target and Akshith, your shoes make a lot of noise to be stealthy." I pointed out.

Shaurya tilted his head slightly, sliding his goggles down, his eyes narrowing."cinnamon fragrance, huh? So you *do* notice me." That wasn't a question but a statement.

My cheeks heated up instantly, and I averted my gaze, suddenly very interested in the bustling market around us. "It's too strong," I mumbled, trying to sound nonchalant.

He leaned in closer, just enough for his words to reach me." It wasn't *that* strong, Ananya." he countered.

That one word—my name, spoken in that smooth, teasing voice of his—sent a shiver down my spine. I clenched my hands into fists to stop myself from doing something crazy, like grabbing his jacket and kissing the smirk off his face which I know was plastered on his lips behind that mask.

Akshith clapped his hands. "Alright, lovebirds, save the banter for later. Let's hit the market before it gets too crowded!"

Choosing to ignore his comment, Shaurya extended his hand toward me, his fingers curling slightly in invitation. Without a second thought, I placed my hand in his, letting his warm grip steady my racing heart.

Though Shaurya's mouth was hidden, his smile was evident from the way his eyes sparkled with amusement. "Lead the way, Ms. Observant," he said, gesturing for me to walk ahead.

As I moved, I couldn't shake the warmth that lingered in my chest. His presence was intoxicating, and consuming, and the playful banter only made me fall deeper into whatever this was between us. Whatever it was, I wasn't ready to let it go.

When we reached a shop, Akshith and I reached for a doll at the same time. I shot him a glare and he stared back, not ready to back off. "Why do you want this doll, Akshith?" I groaned.

"Because you want it?" He cocked a brow, clearly enjoying my irritation.

"Idiot!" I muttered, loud enough for him to hear.

"I heard that!" He exclaimed, his eyes enlarged in anger.

"That was meant to be heard." I countered without missing a beat.

"Shaurya, you found her of all?" Akshith pointed a finger at me, and my brain instantly went on defense. What did he mean by that?

"Excuse me! What's wrong with me?" I snapped, flipping my hair in exaggerated defiance as I glared at him. "Unlike you, I'm smart," I added with an extra sass, not letting him get away with that comment.

Akshith raised an eyebrow, clearly offended. "Excuse me?" he asked as if I'd just insulted his very existence.

"Excused. Let's go, Shaurya," I said, turning to Shaurya and tugging at his hand, ready to leave. No way I was going to give Akshith the satisfaction of a retort.

Akshith stood there, mouth opening and closing like a fish out of water, but I didn't spare him a second glance. I squeezed Shaurya's hand a little tighter, feeling the embarrassment creeping in as I pulled him along.

"Hey! You can't just leave like that after passing that comment about me! I am the smartest all-rounder in the team!" Akshith snapped as he joined us.

"Glad to know," I said, not in a mood for further embarrassment.

"Shaurya, control your girl man!" Akshith whined, sounding like a toddler.

"He won't. Shaurya is on my team." I declared. "Right?" I craned my neck to look at him. Shaurya stared at me for a moment before nodding his head.

"You two are insufferable. And Ananya, you can leave Shaurya's hand. He won't run away," Yuvaan commented with a shake of his head.

I quickly released Shaurya's hand and looked up at him, trying to gauge his reaction to my little stunt. To my surprise, Shaurya was still staring at me, his eyes wide and his ears tinged pink. He looked just as embarrassed as I felt.

Oh, God. Ananya, you idiot! What was the need to drag him like that?

I was busy cursing myself when suddenly, someone shoved me from behind, and before I could brace myself, I found myself pressed against Shaurya's chest. My breath hitched as my chest collided with his, and I could feel his heart racing under my touch. His hands instinctively moved to the sides of my waist, holding me closer as if he didn't want to let go.

The world seemed to stop as I felt his minty-hot breath against my ear, sending shivers down my spine. My skin tingled, and every inch of my body was hyper-aware of the closeness. The warmth of his body seeped into mine, and I felt like I could melt right into him. My heart pounded erratically, and the only thing I wanted at that moment was to hold him tight, never letting go.

I slowly moved my shaky hands from my sides, the desire to be closer to him overwhelming. My fingers grazed his torso, and I was about to wrap my arms around him when suddenly, a faint cry pierced the air, shattering our trance.

I jumped back instinctively, pulling away from him to see what was happening. My heart was still racing, but I couldn't ignore the panic in the air.

"Leave me!"

CHAPTER NINETEEN

Shaurya

Ananya was in the middle of her fiery arguments with Akshith, her energy captivating as always. But what left me utterly spellbound was how she reached out and grabbed my arm, dragging me along without a second thought.

The world seemed to blur for a moment, her voice the only thing I could hear. My name never sounded this sweet, this magical, not even when chanted by a stadium full of fans. *Shaurya.* It felt like she was summoning my soul at that moment. And the way she said it—it was how she owned it as if I belonged to her and no one else.

I let her lead me, my body moving on autopilot while my mind replayed her words in an endless loop. The warmth of her touch burned through my skin, but it was nothing compared to the fire raging inside me at the thought of being hers, even if just at that moment.

In those few seconds, she led me, I wasn't just Shaurya, the cricket captain. I was *her Shaurya.* Her action felt like a claim, a promise, and I could hardly believe how much it meant to me.

Seeing her reaching out to me with such authority made me want to grab her and hold her close, to tell her she could do that forever.

I had no idea how my friends reacted to her move, and frankly, I couldn't care less. My entire world narrowed down to the beautiful woman standing before me, her cheeks tinted with the most delicate blush, her wide eyes betraying the realization of what she had done.

And then, the way her blush deepened at Yuvaan's comment, blooming across her milky cheeks, made my heart thrum in ways I never thought possible. She looked so adorably flustered, and all I wanted at that moment was to pull her into my arms, to hide that precious blushing beauty from the world.

As if the universe itself had heard my silent wish, someone bumped into her, sending her stumbling right into me.

Her soft, warm body collided with mine, and I felt a thousand sensations ignite under my skin, sparking through my veins like fireworks. She fit so perfectly against me, as though she was meant to be there. My hands instinctively moved to her waist, hovering for a moment before finally settling over the soft curves over her top.

The feel of her silken skin beneath my fingers sent a shiver of raw exhilaration through me. She gasped softly, her stomach pulling in as my touch seemed to steal her breath away.

Leaning in, I inhaled deeply, the scent of her hair and skin flooding my senses. Her body trembled, and I could feel her heartbeat racing, echoing the wild rhythm of my own.

Her hands twitched at her sides, hesitating for a moment before she began to lift them as if she was about to hold me too. My chest tightened at the thought of her hugging me back, and I felt like I could live in that moment forever.

But then, a plea, low but desperate, shattered our little bubble of magic. She froze, her body pulling away from mine as reality came crashing back.

The loss of her warmth made my blood boil with frustration, my jaw clenching at the intrusion. For just a moment, she had been mine—entirely mine—and I wasn't ready to let her go.

"Leave me!" a desperate plea tore through the air, yanking us both out of our moment. For a second, I thought it was my imagination, but the look on Ananya's and others' faces told me it wasn't. Someone was in trouble.

Our heads whipped around to see the source of the commotion. A man was dragging a girl by her hair, her pleas muffled by his iron hand. Behind him, four other men followed, their sinister smirks painting an ugly picture of what was to come. Before we had time to grasp the situation, Ananya was already running behind them.

In the middle of the crumbling, desolate walls stood a terrified girl, trembling as tears streamed down her face. Her hands were clasped together in desperate supplication, shaking uncontrollably as she begged the brute in front of her.

The man was built like a fortress—thick muscles straining against his shirt, a jagged scar cutting across his left eye, and a gleaming silver earring dangling from one ear. His presence was terrifying, his every step radiating menace as he advanced toward her, like a predator approaching its prey.

The girl, fragile and shaking in fear, tried to crawl away on the dusty ground, her knees scrapping against the broken terrain. But the brute advanced towards her slowly, deliberately, as if he was enjoying every bit of her dread.

Every fiber in my body tensed at the sight, anger bubbling in my chest like molten lava.

"I'll call the police," Akshith said, pulling out his phone, his voice barely steady as the tension in the air thickened.

Ananya took a step forward, her instinctive need to help evident in the determination blazing in her eyes. But before she could move further, I grabbed her hand, my grip firm yet gentle.

"It's too risky," I whispered, my voice low but urgent. "Let's wait for the police."

Her gaze flickered between me and the helpless girl, her inner turmoil etched clearly across her face. Her lips parted as if to argue, but she must have seen the seriousness in my eyes, because she nodded hesitantly and stepped back.

But as we waited, the scene in front of us became unbearable. The brute had closed the distance between himself and the girl, his massive hand tangling in her hair and yanking her up with cruel force.

The girl cried out in pain, her sobs tearing through the air, and that was it. My blood boiled, fury coursing through my veins like wildfire.

Bastard!

The word echoed in my mind as I clenched my fists, every muscle in my body screaming to act.

"Scream all you want. No man is going to come and save you," the brute sneered, his voice dripping with twisted pride.

I took a step forward, my instincts screaming at me to intervene before the girl suffered any more of this nightmare. But just as I moved, I felt a soft yet firm grip on my hand.

Turning, I saw Ananya clutching me, her eyes burning with a mix of determination and something deeper—something resolute. She shook her head gently, her silent plea for restraint clear. And then, to my utter shock, she stepped forward.

"I will handle them," she said, her voice calm yet charged with an undercurrent of steel.

I blinked at her, flabbergasted. *What does she mean she'll handle them? Did she not see the size of those men?* They looked like they were carved out of stone—hulking bulls with pure menace in their stance. And here she was, my fragile, delicate doll, standing there, ready to take them on.

"Ananya, but—" I began, my voice laced with panic and disbelief.

Before I could finish, a sharp, agonized scream tore through the air. Our heads snapped back toward the girl just in time to see the brute strike her across the face with a resounding slap. She crumpled to the ground, her sobs growing louder, echoing in the eerie silence of the ruins.

That was all it took for Ananya.

With a determination that left me rooted in place, she gently removed my grip from her hand, her touch lingering for the briefest moment before she pulled away. She turned to me, her eyes meeting mine with an unspoken assurance that somehow calmed the storm raging inside me. And then she ran.

"Ananya!" I shouted, my heart seizing in fear as she darted toward the group. I couldn't let her face them alone—not her.

I surged forward, chasing after her, my pulse pounding in my ears. My friends, catching onto the gravity of the situation, didn't hesitate and followed close behind.

"Leave her!" Ananya's voice thundered, cutting through the air like a sharp blade. It wasn't the sweet, gentle tone I knew—it was raw, fierce, and commanding. My breath hitched as I watched her, this unfamiliar fire burning in her eyes. They weren't the soft pools I was used to; they were blazing fireballs, daring anyone to defy her.

A shiver ran down my spine, goosebumps rising on my skin as the sheer intensity of her fury washed over me.

"Or else? What will you do?" the brute sneered, his voice laced with mockery. His taunting tone made my hands curl into fists. I wanted nothing more than to launch myself at him, to make him regret ever crossing our path.

"You'll see," Ananya retorted, her voice as cold as steel. Without breaking her glare, she strode forward, her every step radiating unyielding resolve.

She reached the girl, who was trembling like a leaf, and gently pulled her to her feet, her protective presence a stark contrast to the chaos surrounding them. Then, with deliberate grace, she placed herself between the girl and the men, her small frame standing tall against their hulking figures.

One of the goons, his ego bruised by her audacity, lunged forward, his hand outstretched to grab her neck. I felt my heart leap in fear.

But Ananya didn't flinch.

With speed and precision that left me stunned, she caught his wrist mid-air, her grip unyielding. Before he could react, she twisted his arm back, the sound of tendons straining and his agonized scream ripping through the air.

The man dropped to his knees, clutching his arm, while Ananya's gaze didn't waver for a second.

"Don't you dare touch me!" Ananya's voice rang out, sharp and commanding, echoing off the ruined walls. It wasn't just a warning—it was a threat, brimming with raw power. The brute who had dared to raise his hand froze, his confidence wavering under her fiery glare.

The other men, who had seemed invincible just moments ago, exchanged uneasy glances. I saw it—fear flickering in their eyes as they realized they were up against something far more formidable than they'd anticipated.

But one of them, bolder—or perhaps more foolish—than the rest, stepped forward, his sneer dripping with arrogance. "Let's see how tough you are," he mocked, lunging toward her.

Before I could even process what was happening, Ananya moved. Her foot shot out in a swift, calculated motion, landing a brutal kick squarely in his stomach. The impact was so forceful that he stumbled back, crashing against the crumbling wall behind him. He doubled over, gasping for breath, the wind knocked out of him.

My heart was pounding, a chaotic mix of pride and worry swirling within me. She was breathtaking—a force of nature unleashed.

Another man tried his luck, charging at her with a roar. But Ananya was ready. She sidestepped his attack with ease, grabbing his arm and twisting it behind his back in one fluid motion. His scream of pain pierced the air as she slammed him down to the ground with a strength I didn't know she possessed.

The third man hesitated, his confidence visibly faltering as he watched his comrades fall one by one. But his hesitation didn't last long. He charged at her with a wild swing, but Ananya ducked effortlessly, spinning around to deliver a sharp elbow strike to his jaw. The crack was audible, and he crumpled to the ground, clutching his face.

The remaining two men, clearly shaken, tried to circle her, hoping to overwhelm her with numbers. My fists clenched as I fought the urge to intervene, but I couldn't tear my eyes away from her.

"Come on, then," Ananya taunted, her voice laced with daring. She stood her ground, fearless, her stance steady and unwavering.

The first man lunged, and she met him halfway, her knee slamming into his ribs with devastating precision. He let out a guttural groan before collapsing, writhing in pain.

The final man, now visibly trembling, made a desperate attempt to grab her from behind. I moved instinctively, ready to protect her, but Ananya didn't need me. She spun around, catching him off guard, and delivered a roundhouse kick that sent him sprawling to the ground.

By the end of it, all five men were lying on the dirt, groaning in pain and humiliation.

I couldn't take my eyes off her. Ananya stood amidst the chaos she had created, her chest heaving, her fiery gaze sweeping over the fallen goons. She was radiant, and her courage and strength left me utterly speechless.

And then the sound of sirens cut through the tension, growing louder as the police arrived. Within moments, the officers were on the scene, cuffing the men and hauling them to their feet.

"Bhai, I irritated her a lot in the past, didn't I?" I heard Akshith whisper nervously from my left. I turned to him, finding him trembling, his hands clasped together in a desperate, almost comical gesture of prayer.

I couldn't help but chuckle, though there was a tight knot of pride in my chest. "Forget the past, Akshu. You were just arguing with her a few minutes ago. Look at her now." I nodded toward Ananya, my voice low but filled with awe. "She looks damn scary, bro."

Akshith's wide-eyed expression was priceless, but it was Yuvaan who made the moment all the more amusing. "If she punches you in the same anger, your fans will be missing your handsome face for a month, bro," he teased, his grin sharp with mischief.

Akshith swallowed hard, wiping the sweat from his brow. Honestly, it was no wonder he was afraid—Ananya had just handled five grown men like they were nothing.

I couldn't help but admire her, a swell of pride filling my chest. She was stronger than I had ever imagined, her determination blazing like fire. My heart swelled as I turned to her, seeing the way she stood among the wreckage of those men, the calm after the storm.

But as I approached her, a wave of concern washed over me. I couldn't help myself. I needed to make sure she was okay. Despite the way she'd dispatched those goons with such force, a part of me couldn't shake the worry. What if she'd hurt herself in the process? What if a stray punch or a kick had left its mark?

I reached out for her hands, my fingers brushing hers in a gentle, almost tentative motion. She turned to me, her expression softening slightly at my touch, but I was too focused on checking her over to care about anything else.

"Are you okay?" I asked, my voice filled with quiet concern, my eyes scanning her for any sign of injury. "None of them got to you, right?"

I knew deep down that she was strong—stronger than anyone I'd ever known. But the sight of her fighting those men, her every movement so graceful yet powerful, made me realize just how much she meant to me.

Her soft chuckle broke the silence, and I met her gaze, the intensity of her stare calming the storm of worry in my chest. "I'm fine, Shaurya," she said, her voice steady, though I noticed the faintest tremor in her hand as she gripped mine in return.

"I'm more worried about you," I murmured, pulling her into me instinctively. "You were incredible, but I couldn't bear it if you got hurt."

She smiled up at me, the warmth in her eyes making my heart skip a beat. "I can handle myself, Shaurya. But I guess I like it when you get concerned about me."

And with that simple statement, I knew. I would always be there for her—no matter what.

"Kuch khaane chale? Bhook lag rahi hai," she whined, her lower lip jutting out most adorably, and her eyes—those innocent puppy eyes—were so irresistible that I felt my heart melt. I couldn't help the overwhelming urge to pull her cheeks, to kiss those soft, pink lips that were teasing me with their cuteness.

Damn! She's breathtaking.

I couldn't stop the smile that tugged at my lips. "Come," I said, gently grabbing her wrist. As I led the way, I noticed Akshith was keeping a fair distance from Ananya. He was practically tip-toeing around her, as though she might turn him into pulp with one wrong move. It made me want to burst out laughing, but I held it in, not wanting to look like a fool in front of my girl.

My girl!

Yes, I'm hers, and she's definitely mine. There was something so grounding about the thought—like everything suddenly felt right in the world.

I shook my head, trying to push away the silly thoughts threatening to distract me. I needed to focus. My girl was hungry, and I was going to feed her.

I scanned the area, my eyes darting over food stalls and small shops, looking for something quick. Then I spotted a momos stall at a distance, the scent of steaming hot dumplings filling the air, making my stomach growl in sympathy.

I turned to Ananya, about to ask if she'd like to stop there, but she was already looking at the stall with those eager, hungry eyes. She caught my gaze and, sensing my question before I could even ask, gave me a grin that could only be described as mischievous.

Without a word, she turned and started pulling me towards the stall, her excitement so contagious that I couldn't help but laugh. "You're dragging me there already?" I teased, letting her lead me with an enthusiasm that matched her energy.

"Well, you were taking too long to decide!" she shot back, her tone playful, and I found myself completely enchanted by her.

I didn't care anymore if Akshith and Yuvaan were following us or if the world was watching. At that moment, it was just me and her—the warmth of her hand in mine, the sound of her laughter, and the joy of knowing that we were together, sharing this little piece of happiness.

I knew I had everything I ever needed right here—my girl, her puppy eyes, and the promise of food that would make her smile even brighter.

"But how will you guys eat? You can't take off those masks, na?" she asked, her voice carrying a hint of disappointment, once we were standing in front of the shop. The concern in her eyes made me pause for a moment, but I shook my head, about to order. But then, before I could, she pulled me back by my sleeve.

I turned, eyebrows raised, to face her. "What now?" I asked, already sensing a mischievous thought brewing behind those eyes.

"What if they recognize your voice?" she whispered, her lips so close to my ear that I could feel her warm breath against my skin. I blinked, but I couldn't catch a single word she was saying. The closeness between us was overwhelming, each breath she took sending shivers down my spine.

Her hand tightened around the sleeve of my shirt, and I could feel the electric spark between us, like a current running through my veins. Goosebumps sprang to life on the back of my neck, my body reacting to her touch even as my mind struggled to stay focused.

I nodded mindlessly, not caring much about the words she was speaking. It was as if everything faded away when she was near. Just the sound of her voice and the soft whisper of her breath were enough to drown everything else out. I was lost in her.

"Bhaiya, 7 plate momos pack kar dena please," she ordered, her tone casual yet assertive. The stall owner smiled and nodded at her, completely unaware of the storm that had just taken place in my mind. His wife added a generous portion of chutney in a silver foil and began packing the momos.

Ananya took the bags and, before I could react, she paid for them online with a quick swipe on her phone.

I opened my mouth to protest—after all, I was supposed to be the one treating her—but she stopped me with a single finger pressed to her lips.

The gesture was so innocent, yet the way she looked at me with those teasing eyes made it feel like I was about to lose all control. Those pink, plump lips... I could almost taste them, and the sight of her slender fingers pressed against them had me questioning my own sanity.

Come out of those thoughts, Shaurya!

I mentally slapped myself back into reality, but my mind wouldn't stop running wild. Every little movement, every look, was enough to keep me tied to her, and in that moment, I realized just how much she had already become a part of me.

"Let's go?" she asked, her voice soft and inviting. It felt like the world paused for a moment as we all nodded in unison. We made our way back to the quiet alley, away from the crowd, and found a few stones to sit on. As we removed our masks and goggles, I couldn't help but glance at her—there was something effortlessly beautiful about her, even in such an ordinary setting.

She handed out the momo packets, and we dug into them, the conversation flowing lightly between us. But every now and then, my attention would drift back to her. The way her lips moved when she spoke, the subtle way her eyes glistened in the low light, the way her laughter filled the air—everything about her felt like magic.

"Water?" she asked, breaking my trance.

Akshith practically lunged for the water bottle she pulled out from her bag, chugging it down like he hadn't seen water in days. He passed it to Yuvaan, who finished the rest, leaving me wondering, now what will she drink?

"I'll get you another bottle," I said, ready to get up, but she stopped me with a gentle tug on my arm.

I glanced at her, and she shook her head. So, I sat back down, my curiosity piqued. She reached into her bag and pulled out a flask, handing it to me. The sleek, polished bottle wasn't what I expected—certainly not water. I twisted the cap off and took a sip, only to find that it wasn't water at all, but my favorite orange juice.

"Orange juice?" I asked, surprised and a little amused.

She shrugged, the smile playing at the corner of her lips. "I ordered it before you came to my room and brought it along."

I couldn't help but smile at the thoughtfulness behind it. She had remembered. Just like that, she always seemed to know what I needed, even when I didn't say a word.

I took a few more sips, enjoying the sweet taste, before handing the flask back to her. She took it with a quick grin, lifting it to her lips, but to my surprise, she didn't let her lips touch the bottle. With a casual flick of her wrist, she tossed the bottle back into her bag. It was such a small thing, but it made me smile—a little gesture, a shared moment of intimacy, one that made me feel closer to her than ever before.

I leaned back slightly, watching her with a soft smile. I wasn't sure if I'd ever get used to how she made even the most ordinary things feel extraordinary.

"Let's go buy some goodies!" Her voice sparkled with excitement, and I couldn't help but smile at her enthusiasm. We all got up, ready to explore the vibrant market, and I noticed how her energy seemed to light up everything around us.

We wandered through the bustling lanes, picking up little treasures. I bought a few sandalwood oils and soaps, along with two intricately designed Rosewood inlay workpieces, which I knew would make great gifts for the family.

She, on the other hand, chose a delicate sandalwood Ganesh Ji idol—something about the way she handled it, so gently, so thoughtfully, made me admire her even more. She also picked up some Coorg coffee powder and a few incense sticks, the sweet scent of which filled the air, adding to the charm of the moment.

Then, as we continued strolling, she helped me select a couple of sarees for Maa and Di. She was so sure about what would suit her family, her eyes sparkling with love as she imagined how happy they would be. It was clear how much she cared for her family, and that only made me appreciate her even more.

While she was busy looking for a saree for her mother, a beautiful piece caught my eye. It was an exquisite shade of deep crimson, with golden threads that shimmered in the light. I could already picture her wearing it—she would look stunning in that saree. Without a second thought, I turned to the shopkeeper.

"Add that saree to my purchases, please," I said, my heart racing just a little as I imagined the look on her face when she saw it.

I couldn't help but feel a sense of pride, knowing I had bought something special for her—something that would bless me with a smile of hers.

CHAPTER TWENTY

Ananya

After bidding farewell to Akshith and Yuvaan, I stood beside Shaurya, the setting sun casting a golden glow over the bustling market. Shaurya and I wandered through the streets, lost in our own little world, until the sky began to fade, transitioning from soft hues of orange to the dusky purple of the evening. It felt as though time had slowed down, allowing me to savor the fleeting moments of this perfect day.

As we moved to the parking, I noticed Shaurya being unusually quiet. Before I could enquire about it, I felt his presence beside me—calm yet filled with an unspoken tension. Shaurya's voice, low and slightly unsure, broke the stillness. "Ananya, will you come to a place with me?"

I turned to face him and found him standing just a few inches away, his posture tense and his hand slightly trembling as he ran it through his hair. His eyes, usually so intense, now appeared almost vulnerable. Something was going on in his mind.

"Is everything alright?" I asked softly, my voice laced with concern. The nervous chuckle that escaped his lips only deepened the unease swirling inside me.

"I'm fine," he assured me, but the uncertainty in his eyes spoke volumes. "Will you come?"

The vulnerability in his gaze tugged at me in ways I couldn't explain. There was something about the way he asked, something raw and honest, that made my heart beat just a little faster. The trust between us had always been there, but now, it felt like it was deepening like we were on the verge of something unspoken.

I nodded, unable to resist his silent plea. "Okay."

A small relieved smile bloomed on his face, a brief but beautiful moment of light in the tension that surrounded us.

As we reached his bike, I felt my pulse quicken. Shaurya, ever the enigma, was a sight to behold—his quiet strength and the way he seemed to move through the world with effortless confidence. He handed me a helmet, his fingers brushing against mine for a fraction of a second, sending an unexpected shiver through me.

I slid the helmet over my head, the cool leather encasing me in its warmth. Shaurya adjusted his own helmet, his movements slow but deliberate, and then, he gestured for me to hop on.

I had no idea where he was taking me, but the cool evening breeze and the fading warmth of the sun made everything feel so serene, so...right. The road stretched before us, a ribbon of freedom that seemed to go on forever. And before I could stop myself, I leaned into him, my cheek resting softly against his back.

The closeness between us, the stillness of the world around us, and the steady hum of the engine under us felt...heavenly. In that moment, it was just him and me—nothing else mattered. I expected him to shift or pull away, maybe even comment on my sudden closeness, but instead, he did something that made my heart flutter in unexpected ways. Without a word, his hand reached up, warm and gentle, guiding mine to his torso.

I hesitated for a fraction of a second, my pulse quickening at the touch, but then, as if drawn by an invisible force, I wrapped my arms around him. The sensation of his body against mine, the warmth of his chest under my hands, felt so right, like I had always belonged here.

I pressed my cheek more firmly into his back, the leather of his jacket cool beneath my skin, and let my helmet fall to the side, my hair now free in the wind. With my eyes closed, I let myself sink deeper into the moment, letting the wind carry away the thoughts that were beginning to overwhelm me.

But even in this perfect serenity, there was something else—a pull, a yearning that I couldn't quite explain. Deep down, a part of me wasn't ready for this moment to end. I wasn't ready to leave him, to slip away from this closeness we had found.

I didn't understand the feelings stirring inside of me, but they were strong, undeniable. A part of me had always known something was different with Shaurya—the way he looked at me, the quiet intensity in his touch, the way he made me feel like the only person in the world. But now, with my arms around him, pressed so close, I couldn't ignore it anymore. There was a bond between us, unspoken and yet so real. It was more than just attraction.

It was something deeper—something I wasn't ready to face, but couldn't deny.

In this moment, I wasn't just holding onto him physically—I was holding onto something I couldn't name, but it was there, pulsing between us, and I was too afraid to let go.

"We are here."

His voice sliced through the quiet, pulling me out of the trance I had slipped into. I hadn't even realized the tears had fallen until I felt the coolness of them against my skin. Hastily, I wiped them away, embarrassed, but the vulnerability in that simple gesture lingered in my chest. My heart raced as I stepped off the bike, my fingers trembling as I ran them through my hair, trying to regain some composure.

Shaurya put the bike on its stand, and I watched him remove his helmet, his movements almost mechanical—too controlled, too still. When he got off, I looked around, trying to piece together where we were.

We were in the middle of nowhere, it seemed—a forest, or something wild like that. The trees surrounded us in every direction, their shadows stretching long in the fading light of the evening. The quiet was deafening, broken only by the distant rustle of leaves and the soft lapping of water. I felt my pulse quicken, a mix of awe and unease swirling within me.

I turned to Shaurya, confusion written all over my face, and that's when I noticed it—the flicker of nervousness in his eyes. It was faint, but it was there, and it sent a ripple of unease through me. Not because I didn't trust him—no, it was something else. A quiet fear, one that had nothing to do with me but everything to do with him.

His lips curled into a small smile, trying to ease the tension between us, but it only deepened my concern. "I own this place," he said, a gesture sweeping towards the small house nestled at the edge of a lake, surrounded by nature. His words felt like a secret, whispered between us, but they also carried a weight I couldn't understand.

The house was breathtaking—modest yet perfect in its own way. It sat on the edge of a tranquil lake, the water reflecting the fading light of the sun like a mirror. I could feel the serenity of the place seeping into me, calming the frantic beating of my heart, but still, something about this whole situation felt...different.

Without another word, Shaurya extended his hand to me, his fingers outstretched, almost hesitant. I placed my hand in his without thinking, and for a moment, everything else faded—the tension, the fear, the questions. It was just us.

We walked together toward the door, and Shaurya unlocked it with a key I hadn't seen him bring. The sound of the door creaking open was surprisingly loud in the stillness, and I stepped inside, my senses immediately assaulted by the coziness of the space.

The living room was small but warm, and inviting. The soft glow of the lamps filled the room with a golden hue, making the wooden walls feel even more intimate. There was a couch in the center, a small kitchen attached to the side, and a dining table tucked near the windows. The space felt like it belonged to someone who cherished peace, someone who found solace in simplicity. But the thing that struck me the most was the staircase leading upstairs, and the photos of Shaurya and his family that lined the wall beside it.

I didn't need to ask the question on my mind. Shaurya must've sensed it, for he answered before I could open my mouth. "There's a bedroom with an attached bathroom upstairs." His voice was low, almost gentle, as though he was trying to make me feel comfortable.

I nodded, my thoughts still racing. I couldn't help but notice how the light from the windows played off the white curtains, casting soft shadows across the room. Everything about the cottage felt like a dream—beautiful, calm, almost surreal.

I looked at him, trying to gauge what this place meant to him. There was something deeply personal about it, something that went beyond the walls and windows. As I stood there, surrounded by the quiet of the space, I couldn't help but feel like I was stepping into a piece of his soul.

"Do you want water? I can't offer anything cold as there's no fridge here," Shaurya said, removing his jacket and draping it over the armrest of the couch. His movements were casual, but there was a quiet grace to them that I couldn't ignore. As he walked toward the kitchen, I couldn't help but watch him, a sense of wonder filling me.

I looked around the space, still trying to grasp the peace this place seemed to hold. The kitchen was simple yet inviting—there was a stove, a few cutlery pieces, and a cabinet stocked with vegetables and food items. The sight of the freshly stocked supplies made it feel even more personal like this was a place he genuinely used and cared for.

"Do you have milk? I'll make coffee for us," I offered, and without missing a beat, Shaurya retrieved a bottle of milk from one of the cabinets. I felt a strange warmth settle in my chest as I turned on the stove, the soft click of the flame breaking the quiet.

He leaned against the kitchen counter, watching me intently, but not in a way that made me uncomfortable—instead, it felt like he was truly present, savoring this moment with me. I carefully poured the coffee powder into the pan, the smell of it filling the space, rich and comforting. It was such a simple thing, making coffee, yet it felt so... intimate.

The scent of the brewing coffee seemed to envelop the room, and I couldn't help but take a deep breath, inhaling the warmth that spread through me. Shaurya moved to the cabinet and took down two cups, his actions fluid, almost rehearsed. I filled both cups, handing him his, and as I did, I noticed the soft, amused smile playing on his lips. It was a small thing, but there was something about the way he looked at the cup that made my heart skip a beat. Why was he smiling at something so ordinary?

I brushed the thought aside, but the quiet smile lingered in my mind. We both walked back to the living room, settling into the couch. There was only one seat, so we found ourselves sitting side by side, the space between us so small, so intimate. I could feel the heat from his body seeping into mine, and a strange, almost electric tension filled the air.

I took a sip of my coffee, and instantly, I felt the warmth spread through me. The taste was perfect—the right balance of milk and sugar, just the way I loved it. It was the best coffee I had ever tasted, but I couldn't help the soft moan that threatened to escape my lips. I stopped myself at the last second, a small flush creeping up my neck as I silently cursed my own reaction.

"You make the best coffee, Ananya," Shaurya said, his voice a low, warm murmur, and I felt my cheeks heat up. His words, simple as they were, seemed to carry so much weight. I wanted to thank him, to say something meaningful, but my words got stuck, tangled in the strange, deep feeling that had taken root in my chest.

"Do you come here often, Shaurya?" I asked, the question escaping my lips before I could stop it. I turned to look at him, only to find that he was already looking at me. His gaze was steady, and intense, like he was waiting for me to say something more.

"Yes, and we can come here whenever you want to," he replied, his voice low, like he was offering me something private, something special. The words settled in my chest, making my heart race a little faster. I just nodded, too shy to speak, my cheeks flushing a soft pink at the thought of being here alone with him, in this quiet, secluded place.

I caught the edge of a smile tugging at his lips from the corner of my eye, but I didn't dare to meet his gaze. The space between us was thick with unspoken words, with feelings we hadn't yet voiced.

A strand of hair fell across my face, and as I reached up to tuck it behind my ear, I felt his hand cover mine. The touch was gentle, but something was electrifying about it, something that made my breath catch in my throat. My eyes shot up to his, and I found him looking at me with such intensity that it made my heart skip a beat.

Without a word, his fingers slid through the strands of my hair, pushing it back behind my ear, his touch lingering a little longer than necessary. His eyes never left mine, his gaze deep, like he was searching for something in me, or perhaps, letting me see something in him. The world around us seemed to fade, the only sound was the beating of my heart, loud in my ears, drowning out everything else.

The tension between us was palpable, so thick that it almost hurt. I could feel it, crawling under my skin, making every nerve in my body come alive. He was close, too close, and yet I couldn't seem to pull away, couldn't bring myself to break the moment. Every inch of me was aware of him, of the way his hand was still hovering near my face, of the heat radiating between us.

"Wh...why did you bring me here?" I stammered, the words slipping from my lips as my heartbeat quickened, pounding in my chest like it was trying to escape. The nervousness mingled with excitement, twisting inside me, tightening my stomach into a knot. As if sensing the turmoil within me, Shaurya moved a little closer. The couch beside me dipped, and my breath hitched at the shift in the space between us.

"I wanted to spend some time with you, alone," he murmured, his voice barely audible, the words almost like a secret meant only for me. The way he whispered the last word, so soft and intimate, sent a shiver down my spine. The warmth of his breath brushed against my ear, and every nerve in my body seemed to come alive. Goosebumps rose on my skin, the heat inside me intensifying. I could feel every inch of him near me, my body responding to his presence in ways I didn't fully understand.

"Wh...why?" I managed to whisper, my voice betraying me, trembling under the weight of his proximity. My fingers fisted the fabric of my kurti, a futile attempt to steady myself. His thighs brushed against mine, a touch so subtle but so electric that it stole the air from my lungs. His forearm brushed against mine, and I felt him closing in, leaving no space between us. I had felt these urges before, when we were close, but now, with him this near, my entire body went into overdrive. My throat felt dry, my pulse racing and I was suddenly too aware of how badly I wanted him.

"Tell me you don't want to spend time with me, we will leave" his voice dropped lower, husky, just for me, his words brushing against my ear like a caress. I could feel the unevenness in his breathing, and it mirrored my own. My hands trembled, gripping the fabric of my kurti tighter, but somehow, I didn't want to pull away. I wanted this closeness, even if it was making me lose control. I was scared, but excited in a way that felt almost wrong.

"I...I didn't...didn't say that," I stammered, my voice barely a whisper, the words fighting to come out as I licked my dry lips. My mouth was parched, my throat tight, but I couldn't bring myself to look away from him. When I finally raised my gaze and locked eyes with him, something shifted. His eyes were dark, and intense, like they were pulling me into a world I wasn't ready to enter. But I couldn't look away. The magnetism between us was undeniable, and the proximity, the way his body was so close to mine, made my heart race out of control. I didn't know what to do, how to breathe, or what to say. All I could focus on was him, his presence, and the overwhelming desire I felt, pounding through every inch of me.

His breaths were now warm against my cheeks, the air between us thick with unspoken words and the weight of the moment. The distance between us was so small, I could feel the heat radiating off of him, and every exhale from him seemed to stir something within me. My eyes fluttered shut for a moment as his rough, calloused palms cupped my cheeks, the sensation sending a ripple of heat through me. The warmth of his touch contrasted against the softness of my skin, making my pulse race.

My hands moved almost instinctively, sliding up to rest on his forearms, fisting the fabric of his shirt, unable to ignore the way his presence was consuming me. I felt the air around us grow heavier, the world outside fading as his lips, those pink, inviting lips, hovered so close. My breath caught as his lips neared my forehead, the gentle touch making my heart skip a beat. I didn't want to move, didn't want to break this moment, yet my body betrayed me, yearning for more.

He moved closer, his body pressing against mine, and with every inch he reduced the distance, my breath became shallower, more desperate. My thighs instinctively clenched together, the pressure building, a mix of anticipation and desire that left me feeling almost dizzy. I could feel the overwhelming weight of his presence, his heat, his need.

"Go upstairs before I lose my control, Ananya," his voice was low, a husky whisper that vibrated against my skin, sending a jolt straight to my core. His lips brushed against my forehead, and I swore my mind went blank, numb to everything but the intensity of the moment. I couldn't think, couldn't move. All I could focus on was him, and the pull between us was magnetic.

"Then lose it," the words slipped from my lips, more bold than I'd ever thought I could be. A rush of adrenaline surged through me, and suddenly, my hands were moving, trailing from his elbows to his shoulders, then around his neck. The weight of his touch, the way his hands slid down my back, was enough to send me into a frenzy of longing. My body pressed against his, unable to break free from the magnetic force that tethered us together.

I felt him pull me closer, our bodies fitting together in a way that felt both natural and electrifying. My hands tightened around his neck as I rested my head in the crook of his, our breaths mingling. His heart beat in time with mine, a steady rhythm that seemed to synchronize our souls. At that moment, I wasn't sure where I ended and he began.

His hands trailed lower, the heat of his touch moving across my back before he cupped my asscheeks, and I gasped, the shock of his touch sending a shockwave of sensation through me. Without a word, he lifted me effortlessly, his strength both surprising and comforting, and I was suddenly straddling him, my legs wrapped around his hips, my front pressed against his, leaving no room for doubt about the intensity of our connection. His hands, firm and possessive, held me against him, as if afraid I might slip away.

Every inch of our bodies was pressed together, the heat, the desire, the need, it all felt so overwhelming. But still, I couldn't stop myself. Every nerve in my body screamed for him, for this closeness, for more. But I couldn't find the words, so I let my actions speak, tightening my hold around his neck as I let my body melt into his.

His hands slid from my backside to my waist, his touch sending a shiver down my spine as he pressed his hands into the curves of my body. A soft gasp escaped my lips, and I couldn't help but lean into him, my breath quickening. I pulled away from his neck slowly, meeting his gaze, and there it was again—those eyes, dark and filled with an intensity that made my heart race.

My lips trembled as his gaze pierced through me, almost as though he could read my every thought. My tongue unconsciously darted out to wet my lips, and I saw him swallow, his Adam's apple bobbing as if he, too, couldn't fight the attraction between us. It was as if a magnetic pull between us was growing stronger with every passing second. I wanted to kiss his Adam's apple. I wanted to suck on it.

His hand gently cupped my face, tilting it ever so slightly, bringing me closer, his other hand still on my waist but now slipping beneath the fabric of my kurthi, his fingers brushing lightly against my skin. The touch was electric, sending goosebumps in its wake.

I fisted the fabric of his shirt above his shoulders, feeling his warmth, his strength, wanting more of it. As he moved closer, the space between us evaporated, my breath hitching in anticipation. My eyes fluttered shut, waiting for the kiss I thought was inevitable, but instead, his lips landed gently on my right cheek, pressing a soft kiss there. His other hand traced my cheek with the gentlest caress, sending a wave of heat rushing through my body.

I stayed frozen for a moment, my heart pounding in my chest, unsure whether to pull him closer or let the moment unfold. The tenderness of his kiss on my cheek made something inside me ache, the softness contrasting with the intensity of everything else between us. But still, I wanted more.

He pulled back slightly, and I felt a strand of my hair catch on his stubble. The sight of him, his jawline shadowed by the mess of tangled hair, only made him look even more irresistible. I could hardly breathe as he leaned in again, this time kissing my left cheek, soft and lingering. Then, his lips moved down to my jawline, each kiss igniting a trail of warmth that sent shivers through my body.

My hands, almost of their own accord, moved from his fingers to the back of his neck, pulling him closer. My head tilted back as his kisses awakened something deep within me—something I wasn't sure I was ready for, but at the same time, I craved it.

His hand left my cheek and moved slowly to the back of my neck, fingers threading through my hair and gripping my nape with a firm yet tender hold. The pressure sent a rush of heat through me, making me gasp. His lips hovered over mine, our foreheads gently touching, breaths mingling in the space between us. My eyes fluttered shut, overwhelmed by the closeness, the intensity, and the electric pull between us.

"Open your eyes, Anya," he commanded, his voice low and filled with a kind of quiet power that made a shiver run down my spine. The words sent a surge of warmth through me, and despite myself, my core responded.

"Ahh..." A soft moan escaped my lips as his fingers pinched the side of my waist, sending jolts of sensation through me. He caressed the skin with his knuckles, repeating his words. This time, I obeyed, opening my eyes.

Our gazes locked, and I could see the heat in his eyes, a fire that matched the one burning within me. But there was something more—something deeper—that made my heart skip. There was a vulnerability there, a feeling I feared to name: love. His eyes held a sincerity that left me breathless.

"I started falling for you, Ananya," he confessed, his voice steady but filled with emotion. My breath caught in my throat, and for a moment, everything around us faded away. My grip around his neck tightened, as if afraid the world would slip away if I didn't hold on.

"Are you sure you're not saying this in the heat of the moment?" I asked, my voice barely a whisper, afraid of what this revelation might mean.

His eyes never left mine, and he shook his head slowly, firmly.

"I'm physically attracted to you, yes. But more than that, Ananya, I'm emotionally drawn to you. I'm sure about my feelings for you. I can see a future with you," he said, his words seeping into my soul like a balm. My heart fluttered in my chest, and for a brief moment, time seemed to stand still. Just hours ago, I was crying, unsure of where we stood. And now, here he was, confessing everything I'd secretly longed to hear.

The happiness that had bloomed in my chest faltered when the realization hit me like a crushing weight. He is falling for the Ananya he met as a host—the version of me that wasn't real. I'm not her. I'm an agent, playing a part. The interviews, the dresses, the questions, everything—none of it was genuine. What if he finds out? Will he still love me when he knows the truth?

I pulled my hands from his neck and stood up, distancing myself from him. Why did it have to be this way? I couldn't tell him the truth—not when he's been falling for someone I'm not. The fear gnawed at me. What if, in the future, he can't accept the real me? What if he resents me for all the lies?

CHAPTER TWENTY-ONE

Shaurya

When Ananya stepped away from me, my heart stopped for a moment. Did I say something wrong? Everything had felt so perfect between us. We'd shared something special. She'd been there with me, not just physically, but emotionally. I could feel it in every shared whisper, every stolen glance, and every fleeting touch. The way her body had softened when I held her. The way her eyes had sparkled when I kissed her forehead. It felt real—felt like we were building something, something genuine.

Did I misread her feelings?

I thought back to the times we spent together, how she seemed happy when we were close, how she let me in. How she'd allowed me to get this close. I couldn't believe I had misread that, but now... I was questioning everything. Maybe I had. Maybe I'd misunderstood her, misinterpreted the signs.

"Ananya, let's talk it out, please?" I requested, my voice low, and sincere.

She nodded silently, tightening her grip around my hand, and for the first time that night, I felt her body relax in my arms. The overwhelming fear I felt earlier started to fade, replaced by the warmth of having her this close, like everything was going to be okay.

"Now tell me. Why did you step away like that?" I asked, holding her hands gently in mine, my thumbs moving in slow, soothing circles across the back of her palms. I needed to understand what was going through her mind.

She seemed lost in her thoughts for a moment, before looking up at me, her eyes filled with a kind of fear and hesitation. "We can never be together, Shaurya," she said, her voice soft but heavy with sorrow.

I frowned, confused by her words, but I didn't interrupt. I just waited, patiently, for her to explain further.

"The Ananya you see daily is not the real me. Those clothes, those intellectual interview questions, none of them are real me. You don't know the real Ananya. You are falling in love with a mirage," she continued, her words full of anguish. My heart clenched as I processed what she was saying. Is this about her profession? The persona she puts on for the cameras? She thinks I like that?

I leaned in slightly, my grip tightening on her hands, though I kept my voice calm. "But I don't care about that, Ananya," I said, speaking slowly, carefully. "I'm falling for the Ananya who jogs with me in the morning, the girl who makes coffee for me, the girl who talks to me for hours under the moonlight, the girl who gets jealous of my female fans though she never admits it openly, the girl who irritates my bestfriend every chance she gets, the girl who fought those goons to save an innocent... I'm in love with that Ananya."

Her eyes filled with tears, and before I could say anything more, they started falling—one after another, like a waterfall. It broke me to see her like this, and without thinking, I gently wiped the tears from her cheeks with my thumb, pressing a soft kiss to her forehead.

"But it is not easy, Shaurya. There are a lot of things I can't say you. Secrets I can never share and the danger that comes along with me. You don't deserve all this." She rested her cheek against my chest, her body trembling slightly as she let out a small sob. I wrapped my arms around her, holding her close, caressing her hair, and whispered soft words of comfort.

"I'm here, Ananya," I murmured. "I don't care about anything else. I love you, just the way you are, with all the secrets and dangers that come along."

Her hands tightened around my waist, and I could feel her breath start to slow as she relaxed into my arms. I wasn't going to let her go, not until she understood that everything about her—the real her—was what I wanted. It always had been.

I would prove that to her, no matter what it took.

"Why don't you understand, Shaurya? It can put your career and your life at risk." Her voice was tinged with fear, and I could feel her hands gripping my shirt tighter as if she was afraid that if she loosened her hold, I would slip away from her.

The fear in her voice stung, but I remained calm. I didn't want her to feel like she had to hold anything back from me. "It is not enough of a reason to let go of you, Ananya." I said, my voice steady but filled with sincerity. "I love you and I know you do too. Please don't fight it, Ananya. Please!" I pled, tears flowing down my cheeks as I held her closer.

I could see her relax a little at my words, though the worry still lingered in her eyes. I understood it. Everyone has their own share of secrets, and I didn't expect her to reveal everything. One thing I was sure about was the beautiful future with her.

"So, are you convinced now?" I asked with a teasing smile, trying to lighten the mood. She slapped my chest lightly, and I couldn't help but chuckle at her reaction.

"Yes," she whispered so quietly that I almost didn't hear it, but in the silence of the room, I caught the soft sound of her affirmation. My heart swelled with happiness, and a smile spread across my face.

I pulled her closer, feeling the warmth of her body pressed against mine, and couldn't resist the urge to tease her just a little. My fingers traced circles on her back, just light enough to send shivers down her spine.

"You know, I still can't believe you said yes," I whispered, my lips brushing against her ear. "You sure about this? Because I might just spoil you rotten."

She pulled back just a little to look at me, her cheeks flushed and her eyes sparkling with that familiar playfulness I adored. "Spoil me, huh?" she said, raising an eyebrow. "I'm not sure you can handle me, Shaurya."

A laugh escaped me, and I pulled her back into my chest, my arms snug around her waist. "Oh, I can handle you. All of you. Your maturity, your childishness, your moodswings, your independence and your strength. Trust me," I said, my voice low and teasing, my lips grazing the top of her head. "You might even like it."

Her breath caught at my words, and I couldn't help but smile as I felt a slight tremor in her body. "You think so?" she asked, her voice teasing now, a hint of challenge in it. "Let's see if you can live up to all that talk."

She looked up at me, her eyes filled with mischief, and I could see that familiar fire burning there. Her fingers traced the lines of my shirt as if she were trying to memorize every inch of me. "But don't think you're the only one who can spoil someone."

I raised an eyebrow, amusement flickering in my chest. "Is that so?" I asked, letting my hands slip around her waist, pulling her even closer, until I could feel her heartbeat match mine. "You plan on spoiling me too? Because I warn you, I'm hard to spoil."

Her lips quirked up at the corners, a teasing smile dancing on her lips. "I'm up for the challenge," she said, her voice light, but I could sense the depth behind her words, the connection we shared growing stronger with every breath.

"Is that a promise?" I asked, my lips inches from hers, savoring the teasing game we were playing.

She leaned in just enough to brush her lips against my cheek, a soft, lingering kiss that had me groaning quietly in response. "Maybe," she whispered, pulling back slightly but keeping her hands firmly planted on my chest. "But I think I'll make you wait for it."

I let out a low chuckle, my arms tightening around her in a gentle yet possessive hold. "You know, I think that might just drive me crazy," I said, my voice thick with desire.

Her eyes locked with mine, and for a moment, there was silence between us. A kind of quiet understanding, like we both knew exactly what the other was feeling. Her smile softened, and she placed her hand over my heart, her touch sending a warmth spreading through my chest. "You already drive me crazy, Shaurya," she said, her voice almost teasing but with an undeniable sincerity underneath.

She sighed, a soft sound of both frustration and desire, and it made my heart race. She was always so damn captivating when she was teasing me, but I was done playing games for now. I wanted her to know exactly how I felt.

I cupped her face, gently lifting her chin, and met her eyes with a look that was all sincerity. "But one thing is for sure, Ananya... I'm crazy about you. I've never been more sure about anything in my life."

Her eyes softened, the teasing edge disappearing as she gazed at me with that vulnerability I'd grown to love. "Shaurya," she whispered, the emotion in her voice making my chest tighten. She closed the distance between us, her lips pressing softly to my forehead as if sealing everything we'd just said without needing any more words.

I smooched her face, letting all the pent-up feelings, affection, and love flow through me, and when we finally pulled away, I smiled down at her. "You're mine, Ananya. And I'm never letting you go."

Her smile matched mine, her hands now tracing the contours of my chest. "I think I'm starting to believe that," she whispered, her eyes full of warmth and love. "I think you might actually be capable of spoiling me."

I raised an eyebrow playfully, brushing a lock of hair from her face. "Capable? Sweetheart, I will spoil you, and you'll love every second of it."

She laughed softly, her fingers gently tracing my jawline. "I'd love to be spoiled by you."

CHAPTER TWENTY-TWO

Ananya

Nestled in the warmth of his embrace, I didn't realize when sleep had claimed me. Only when I felt myself floating, weightless, and cradled by something firm yet gentle, my eyelids fluttered open. His face greeted me—the sharp lines of his jaw softened in the dim light, his eyes holding a tenderness that made my heart ache in the best way.

I was in his arms. Shaurya had lifted me as if I weighed nothing, carrying me as though I were the most precious thing in his world.

"Sleep, baby," he murmured, his voice so soft it felt like a lullaby. "I'm just taking you upstairs."

The gentle rumble, of his voice and the way he called me *baby* made me melt. Without thinking, I tightened my arms around his neck, tucking my face into the crook of his shoulder. His scent—comforting and familiar—enveloped me, and I allowed myself to sink into it, trusting him completely.

He laid me down on the bed with the utmost care, like I were fragile, a porcelain doll in his hands. The moment his arms left me, I stirred, the absence of his touch waking me fully.

"Where are you going?" I asked, my voice drowsy and barely above a whisper.

He paused and turned to face me. His smile was gentle, almost shy.

"I'll be sleeping on the couch downstairs," he mumbled, a faint blush coating his cheeks.

"You're seriously thinking of sleeping on that couch?" I asked, incredulous, my voice a little sharper than I intended. That couch—small, rigid, and utterly unfit for someone his size—flashed in my mind, and the thought of him trying to contort his tall frame onto it troubled me.

He didn't respond right away, just closed the cupboard and nodded with a small smile.

"But you won't fit on it," I argued, sitting up straight, my voice laced with concern.

He chuckled softly, the warm, rich sound sending a flutter through my chest as he walked over to the bed.

"I know," he admitted, the teasing lilt in his voice unmistakable. "But back when I bought it, I never imagined I'd be bringing my girlfriend here one day, let alone arranging extra bedding."

That one word—girlfriend—wrapped around my heart like a soft whisper. Heat bloomed across my cheeks, and I ducked my head, too flustered to meet his gaze.

"You can...you can sleep here," I offered quietly, staring at my hands. My voice wavered slightly but my resolve was firm. "If you don't mind, that is."

His eyes softened, the teasing gone, replaced by something deeper, more intimate. "Are you sure?" he asked gently. "I can sleep on the ground or something. You don't need to worry about me."

That angered me further. I shot him a glare, all my sleepiness vanishing as irritation bubbled up.

"Shut up and sleep here!" I snapped, my voice sharper than intended. "It's not like we're going to... you know... do the deeds or anything!"

The words tumbled out before I could stop them, and I instantly regretted how blunt I'd been. My cheeks flared again, hotter this time, and I refused to meet his eyes.

But Shaurya, of course, didn't make it any easier. His lips quirked into a crooked smile, his amusement barely contained. "The deeds, huh?" he repeated, his tone mischievous yet affectionate.

I groaned, flopping back onto the bed and yanking the blanket over my face. Why was this man so insufferable? And why did my heart keep doing flips every time he so much as breathed?

"Fine, I'll sleep here," he said finally, his voice tinged with amusement. "But only because you insist."

I peeked out from beneath the blanket, catching the faintest glimmer of something tender in his eyes before he turned away to settle on the other side of the bed.

"By the way, we can do the deeds... if you want us to," he teased, his voice playful yet daring. I sunk more into the mattress, clutching the blanket as if my life depended on it.

From behind, I heard his laugh—a deep, rumbling sound that made my heart skip despite my mortification.

My cheeks burned hotter with every second that passed. I couldn't move, couldn't face him. Why did I say something so ridiculous?

"It's okay, Anya," he murmured, his voice closer now, filled with a warmth that melted some of my embarrassment. "I know you didn't mean it. No need to feel embarrassed."

Before I could even peek out, I felt it—a hand sliding over the comforter, resting lightly on my waist. My breath hitched as his touch sent shivers up my spine. His presence hovered near, his breath brushing against my face through the thin barrier of the sheet.

I peeked out hesitantly, my gaze meeting his, and the soft expression in his eyes stole whatever words I might've found.

His hand still rested on my waist, his touch steady yet comforting. There was no teasing now, no playful smirk—just an unwavering tenderness that made my heart ache in the most beautiful way.

Gathering courage, I nodded slowly, letting the comforter slip down further. Without breaking eye contact, I turned toward him, seeking the comfort I knew only he could give.

Tentatively, I wrapped my arms around his torso, pressing myself into the steady strength of his frame. His arms came around me instantly, pulling me closer, and the comforter shifted as he joined me beneath it, cocooning us together.

The world outside faded away as I rested my head against his chest, listening to the steady rhythm of his heartbeat. His arms enveloped me completely, shielding me from every worry and every thought.

In his embrace, there was nothing but peace, nothing but us.

"Good night, Anya," his voice whispered above my head, soft and velvety, like a gentle caress in the quiet night.

Before I could process the warmth in his tone, I felt it—a feather-light kiss pressed to my temple. My heart stilled for a moment, only to take off in a wild rhythm that left me breathless.

Anya.

He called me Anya. Not Ananya—formal and distant—but Anya. His Anya.

The realization sent a swarm of butterflies swirling in my stomach, their delicate wings brushing against every inch of my being. I bit my lower lip to hold back the ridiculous grin threatening to take over my face, pressing my cheek against his chest to hide my flushed cheeks.

His heartbeat was steady, and soothing, yet somehow it matched the flutter in my own. I closed my eyes, letting the warmth of his embrace wrap around me like a cocoon.

"Good night, Shaurya," I murmured, my voice barely above a whisper, afraid to break the magic of the moment.

His arms tightened around me slightly, as though he, too, found comfort in this closeness.

And just like that, as his steady breathing became my lullaby, I let myself drift off, safe and cherished in the arms of the man who was slowly becoming my everything.

I felt the sun's warm rays sneaking through the curtains, dancing on my face, nudging me from my sleep. Groaning softly, I turned my head and snuggled deeper into the comfort of my pillow. But something was different. My pillow was firm, strong... and radiating warmth.

Frowning slightly, I burrowed further into the inviting cocoon, pulling the duvet over us. It felt too comforting to leave, as if this warmth was meant to shield me from the day's worries.

"Anya, wake up, baby. We need to leave," a soft, familiar voice murmured near my ear, laced with affection.

I wasn't ready to wake up—not today. My body resisted the pull of reality, clinging stubbornly to this stolen peace. Ignoring the voice, I sighed and pressed closer to the warmth.

Fingers—gentle and soothing—trailed through my hair, and then I felt it. A kiss. Featherlight, placed on my temple with such care it made my heart skip even in my half-asleep state.

No one had ever woken me up like this. Not my family. Not my friends.

A curious tug at my heart made me crack open one eye. I peeked beside me, only to freeze when my sleepy gaze landed on him.

Shaurya.

The thing I had been clinging to wasn't just my pillow—it was him.

My eyes shot open, and I jerked back instinctively, my movements fumbling as the duvet tangled around me.

But then the realization struck me like a lightning bolt.

This wasn't my bed. Not my room.

"Don't tell me you forgot everything that happened yesterday," Shaurya said, his brow quirking in mock confusion, though the teasing glint in his eyes betrayed his amusement.

His words snapped me back to reality. Of course, I remembered. My sleepy mind just needed a moment to catch up.

"Of course, I do, Shaurya," I mumbled, sitting up and rubbing my eyes, trying to look composed.

"Thank god!" He let out a relieved chuckle, his lips curving into that devastating smile that could melt glaciers. Before I could react, he leaned in and placed another kiss on my forehead—soft, lingering, and entirely too distracting.

And then he stood up.

I blinked, and my breath caught as my eyes drank him in. The soft morning light framed him like a scene out of a dream, his hair, messy and adorable fell onto his forehead in lazy strands. His sharp jawline, a masterpiece sculpted by the gods themselves, moved subtly as he ran a hand through his hair.

And those eyes. Oh, those mesmerizing, deep eyes that seemed to hold galaxies within them. They were still slightly heavy with sleep, but the way they glinted with humor as they caught me staring...

Then there were his lips—soft, pink, and inviting, like they held secrets meant only for me.

And don't even get me started on his body. His broad shoulders, the ripple of muscles as he stretched, the way his shirt clung to his chest just enough to hint at the strength beneath.

Uff!

This man was walking sin.

My cheeks flushed as my thoughts took a decidedly naughty turn, my sleepy brain clearly lacking any filter. Morning Ananya, stop being such a menace!

"Anya?" His voice broke through my spiraling thoughts, his brow quirking again, this time in genuine curiosity.

I blinked rapidly, snapping my gaze up to meet his, praying he couldn't read my mind.

"Uh... yeah, what?" I stammered, my cheeks burning as his smirk deepened.

He leaned casually against the bedframe, crossing his arms, looking every bit the confident man who had caught me red-handed in my little moment of admiration.

"Nothing," he said with a teasing glint. "Just wondering why you're looking at me like I'm your morning coffee."

"But it's okay," Shaurya said, his smirk deepening as he caught me mid-stare. "I'm all yours to ogle at, so I don't mind. But we are getting late, my adorable sleepyhead."

His words snapped me out of my shameless boyfriend-appreciation session, and I quickly grabbed my phone. The screen flashed 8:00 a.m.

"Freaking 8?!" I bolted upright, panic surging through me. "Shit!"

I dashed into the bathroom, hastily brushing, washing up, and doing whatever I could manage in record time. I realized I didn't have any spare clothes, so I emerged wearing my previous day's outfit after freshening up a bit.

But my eyes fell on a neatly placed bag lying on the bed.

It hadn't been there when I ran into the bathroom. Did Shaurya bring it? But how? He'd only left the room ten minutes ago.

"Shaurya, this bag?" I called out, descending the stairs. I found him standing in the kitchen, his back to me, casually chopping something on the counter. The domesticity of it all—the man I loved in his kitchen, doing something so mundane yet utterly captivating—made my heart skip a beat.

He turned around with a smile, a knife in one hand, and said, "That's for you. I asked someone to bring those over."

His words eased my worries, and I nodded, ready to retreat upstairs when his voice stopped me mid-step.

"Anya," he called softly, scratching the back of his neck in what looked like rare awkwardness.

"Yeah?" I asked, turning around.

"I didn't, uh... I didn't arrange for the innerwear," he admitted, the tips of his ears turning slightly pink.

Heat rushed to my cheeks faster than I could process his words. My embarrassment shot through the roof, and I hastily nodded, mumbling something unintelligible before rushing upstairs like my life depended on it.

After a quick shower, I slipped into the clothes he'd thoughtfully arranged for me. While I had to make do with my old innerwear, the absence of any new ones felt like a relief. The thought of Shaurya handling that just yet would've been mortifying.

"You go and take a shower, Shaurya. I'll handle the rest," I suggested, my voice a bit more breathy than usual as I descended the stairs. He nodded, but before I could turn around, I felt him behind me, a sudden warmth enveloping me.

Without a word, he removed his apron, and before I could even react, he slid it over my head, pulling the straps tight behind me. His hands lingered on the fabric, and then—oh god—he hugged me from the front, his chest pressing against my back, making my heart skip a beat. His breath against my neck and the feeling of him so close made butterflies erupt in my stomach.

"I'll be back in 15 minutes," he murmured, placing a soft kiss on the top of my head.

But before I could say anything, I found myself unable to resist.

"Don't you think you're kissing me too much?" I raised an eyebrow, a teasing smile curling on my lips.

He froze in his tracks, a grin playing on his lips. Slowly, he turned around and started toward me, each step drawing him closer. In reflex, I took a step back, a playful smirk matching his.

"Do you have a problem, sweetheart?" His voice was low, warm, and dripping with that irresistible charm. He tucked a strand of hair behind my ear, his fingers grazing the delicate skin of my neck. His face was so close, his lips nearly brushing my skin, and I could feel his breath dance across my cheek. A shiver ran down my spine.

"N...no," I stammered, my pulse racing.

His eyes never left mine as he leaned in, brushing his rough stubbled cheek against mine, and I couldn't help but close my eyes, my body flooding with heat.

"Good," he whispered in my ear, and the shivers came back, stronger this time, as his lips lingered just at the edge of my earlobe. He was so close, I could feel his words like a pulse against my skin, each syllable lighting a fire inside me.

His body caged me in—between the kitchen counter and him. I grabbed the edge of the table behind me, my knuckles white with tension.

"And we just started, sweetheart," he murmured, his voice a low growl. "I want to kiss and worship every inch of this beautiful body of yours, only yours."

His hands slid down to my waist, gripping tightly, pulling me closer, and I felt my breath catch in my throat. Every nerve in my body screamed as his words sunk in. My thighs involuntarily clenched, and I could feel him noticing, his gaze sharpening.

His grip tightened on my waist, pulling me even closer, and a soft whimper escaped my lips. My chest felt tight, my heart racing, as I found myself lost in the intensity of the moment. Then, as quickly as it began, he pulled back, pressing one last, lingering kiss to my cheek.

I stood there, breathless and flushed, my fingers touching the spot he kissed as my heart hammered in my chest. I could still feel the heat of his touch, the lingering effect of his words, and I knew I'd be blushing like a fool for the rest of the day.

My thoughts scattered, broken by the sudden ding of the toaster. I flinched slightly, my heart racing for a moment as I snapped back to reality. Slowly, I steadied my breath, my pulse still erratic, as I reached for the bread and pulled it out of the toaster. The crisp warmth of it in my hands seemed to ground me, but I couldn't shake the lingering thoughts from last night. As I poured the orange juice into the glasses, my mind wandered back to him—Shaurya.

After everything we'd shared, after everything we were, I couldn't help but feel a tightness in my chest as I carried everything to the dining table. The thought of us being apart from the day after felt like a physical ache.

The quiet anticipation that hung in the air seemed to thicken as I set everything down, and just as I finished, Shaurya walked in. His presence filled the space, and suddenly, everything felt right again. We settled into breakfast, eating in silence for a few moments, both lost in our own thoughts.

But then, as I sat there, the realization hit me again, a heavy weight pressing down on my chest. The thought of us being apart... it made my hands shake slightly as I reached for the butter, my fingers brushing against the smooth surface, but all I could think about was how I would miss him. How I'd miss the way his laughter filled the room, the warmth of his body close to mine, the quiet moments and those night talks we shared.

The morning sun kissed my skin as we made our way to the hotel, the familiar rumble of the bike beneath us keeping me grounded. But with every twist and turn, I couldn't shake the overwhelming feeling of needing him. As his body pressed against mine, my arms wrapped around him instinctively, holding him tighter, not wanting to let go.

I buried my face into his back, feeling the cool wind brush past us. But the warmth I craved was only from him. The thought of us being apart for the next few days filled me with a sudden panic like the air had been knocked from my lungs. How would I survive without him this close?

I tightened my hold around him, my fingers digging into his shirt, the rhythm of his heartbeat almost in sync with mine. The bike roared on, but the only sound I cared about was the steady hum of his presence, the undeniable connection we shared.

I couldn't shake the tightness in my chest, that heavy feeling in my heart. Being with him every day for the past few months had made me crave his presence like an addiction, a sweet kind of dependence that was impossible to ignore. Now, I didn't know how I would manage without him, without the warmth of his touch, the comfort of his presence.

"What happened, Anya? Why are you crushing me with your hug?" Shaurya chuckled, his voice vibrating through his chest as he caressed my hands around his torso with one hand, the other steadying the bike with expert ease.

"I will miss you from tomorrow," I pouted, rubbing my cheek against his back, my heart tightening just thinking about the days apart.

"I will miss you too, Anya," he replied softly, his voice carrying a mix of affection and sadness. "But I'll try to contact you whenever I can. And you too, leave me a text whenever you can. We'll meet whenever we can." I could hear the heaviness in his tone, and I immediately regretted bringing it up. Why did I have to mention it?

I snuggled closer to him, my arms tightening around him as if to reassure him, and whispered against his back, "We'll make it work, Shaurya." I felt him relax a little, the tension easing from his body. I planted a soft kiss on his back, feeling the warmth seep through his jacket.

"Not fair, madam," he teased, his voice playful again. "You kiss me rarely, and my jacket got it instead?" He whined cutely, and I couldn't help but giggle at how adorable he sounded.

"Fine, fine, I will give you one once we reach the hotel," I murmured, giving his back another quick kiss, a playful spark igniting between us despite the bittersweetness in the air. "Better now?"

"Much better," he smiled, his tone light, and I could feel the warmth of his grin through his back.

We continued the ride, both of us lost in the rhythm of the road, our minds at ease with the promise of staying connected, of making the distance feel smaller with every message, every call. The remaining distance between us was filled with quiet smiles, the kind that spoke volumes even when words couldn't. And in that moment, I realized that no matter how far apart we might be, I'd carry the warmth of this hug, this moment, with me.

CHAPTER TWENTY-THREE

Shaurya

The tour ended 15 days ago, bringing us back to the ever-bustling Delhi. The team dispersed to their respective adobes in Mumbai, but I decided to stay here with Maa. It's been a while since we had uninterrupted time together, and I cherish these moments with her whenever I'm off the field.

The past 15 days were match-free—a rare pause in my otherwise relentless schedule. The days flew by in a whirlwind of brand commercials and overseeing projects for my company. Over the years, I've ventured into investments and built something I'm proud of—my clothing brand, **StyleSculpt,** and the chain of fitness centers I named **StriveEdge.** Each carries a piece of me, my passion, and my drive. There's a spark in the idea of expanding into the hospitality business, too, though for now, it's just a thought.

Amid the busy schedules, one constant remained—my Anya. We met twice in these 15 days, though our schedules barely allowed for more. But even in quiet moments apart, her presence filled my days through messages and brief video calls. Something is comforting, something grounding, in hearing her voice and seeing her smile even if it's through a screen.

I know she can't follow me to every corner of the world, and I wouldn't ask her to. She has her own dreams to chase, her own world to nurture. And I am not selfish to ask her to throw everything she worked hard for into fire to be with me. We've learned to treasure the distance and to trust that the love we share is enough to span every mile.

But I miss her, more than I let on.

Tonight, I'm taking Maa to her nutritionist's place for dinner. Maa and her nutritionist have become more than clients and consultants over time—they're friends now.

When the invitation came, Maa insisted I join her, her excitement practically bubbling over. I didn't have the heart to say no, though I couldn't quite figure out why she seemed so thrilled about this particular dinner.

Dressed in an Oxford blue button-up shirt and light green pants, I gave my reflection a quick once-over. I tied on my watch, slipped into my polished brown shoes, and adjusted my matching belt. After setting my hair with care and spraying my favorite cologne—an understated but confident scent—I picked up my wallet and headed out.

"Shaurya, we are getting late!" Maa's impatient voice echoed from the living room. She has a way of turning every outing into an event. Her excitement was almost contagious as she stood, ready to go the moment she saw me descending the stairs.

"Radha, we're leaving now," she called out to the head help, her voice carrying that no-nonsense tone she always adopts when giving instructions. "Take care, and don't forget to hand the keys to Mohan before leaving."

Radha nodded, offering a crisp "Ji, Ma'am," and we stepped outside into the cool evening air.

I walked over to the driveway and unlocked the sleek, black Bentley Continental GT—my latest indulgence. The car gleamed under the porch lights, a testament to my love for vehicles. With a collection of 18 cars—Audis, Benzes, and this beauty among them—not to mention my eight bikes, it's fair to say I have a weakness for speed and style.

Sliding into the driver's seat, I felt a familiar thrill as the engine purred to life. Maa settled beside me, her excitement palpable. As we pulled away, the city lights reflected off the windshield, the promise of the evening ahead lingering in the air.

"Stop at some sweet shop or bakery, Sonu. We should take some sweets for them," Maa said with that affectionate tone only she could manage. Yes, Sonu—that's the name she's always called me, her way of keeping me her little boy no matter how far I've come.

I smiled, nodding without a word, and pulled over at one of the renowned sweet shops on the way. The warm scent of freshly made sweets filled the air as we stepped inside. Maa browsed the shelves with the expertise of someone who knew exactly what would impress, selecting a variety of treats.

Once the box was wrapped, I carried it out and placed it carefully on the back seat. "Anything else, Maa?" I asked, glancing at her as I settled back behind the wheel.

"No, beta. That's enough," she replied with a satisfied smile.

The hour-long drive that followed was peaceful, filled with occasional hums of a favorite tune from Maa and the faint murmur of the city fading into quieter streets.

We finally arrived at our destination—a charming bungalow nestled in the heart of a lush green garden. The house was surrounded by vibrant flower beds and tall trees, their branches swaying gently in the breeze. In the garden, four wooden chairs and a matching table were arranged under the open sky, while a swing sat invitingly a little further away. It was the kind of home that exuded warmth and tranquility.

I parked the car on the spacious patio and stepped out, taking a moment to admire the serenity of the place. It wasn't often I found homes that resonated with me, but this one did.

Walking around, I opened the door for Maa with a slight bow, earning a chuckle from her. "Thank you, Sir," she teased.

Grinning, I reached for the box of sweets from the back seat. The evening air was crisp, carrying the faint scent of flowers from the garden.

We pressed the bell and waited, the soft chime echoing beyond the door. Maa, ever the perfectionist, adjusted her already impeccable pallu once more, her fingers deftly smoothing the fabric into place.

A moment later, the door opened, revealing a woman in her early fifties. Dressed in an elegant navy blue suit, her face lit up with a warm, welcoming smile. She stepped out, and before a word could be exchanged, she pulled Maa into a gentle hug. The affection between them was palpable, and Maa reciprocated with equal enthusiasm.

"We were just talking about you," the lady said, her voice filled with delight as they pulled back from the embrace. Then her gaze shifted to me, her smile softening with maternal warmth.

"Welcome, beta. How are you?" she asked, her hands still holding onto Maa's while Maa's hands clung fondly to her elbow. Watching them, I couldn't help but smile—it was as if they'd known each other for years instead of a few months.

"I'm good, Aunty. How are you?" I replied politely, leaning forward to touch her feet in greeting.

"Oh, I'm good too, beta," she said, her hands reaching up to caress my head in a gesture so kind it felt almost familial. "I've seen you a lot on TV. My son talks about you all the time—he's playing for the Junior team, you know."

Her pride was evident, and I offered her a genuine smile, imagining the joy her son must feel hearing his mother speak about him with such admiration.

"That's wonderful, Aunty," I said, meaning it.

She gestured for us to come inside, leading us to a cozy living room filled with warm lighting and tasteful decor. The couch she pointed to looked inviting, its cushions plump and inviting in soft shades of cream and gold. Maa and I took our seats as she disappeared momentarily, returning with water and an eagerness to make us feel at home.

"Vijay, the guests are here!" Aunty called out, her voice carrying a subtle note of authority as she turned toward the hallway.

Moments later, a tall, fit man entered the living room. Dressed in a crisp black shirt paired with brown trousers, he exuded an effortless elegance. The subtle silver in his hair added an extra layer of charm to his already commanding presence. I instantly recognized him—Vijay Shergill, the former Indian Badminton champion, a name synonymous with brilliance and discipline.

"I'm here too!" he declared with a grin, his tone laced with mischief. "Now, where are our little minions?" His playful words hung in the air, clearly directed at someone unseen.

Aunty, however, didn't seem as amused. She shot him a pointed glare, her tight-lipped smile doing little to mask her mild exasperation. "Vijay, behave," her eyes seemed to say without a single word spoken.

Uncle cleared his throat, the glint of mischief in his eyes dimming slightly as he straightened up. Folding his hands, he greeted Maa with a respectful nod and a warm smile. "Namaste, Didi," he said earnestly.

After a brief exchange, his attention shifted to me. "Hello, Shaurya! It's an honor to have you," he said, extending a firm hand in my direction. His handshake was strong but friendly, a silent testament to his years as an athlete.

"Hi, Uncle. It's my honor to meet you," I replied sincerely, matching his smile as we shook hands.

Uncle eased into the single chair nearby, his posture relaxed yet poised. His presence had a magnetic quality, effortlessly drawing everyone into the conversation.

"You all continue chatting. I'll check with the maids about setting the table," Aunty said with a warm smile, gracefully excusing herself. It struck me that I still didn't know her name.

Uncle turned toward me, his sharp yet kind eyes twinkling with curiosity. "So, how is captaincy treating you? Are you finding it challenging?"

I returned his gaze, offering a small, genuine smile. "It is challenging, but I'm enjoying the new responsibilities," I admitted. "Every match feels like a test, and the adrenaline of making decisions on the spot keeps me motivated."

He nodded, an approving smile spreading across his face. "That's a great perspective. Vansh says something similar. That boy has been a fan of yours since he was a child. His sister introduced him to cricket, and now he's completely hooked. He practically eats, sleeps, and breathes cricket!" His pride was palpable, his chest almost swelling as he spoke about his son.

For a fleeting moment, my mind wandered. Would Dad have looked at me with the same pride if he were still here? That thought stirred a mix of emotions in my chest—pride, longing, and a touch of sorrow.

Pushing those thoughts aside, I refocused on the conversation. Uncle's warmth and genuine interest made it easy to engage. "Vansh is fortunate to have such support. Passion, when nurtured, leads to greatness," I said, meaning every word.

Uncle smiled deeply at that. "That's true. He's lucky to have his sister cheer him on, and I've made it my mission to ensure he has every opportunity he needs."

As the conversation flowed, I learned more about him. He co-owned a prominent IT company with branches across the country, and as if that weren't impressive enough, he also ran his own coaching institute with two thriving branches.

Before we knew it, the topics shifted effortlessly—from cricket strategies to the intricacies of business management, and finally, a fascinating discussion on global economics. It felt surprisingly refreshing to converse with someone who could match my enthusiasm in so many areas.

"Vijay! Call Vansh once. They left two hours ago to get ice creams and haven't returned yet," Aunty's voice carried from the kitchen, her tone a mix of worry and mild annoyance.

Uncle immediately grabbed his phone, dialing with the ease of someone accustomed to such instructions. His conversation was brief, his voice calm yet slightly authoritative.

"They'll be here in a few minutes, Rashmi," he yelled back, slipping the phone into his pocket before turning to me with a smile. "Kids these days, always losing track of time."

I nodded, laughing softly, though my mind was now preoccupied with a strange sensation bubbling inside me. As Uncle and I shifted to random topics—his coaching experiences, my team's latest adventures—I found myself distracted by a faint hum of anticipation.

Then, the distant roar of a car's engine cut through the quiet evening. The sound grew louder as it neared, and I instinctively turned my head toward the door. Uncle noticed and smiled knowingly. "That must be Vansh. Always making an entrance," he joked.

Vansh? The name echoed in my mind, triggering a faint but unmistakable connection. Vansh... Could it be?

And then it clicked.

Vansh. Anya's brother, Vansh. My Anya.

The realization hit like a bolt of lightning. My gaze darted to Uncle—no, Vijay Shergill. Vijay Shergill, father of Ananya Shergill, my Anya.

My grip on the armrest tightened as the puzzle pieces fell into place. The easy laughter, the shared warmth between our families, the familiar vibe that I couldn't quite place until now—it all made sense.

What were the odds? Out of all the people, and all the places, I had unknowingly walked into her house. And she had no idea.

A slow, amused smile began to form on my lips. This night was about to get very interesting.

"Mumma, before you scold us for being late, your favorite black raspberry chip ice cream was not—" Vansh's words froze mid-sentence the moment his eyes landed on us in the living room. His initial surprise quickly morphed into a sheepish grin as his gaze flickered between Maa and me.

Recovering quickly, he stepped forward and touched Maa's feet, his ears tinged a deep red. "Namaste, Aunty," he said softly, clearly a little embarrassed but trying to compose himself.

Maa blessed him warmly, her smile as gentle as ever. "God bless you, beta."

He then turned to me, his boyish charm shining through as he waved like an excited child. "Hi, Shaurya sir!"

I couldn't help but chuckle, getting up to greet him. "Hi, Vansh!" I said, pulling him into a quick hug. He hugged me back firmly before stepping away, his usual energy bubbling back.

"I'll just go put this in the freezer," he blurted out before dashing toward the kitchen, not giving anyone a chance to react.

As I sat back on the couch, the sound of footsteps caught my attention. My gaze shifted toward the hallway, and there she was—my Anya.

She walked in absentmindedly, tossing a set of keys into the air and catching them skillfully. There was a casual ease to her movements, a grace that seemed almost unconscious. But the moment her eyes landed on me, everything changed.

The keys slipped through her fingers, falling to the ground with a soft clink as her wide, startled eyes locked onto mine.

Her expression was a mixture of shock and disbelief. Her lips parted slightly as if to say something, but no words came out. I could see her struggling to process the sight of me sitting comfortably between her father and Maa, as if this were the most normal thing in the world.

She bent down quickly, snatching up the keys from the floor, her movements suddenly stiff. I fought the urge to laugh at her panic, finding it both endearing and amusing.

Straightening herself, she approached us with a nervous energy that she was clearly trying to mask. Her gaze darted from her father to Maa, carefully avoiding mine, as if looking at me would somehow confirm her worst fears.

"What are you doing here?"

Her voice was soft but sharp, the words tumbling out before she could stop them. Her eyes were wide, the kind of shock that only came from seeing the unexpected. She stood frozen for a second, her hands trembling just slightly, and I couldn't help but notice. Why was she shaking? Did I look that intimidating? Or maybe... I was just too irresistible for her to handle.

I watched her hand rise to the back of her head, as Aunty stepped in with a smack to her head, the sound sharp but the affection behind it undeniable.

"Behave," Aunty muttered, her voice laced with playful authority.

Ananya pouted and rubbed the spot where Aunty had hit her, giving her mother a look of mock indignation. The sight was so ridiculously adorable, that I almost let my laughter slip, but I caught myself in time, biting down on the inside of my cheek to keep it under control.

Her gaze darted around the room, as though she had no idea what to do next. I couldn't hold back anymore and let out a quiet chuckle.

"Mrs. Singhania is your mother's friend, dear. And you know Mr. Singhania too," her father's calm voice cut through the air, putting an end to her bewilderment.

Her mouth fell open in surprise, her expression changing from confusion to realization in a flash. An 'O' shape formed with her lips.

She quickly turned toward Maa and took her blessings, her smile a little uncertain but still warm.

I couldn't resist. As the others were distracted, I caught her eye and winked. Her cheeks flushed a deeper shade of red, a shade I adored, and she quickly looked away, pretending not to notice. But her attempt at glaring at me only made her look even cuter.

Aunty whispered something in her ear, and with a small smile, Ananya walked toward the stairs. Vansh followed her a few moments later, leaving me with a quiet moment to reflect.

I sat back, mentally preparing myself. I had to make a lasting impression on these people. I couldn't afford any slip-ups if I was going to ask them to let me marry Ananya. The stakes were high, but the game was just beginning.

CHAPTER TWENTY-FOUR

Ananya

"Di! Seriously, do we have to drive 20 more kilometers just to buy this ice cream?" Vansh grumbled from the passenger seat, his irritation palpable. The shopkeeper informed us that the ice cream we requested wasn't available and asked us to visit another branch of theirs for the same.

I rolled my eyes but couldn't hide the smile tugging at my lips. "Vansh, you know Mumma's going to give us *that* look, the one that makes us regret everything... Please, bear with me for a few more minutes."

Muttering something incoherent under his breath, he slouched back into his seat, but didn't argue further. The drive to the other branch was a blur of impatience and a little annoyance, but the moment we finally grabbed the ice cream and started heading home, the frustration faded away.

It took longer than expected to get back, and by the time we reached home, the evening sky had deepened into that soft shade of twilight.

"You go in first, Vansh," I said. "I'll just park the car and catch up."

He nodded, barely acknowledging me as he stepped out of the car. With the keys in my hand, I slowly walked up the driveway, my fingers absentmindedly toying with the keys. But something, or rather someone, was different today.

I hadn't expected the unexpected.

The keys slipped from my grip and clattered to the floor, the sharp sound echoing in the quiet of the room. I froze, my heart stumbling over itself as my eyes locked onto the man sitting there, casually nodding at something my father was saying. His presence hit me like a wave, and before I could fully process what was happening, I noticed the woman beside him—his mother, I presumed, given how she shared the same honey-brown eyes. Those eyes... the ones that haunted my thoughts just the other day.

What the hell was he doing here? With his mother? In my house?

I quickly bent down to pick up the keys, my hands shaking just a little, the cool metal sending a shiver up my spine. The air in the room felt thick, like something was about to happen, something I didn't want to face.

What if this was it? Was this why he was here? My heart pounded as a terrifying thought crossed my mind: Was he here to ask my father for my hand in marriage?

No. He couldn't be. We hadn't even talked about anything like that. But... but what if Shika—being the little detective she was—had spilled the beans? What if she told Dad about us, and now they were here for this very reason?

I had to stop. My thoughts were spiraling out of control.

I forced myself to move, walking toward them, though my legs felt as if they were made of jelly. My eyes were wide with confusion, my pulse racing with panic. I wasn't sure whether to be happy or terrified. But as I opened my mouth to ask, it came out all wrong.

"What are you doing here?" The words slipped out before I could catch them, harsher than I intended. The instant they left my lips, I felt a sharp smack on the back of my head.

"Ouch!" I yelped, rubbing my scalp, completely thrown off by my mum's swift action. "Mumma!"

"Behave!" she hissed, her face flushed with some quiet embarrassment. I watched, dazed, as she leaned in to whisper something in Aunty's ear, before turning away.

I stood there, completely caught off guard. What the hell was going on? My eyes darted around, trying to find any sign, any clue, to make sense of the situation. The tension hung in the air like a storm, thick and unrelenting.

"Mrs. Singhania is your mother's friend, dear. And you know Mr. Singhania too," Dad finally spoke up, his voice cutting through the awkwardness like a lifeline. I forced a smile, my heart still racing, and went over to touch Aunty's feet. Her hand was warm and comforting as she pulled me into a hug, and I could feel my nervousness start to ebb, just a little.

But then, as I straightened up, my gaze met his—Shaurya. My heart skipped a beat, as if it had gotten tangled in the chaos of the moment. I gave him a small smile, but it wasn't natural. I was too embarrassed, my cheeks blazing with the heat of the situation.

And then, he winked at me. That damn wink. That mischievous, teasing wink of his.

It was like he knew exactly how to unravel me, how to make my face go from warm to fire-engine red in seconds. I glared at him, my insides twisting with a strange mix of irritation and... something else. Was it shyness? No. Not now. Not when my mum was in the other room, not when this was happening.

"Are you planning to stand here? Go and change," Mumma's voice was a whisper in my ear, pulling me out of my thoughts. Her words were stern, but there was an underlying warmth, a knowing. She was used to my antics by now. With a final, tight smile to everyone in the living room, I made my way upstairs, my feet feeling heavier with every step.

Why didn't he tell me he was coming? We had talked earlier, and he had mentioned dinner at his mother's friend's place, but this? This was a twist I hadn't expected. I thought we were talking about some random family friend, not... this.

As I reached my room, I closed the door behind me and leaned against it for a moment, my chest heaving with unspent emotions. Why didn't I put two and two together? I had told him about Mumma's friend and their dinner plans, but neither of us had thought it through. And now here I was, on the verge of losing my mind because of this unexpected twist of fate.

Why doesn't my brain ever work when it comes to him?

I exhaled sharply, trying to steady my thoughts. But there was no escaping the burning curiosity, the unrelenting pull I felt toward him. Shaurya was always able to get under my skin, to turn my world upside down with a single glance, a wink, a smile.

"Di! What is Shaurya sir doing here?" Vansh's voice floated through the door before he barged into my room, his eyes wide with confusion.

I didn't even have the energy to form a response, so I just shrugged, my hands flying up in helpless surrender as I collapsed onto my bed. The man downstairs, the very man who somehow made my heart race every time he looked at me, had the audacity to wink at me like it was the most normal thing in the world. Meanwhile, I was two seconds away from combusting with nerves.

If my parents found out anything about us... God help me. They would have us married faster than you could say "muhurat."

I shot a look at Vansh, raising an eyebrow. "I am warning you, Vansh, if you do something to tarnish my image in front of them, I will kill you."

Vansh threw his hands up in defense, nodding furiously, though I could see the mischief in his eyes. "The same goes for you, Di! Shaurya sir is my idol! Don't say something that makes me look stupid in front of him."

I blinked. I hadn't expected that. Oh yes, Shaurya is his idol. We were in this together now, weren't we?

I nodded at him in complete agreement. "Exactly. No one touches each other's image in front of guests, alright? We have to keep our cool, even if I'm about to die of embarrassment. Got it?"

Vansh gave me a thumbs-up, his expression dead serious as if he were agreeing to some top-secret sibling pact.

He continued, lowering his voice to mock seriousness. "I won't make you look stupid in front of Shaurya sir... but if you do anything embarrassing, I swear I'll tell him all your embarrassing stories."

I narrowed my eyes at him. "Don't even think about it."

"Don't worry, Di, it's all under control." He grinned.

"Now go and change," I pushed Vansh out of the room with a dramatic sigh, locking the door behind me.

I sighed, flopping back on my bed. The battle was far from over. Here I was—completely out of my depth, trying not to lose my mind at the fact that Shaurya was downstairs, with his mother, in my house.

Time to make myself presentable.

I grabbed one of my precious Kurthi sets—no, really, I didn't own a lot of clothes—and slipped into it. The soft fabric calmed my nerves, but my heart still felt like it was about to break free from my chest.

I brushed my hair quickly, letting it fall in waves around my shoulders, then popped in my favorite earrings. A little makeup, just a touch, to look decent—I couldn't show up looking like a ghost freshly out of grave. I finished with a spritz of his favorite perfume. I didn't know why I did it; maybe it was just instinct. But somehow, I couldn't help myself.

Finally, I slipped into my heels. Heels. I had always joked with Vansh that they weren't necessary for me, but when you have a tower of a brother and a... well, another tower of a boyfriend, wearing heels becomes essential.

I took a deep breath and walked out of my room, my feet clicking down the hall as I made my way to Vansh's door. I knocked softly, and of course, he opened it with that ridiculously smug grin of his.

"You're lucky I'm not taller than you already," I muttered under my breath, looking up at him with a scowl.

Vansh had always been a little shorter than me until high school, but now... well, I was no longer the older one. Without heels, I reached his shoulders. With them, though? I was eye to eye with his nose.

He chuckled, clearly delighted with the difference, his smile getting wider. "If you're done cursing my height, can we go down, Didu?"

I rolled my eyes, crossing my arms. "Oh, I'm so happy for you, really."

Vansh's laugh filled the air, and in the next moment, his hands were on my shoulders, gently but firmly guiding me toward the stairs. He was taller than me now—no surprise there—but I could still hold my ground. I shot him one last sarcastic smile before we both descended the stairs, the sounds of the lively chatter below growing louder.

When we entered the living room, I couldn't help but notice the easygoing vibe between the women. They were discussing the latest event they had attended, while my dad and Shaurya were in deep conversation about the changes in sports, from his time to now.

I caught Vansh's eye, and the two of us shared a perfectly synchronized roll of the eyes. It was like a language we both understood all too well, something only siblings could share in moments like this. With that silent understanding, we made our way to the couch, and as usual, Vansh claimed the seat, leaving me with my usual spot on the armrest.

But as soon as I settled, I could feel Shaurya's gaze on me, and it wasn't just any gaze. His eyes practically shaped the air around us, and I couldn't help but smile shyly.

The conversation around me seemed to swirl in a blur. Dad and Shaurya were talking sports—again—and my brother was caught in the middle, playing the role of the dutiful son, answering their questions about his matches with a level of focus that only someone who genuinely enjoyed the sport could give. But me? I was lost in my thoughts, counting the seconds until this unbearable boredom would end.

Thanks to my years of training, I kept my face neutral, pretending to care about the discussion, but I could feel my patience fraying. The worst part was that I knew Vansh could see right through me. He squeezed my hand, a silent reassurance that it would end soon. At least, that's what he said.

I wasn't so sure.

Finally, my brother broke the silence, and I nearly jumped when he asked Mumma if we could finally eat.

"Mumma, shall we eat? We can talk after dinner too," Vansh suggested, the words dripping with sweet innocence that made me want to hug him for finally ending this charade.

Mumma's answer left me stunned. "Ha, we were waiting for you both only," she said with a smile, but the words made my mind spiral. We've been sitting here for the past hour! She was too busy discussing Mrs. Sharma's new house to even notice time passing, and now, as if on cue, she was blaming us for not being ready.

I shot a glance at Shaurya, half-expecting him to be caught up in the awkwardness of the moment, but to my surprise, he was chuckling. I tried to ignore the warmth that spread across my face as I glared at him.

The audacity.

His chuckles only grew louder, and my frustration bubbled to the surface, though I managed to hold back from giving him a piece of my mind.

"Stop laughing," I muttered under my breath, but as if he could read my thoughts, he winked at me, his eyes full of mischief. That damn smirk—he was enjoying this too much. I couldn't help it. I huffed and turned away, my patience officially gone.

But deep down, I was enjoying it, more than I cared to admit.

Everyone rose from their seats, and the hum of the room shifted to the comforting sounds of plates clinking and chairs scraping as we all moved toward the dining table. My eyes immediately widened at the spread before me. Mumma really went all out today. It was like she'd prepared for a royal feast—five curries, fragrant pulao, naan, roti, and chapati... And for dessert? Rasagulla, Gulab Jamun, and even ice cream. She never does things halfway.

As Mumma and Aunty immediately dove into their endless chatter about the latest neighborhood gossip, Dad took his turn to grill Vansh and Shaurya about their sporting achievements. Meanwhile, I sat quietly, trying to savor my food, but my attention kept slipping to the two men at the table—the ones who were just a little too close to my heart.

Shaurya was answering Dad's questions with that characteristic enthusiasm of his, while Vansh, on the other hand, was leaning back, a quiet observer, his focus darting between Dad's questions and Shaurya's composed answers. I caught myself sneaking glances at Shaurya, only to find his eyes already on me, making me blush a little deeper each time. But I had to focus—there was too much going on, and I couldn't let my mind wander too far.

"Um... I need to use the bathroom," Shaurya suddenly said, and I looked up just in time to catch the unmistakable look of desperation in his eyes. That was the moment—he was trying to escape the interrogation that my dad had started after we'd finished our dinner. I couldn't help but smirk internally. Poor guy—he was trapped in Dad's endless sea of questions.

I raised an eyebrow at him, but the thought of saving him crossed my mind before the words even formed. I quickly turned to Mumma with a pleading look.

"Please, can you...?" I mouthed, hoping she'd take the hint.

She caught my silent plea and gave me a slight nod. For a moment, I felt a wave of relief. Indian parents... could be relentless when it came to their questions, especially when it was about the careers their children wanted to pursue. And when they were about someone else working in the same field? It was like he had an endless arsenal of questions lined up. I swear, sometimes I think Dad was planning to turn every meal into a job interview.

"Anu show him the guest room beta," Mumma instructed me with a smile.

I glanced at Vansh, who was already escaping from the scene with the stealth of a ninja, his phone glued to his hand.

I shot my mother a quick look, silently pointing to the way Vansh escaped, and she gave me a reassuring nod, mouthing, "I'll handle it." Sighing in relief, I turned toward Shaurya, who was getting up from the couch as if it had just caught fire.

I fought hard to suppress my smile but couldn't hold it in as soon as we stepped inside the guest room. Shaurya's expression was so priceless, that I could barely keep it together. He looked like a kid who managed to escape a meal he didn't fancy.

And that's when I lost it. A soft laugh bubbled up, and I couldn't hold it in any longer.

"You're enjoying my plight, aren't you?" Shaurya's voice was a mixture of mock annoyance and amusement, his eyes narrowing at me like he was plotting some kind of revenge.

I grinned, barely containing my giggles. There was something irresistibly cute about his playful glare, the way his lips pressed into a pout. Without thinking, my hands reached for his cheeks, giving them a playful pinch.

He squatted my hands away with a small growl, but his eyes were still mischievously twinkling. His expression made me laugh even harder, and I pressed my hand to my stomach to steady myself.

"Stop laughing at me, Ananya!" he said, though his voice was filled with more amusement than anger. He was fighting a losing battle against that smile of mine.

My laughter died in my throat the moment Shaurya placed his hands on my waist. The warmth of his touch sent a jolt through me, and before I could even process what was happening, he pulled me closer. His grip on my waist tightened, and the space between us became a breathless void. Our noses were almost touching, the air between us crackling with something electric.

I couldn't breathe. I couldn't think. All I could focus on was the way his presence consumed me. He bent just enough so that his lips were dangerously close to my ear.

"Ab hasi nahi aarahi?" His voice was low, and husky, sending a shiver down my spine. His nose brushed against my cheek, soft yet possessive, and I inhaled sharply. The warmth of his breath fanned over my skin, making my heart skip a beat.

I couldn't bring myself to look at him, my gaze dropping to his chest, my throat dry as I shook my head, the wordless "no" caught in the back of my throat. His nose moved slowly, delicately, from my cheek to my jawline, and I couldn't stop myself from squirming in his hold. Every nerve in my body was alive, humming with a strange, intoxicating heat.

"Good," he whispered, his lips brushing my cheek in a soft, almost teasing kiss. And just as quickly as he had pulled me in, he released me, stepping back with a satisfied smirk.

I placed a hand over my chest, my heart racing so fast I thought it might burst out of me. My cheeks were on fire, burning with a warmth I couldn't explain, and I dared not meet his eyes, terrified of what I might see there—what I might feel.

Shaurya stood across from me, leaning casually against the door as if he hadn't just reduced me to a breathless, heart-thumping mess. His arms were crossed over his chest, and that damn smirk was still there, taunting me.

"What if someone came in?" I finally managed to ask, my voice thick with a mix of annoyance and... something else. Something I couldn't quite name yet.

But he just chuckled softly, his fingers reaching out to pinch my cheeks—playfully, tenderly, like he knew he had me wrapped around his finger.

Before I could react, he bumped his forehead gently against mine, his smile softening just for a moment. Then, he placed a kiss on my forehead, his lips lingering for the briefest of moments before he pulled away and walked out of the room, leaving me standing there, completely flabbergasted.

I stood frozen, my head still spinning, my heart still racing. Is he for real? I couldn't decide if I was angry, embarrassed, or just... overwhelmed by the way he had looked at me—like he knew the effect he had on me, and he enjoyed every second of it.

After Shaurya walked out, leaving me in a dazed state, I barely had time to collect myself before Mumma called me from downstairs.

"Ananya, beta, could you please give Shaurya some company? Your father's on an important call, and Vansh is MIA." Her voice carried the usual sweetness, but the tone left no room for refusal.

I sighed, adjusting myself before heading downstairs, where I found Shaurya lounging lazily on the couch, looking as composed as ever. The nerve of that man—acting like he hadn't just completely scrambled my thoughts.

"Come on, Mr. Singhania," I said with a small smirk. "Mumma wants you to see our lawn. I guess it's my duty as your temporary tour guide."

He lifted his gaze from his phone, his lips curving into that signature, teasing smile. "Lead the way, Ms. Shergill. You're the expert on this tour."

I rolled my eyes but walked ahead of him, taking in the way his eyes followed me as I led him outside. The evening air was warm, a gentle breeze playing with my hair as I guided him to the swing in the corner of the lawn, the very same swing I had spent countless hours on growing up.

We both sat down, the swing creaking under our weight, and for a moment, neither of us spoke. I could feel the tension from before still lingering in the air between us, thick and unspoken.

Shaurya broke the silence first, his voice low and amused. "I think this is the first time I've seen you so quiet. Usually, you can't stop talking."

I laughed softly, feeling the warmth of his presence beside me. "Maybe you've just caught me off guard."

"Mm, I've noticed that happens a lot around me." He said it casually, like he had every right to tease me, and I couldn't decide whether to be annoyed or... intrigued.

I narrowed my eyes at him. "You know, you're getting really good at making me blush. It's getting a bit annoying."

He chuckled, a rich sound that seemed to reverberate through my chest, and he shifted closer, making the swing sway slightly under us. "Annoying? I don't think so, Ananya. I think you like it. You like my attention, Anya."

I shot him a glare, but it lacked any real heat. "Don't get ahead of yourself."

The swing creaked again as Shaurya leaned in just slightly, his arm brushing against mine. "You know, for someone so clever, you sure are easy to read."

I stiffened, trying to keep my composure. "I'm not easy to read."

He smiled that infuriatingly perfect smile, his eyes locking with mine, daring me to deny it. "You're right," he said, his voice softer now, almost teasing. "I guess I'm just getting better at understanding you."

I wasn't sure if I liked the way he said that or if it made me a little... nervous. "Well, you'll have to try harder, because I'm full of surprises."

"Is that so?" Shaurya leaned in slightly, and for a moment, I could feel his breath on my neck. "I'd love to see what surprises you have in store, Anya."

I felt my breath catch at his proximity, my heart thudding loudly in my chest. His eyes were so intense now, like he was studying every little movement I made, every breath I took.

I swallowed, trying to sound unaffected. "You're getting way too comfortable in my home. My parents and your mother are in there,"

"Am I?" His voice was low, and playful, but there was something deeper in it, something that sent a shiver down my spine. "Maybe I'm just getting comfortable with you despite the location."

The air between us shifted, and I could feel my cheeks heating up, but I refused to let him see how much his words were affecting me. Instead, I leaned back a little, pretending to ignore him as I stared out at the stars starting to dot the sky.

But Shaurya wasn't having any of it. He leaned forward again, his face inches from mine, and I could feel his gaze on me, intense and unrelenting.

"You're still not going to admit it, are you?" he asked, his lips almost brushing my ear as he spoke.

I bit my lip, trying to hold back the smile that was threatening to break through. "Admit what?"

"That you like my attention," he whispered.

I turned to face him, my lips curving into a half-smile. "Maybe I do. But I'm not saying it out loud and boosting your ego."

"Good," he murmured, his thumb brushing lightly across my hand. "I like it when you're a little difficult. Makes it more fun."

Before I could respond, he pulled me back towards him, causing the swing to rock gently. Our faces were mere inches apart now, the space between us charged with an undeniable energy.

I couldn't help myself. I gave in, just for a second. I let myself feel everything. His warmth. His presence. His smile made my heart race.

But then, just as quickly as he had drawn closer, he pulled back, flashing that same teasing grin. "But we're not done yet, Ananya. Not by a long shot."

I was left breathless, my heart still fluttering as I tried to catch my composure.

"You're impossible," I muttered, though I couldn't hide the smile tugging at my lips.

"Impossible to resist, you mean," Shaurya corrected, his eyes sparkling with mischief.

"Shaurya!" I narrowed my eyes at him in mock seriousness. Shaurya chuckled, throwing his hands up in mock surrender.

The night air was cool, and the scent of fresh grass lingered around us as the swing creaked under our weight. Shaurya's hand had found mine again, his fingers brushing lightly against my skin, sending waves of warmth through me despite the cool breeze.

"You know," he said casually, breaking the comfortable silence, "you're really something else, Anya."

I tilted my head, curious. "Something else? What does that mean?"

He turned his head towards me, his eyes dark with affection and something else I couldn't quite place. "You've got this perfect balance of being sweet and stubborn. It's... intriguing."

I raised an eyebrow, unable to hold back the smile that tugged at my lips. "Intriguing, huh? I'll take that as a compliment."

He chuckled softly, his thumb tracing circles on the back of my hand, making my heart skip a beat. "Oh, it's definitely a compliment, babe. You're the only one who can make me lose my focus without even trying."

I leaned in, resting my head against his shoulder, the familiar warmth of his body making me feel safe and content. "I don't know if that's a good thing or a bad thing."

Shaurya's arm wrapped around my waist, pulling me closer until I was practically sitting on his lap, my back against his chest. "It's a good thing. You make everything feel better, Anya." His voice was softer now, the teasing edge replaced with something deeper, more sincere. "You know that, right?"

I couldn't help but smile, feeling my heart swell at his words. "I know," I whispered back, turning my head to meet his eyes. "I feel the same way."

He stared at me for a moment, his gaze flickering from my eyes to my lips. There was a vulnerability in his expression that made my chest tighten. "Anya..." he murmured, his voice low and intimate. "Do you ever get scared of how much I care about you?"

I blinked in surprise, not expecting such a question. "Why would I be scared?" I asked softly, genuinely curious.

He exhaled a breath, leaning his forehead against mine, his hands still holding me close. "Because sometimes, it scares me. How much I care about you." His words hung in the air between us, thick with emotion.

I reached up to touch his face, tracing the line of his jaw with my fingers. "Shaurya... you don't have to be scared. I'm here, and I'm not going anywhere."

He closed his eyes for a brief moment as if he was savoring the sound of my words. Then, with a soft smile, he opened his eyes and whispered, "You really know how to make me feel safe, Ananya."

"Good," I said, my voice barely above a whisper. "Because I'm not going anywhere either."

I smiled softly, cupping his face in my hands. "You make everything feel like it's right in the world, Shaurya."

His lips curled into a smile, his hands still holding me firmly. "I think you do the same for me, Anya."

Shaurya pulled back slightly, his lips brushing against my ear as he whispered, "I'm not letting you go, you know that, right?"

I smiled against his lips, brushing our lips together. "I wouldn't want you to."

CHAPTER TWENTY-FIVE

Ananya

It's been a week since that dinner. That night lingers in my mind, like a melody that refuses to fade. Shaurya and I haven't had a chance to meet since then. He's busy with his commercials and companies, the responsibilities weighing heavy on his shoulders, while I've been free from the time we returned. There's nothing on the horizon right now, no new mission to keep me occupied, so I'm left with these endless days of waiting.

I spend most of my time at home, or else talking to Shaurya—our conversations an unspoken escape, a brief moment of connection in a world that keeps us apart. There's something so comforting about hearing his voice, but the silence between us also makes the longing grow.

"Di, chale?" Vansh's voice snaps me out of my thoughts. He's standing at the door, dressed in his tee and tracks.

"Yes," I replied, grabbing my phone and slipping it into my pocket before heading out the door.

Vansh led the way, and I followed, clutching his cricket kit as I hopped onto the scooty. It's heavy—far heavier than I thought it would be—and it digs into my arms, making me huff with the effort of holding it. How do they carry these things around, I wonder? It's like carrying a part of the game itself—solid, weighty, demanding.

He parked the scooty in the lot, and before I could even step off, he snatched the bag from my hands. Without a word, he swung his arm around my shoulders, pulling me closer in a playful yet possessive move.

We reached the coach, and Vansh was quick to disappear, darting off to change. I stood there, alone, with nothing but the distant sound of the team getting ready for practice. The coach and I exchanged a few words about Vansh and the others, but soon, he was off too, leaving me standing amid the energy swirling around the field.

The air was thick with the scent of fresh grass, the sound of shoes scraping against the dirt, and the quiet hum of anticipation. It was odd, though—I wasn't here to watch the game, to analyze, or even to cheer on my brother. No, I was just here... to fill the silence that had been growing inside me. And maybe, just maybe, to take my mind off someone I couldn't seem to stop thinking about.

Vansh returned, dressed in his sleeveless tee and shorts, his muscles flexing as he moved, a sight I had no intention of commenting on. I may have noticed that he looked quite handsome, but there was no way in hell I was going to say that to his face. If I did, he'd be insufferable—his head would literally float into the clouds, and I'd never hear the end of it.

The team scattered, and the practice began. Some of the guys were engaged in a game of football, their laughter echoing in the background, while others took to the nets. My gaze drifted, following the chaos of activity until I saw Sid, standing in the middle of the field with a stump in hand. I blinked, confused at first, then frowned as he swung it at the ball. It was bizarre—he was supposed to be batting with a proper bat, wasn't he?

Ved was bowling to him, and yet Sid seemed more interested in using a wicket than the bat, the oddity of it pulling my attention even more. I couldn't help but smile at the ridiculousness of it all.

Are they short of bats? I wondered, my gaze still lingering on Sid and his strange use of a stump.

Before I could think much more about it, a voice that was far too familiar for my own peace broke through my thoughts. "It's part of the training," it said, smooth and effortless, sending a ripple of warmth through me. My heart skipped a beat as I turned toward the sound, and there he was, standing beside me, looking like he owned the world.

Shaurya.

He was dressed in a navy blue tee with track pants, the color so perfect it seemed like it was custom-made for him. His tracksuit, the same shade, draped over his broad shoulders with a casual elegance that only he could pull off. Honestly, I wouldn't be surprised if the sales for that exact outfit skyrocket once people start spotting him wearing it. He had that effect on everything he touched.

He noticed me staring, and of course, his lips curved into that trademark smirk. "Hello?" He waved his hand in front of my face, the motion teasing, his gaze locking with mine like a challenge.

It took me a second to realize what had happened. My eyes had been... on him—again. I blinked, suddenly feeling like I'd been caught in a moment of weakness. My cheeks flushed, and I cursed inwardly. Oh God, I've been ogling him again!

"What are you doing here?" I blurted out the first question that came to my mind, desperate to divert his attention from the teasing glint in his eyes. My cheeks were already on fire, and I could feel the heat spreading across my face as he casually settled beside me, his forearm brushing against mine.

"Finding you here is more surprising than finding me here, isn't it, sweetheart?" he teased, raising a brow in that infuriatingly perfect way. That look—it was a lethal combination of confidence and charm, and why did it have to be so drool-worthy? Kill me already, please.

I tried to regain my bearings, shifting uncomfortably as the warmth in my cheeks intensified. "I...I came here with Vansh. I was getting bored at home," I said, trying to sound casual, but the stutter in my voice betrayed me.

Why did I even stutter? It's not like I came here to see him. It's not like I knew he'd be here, right?

Liar.

Okay, fine. Vansh had told me earlier that Shaurya and Akshith were coming today to talk to the coach, but that wasn't the reason I decided to come here. I just... I needed a change of scene. I was genuinely bored. The thought of spending another day staring at four walls was enough to drive me insane.

"And I'm here to meet their coach. It's been a while since I met him," Shaurya said casually, his gaze flicking to the field, and I nodded in acknowledgment. A soft silence fell between us, the kind that wasn't awkward but instead comfortable, like two people who understood each other's presence without needing words to fill the space.

He was watching the team now, his focus intense, his eyes scanning every move with the keen precision of someone who knew what it meant to be at the top. I, on the other hand, found myself stealing glances at him, unable to help it. I couldn't take my eyes off the way his jaw clenched when he observed the players, the way his fingers flexed as if itching to step in and correct something. There was something so deeply... captivating about him in these moments, so much more than just the cricket star that everyone else saw.

I had always enjoyed watching my brother play. His dedication, his relentless effort to improve, made me proud beyond words. But there was something different about seeing Shaurya like this, so at ease in his world. He wasn't just the captain of a team; he was an embodiment of everything I admired—determination, strength, and a quiet intensity that had nothing to do with his fame.

After a few minutes, I heard his voice again, softer this time, but no less certain. "I can imagine seeing you a lot in the stadiums in the coming years."

The words tugged at something deep inside me, a warmth blossoming in my chest. I smiled at him, nodding slowly, agreeing with a sense of calm certainty. "It's bound to happen when two important men in my life spend most of their time in stadiums."

I said it lightly, but the truth in my words hung there between us, settling comfortably in the silence. I could easily picture it—spending my days in stadiums, cheering for Shaurya and Vansh, watching their journeys unfold. I wanted to see them play together. I wanted to see them push each other, for Vansh to learn from Shaurya, and to rise under his guidance. I was proud of both of them, even if I'd never be the one to say it out loud.

"Do you realize you just called me an important person in your life?" Shaurya asked, his lips curling into that mischievous grin I could never resist. I couldn't help but smile back, warmth blooming inside me.

I nodded with a playful smile, then reached up to snuggle closer, sliding my arms around his bicep. Resting my head against his shoulder, I allowed the moment to settle between us like a quiet, shared secret.

"We wouldn't be dating if I felt otherwise, Mr," I said lightly, a teasing edge to my voice. I pulled away as I noticed Vansh emerging from the nets. He was gulping down water, lost in his own world, before returning to his team. I watched him for a moment, my mind momentarily distracted, but Shaurya wasn't far behind.

I felt his hand slide around my back, warm and strong, pulling me closer to him. He held me against his chest with a possessiveness that made my heart flutter.

"And I feel lucky to be dating you, Ms." His voice was low and intimate, and I could feel the warmth of his breath against my ear, sending a shiver down my spine.

I grinned like a fool, my cheeks lighting up in a soft pink hue. I knew I was blushing, but I couldn't stop it.

Shaurya, the captain of the Indian cricket team, a man with millions of fans, never once made me feel like I was beneath him. He never flaunted his fame and never acted like he was above anyone. With him, I was always just Ananya, equal in every way. And it was that quality of his—the humility, the genuine care he showed—that had pulled me in and kept me captivated. It was more than his looks, more than his achievements. It was the way he made me feel seen, valued, cherished. And that... that was what truly made him irresistible.

"What are your plans for the evening?" Shaurya's voice was soft, his hand still gently drawing random patterns on my skin. I felt his left hand resting against my waist, his touch warm and comforting.

"Vikram and Rakshith haven't responded to our calls or texts since yesterday," I said, my voice filled with concern. I let out a sigh, and he gave my hand a gentle squeeze, his reassuring smile melting away some of the unease in my chest. "They will be fine."

I hated not knowing what was going on with my friends. What if someone took them? The thought gnawed at me, and I couldn't shake it off.

"What about you? Same company stuff?" I asked, trying to push the worry aside for a moment, though I couldn't fully hide the irritation in my voice. Shaurya chuckled, catching my expression.

He's been a bit more involved than usual in his office stuff. He said the CEO of his clothing brand resigned recently after Shaurya caught him tampering with some data. Now, he's to go through everything, checking the numbers, looking for a new trustworthy CEO.

I knew he didn't like being involved in the company's day-to-day affairs. He preferred to focus on cricket—but now, with the situation at hand, I could see how much it was weighing on him. His jaw clenched slightly, and there was a rigidness in his posture at the mention of it, that made me want to pull him closer, to ease his burdens, even just for a moment. I squeezed his hand a little and he turned to me with a smile, squeezing my hand in return.

"No, I'm going out with the team today," Shaurya said, his voice steady but there was a hint of something else—maybe excitement, maybe anticipation. "We're leaving for the England tour in ten days, and training starts the day after."

I made an "O" with my lips, absorbing the information, but my mind was still on him, on us. The silence between us stretched comfortably as I absentmindedly played with his fingers. The way our hands intertwined felt like an unspoken promise, something simple yet profound.

"Wait," I suddenly blurted, feeling the urge to capture the moment. I pulled out my phone and clicked a few pictures of our hands, the soft sunlight catching the curves of his fingers and mine. I looked at the pictures and couldn't help but smile.

Shaurya looked at them, raising a brow, a playful glint in his eyes. "You're capturing our hands, huh?" he asked, a smirk tugging at the corner of his lips.

I shrugged, a little embarrassed but enjoying the sweet simplicity of the moment. "They look good together," I said softly, showing him the photos.

He gave me a small smile that lit up his face, and for a moment, the whole world seemed to fade away. But then, he glanced around, as if checking if anyone was watching. His eyes locked with mine, mischievous, as he leaned in and kissed my cheek, right there, in the middle of all the empty stands.

My heart raced at the sudden affection, and I turned quickly, looking around frantically to make sure no one had witnessed the kiss. I let out a quiet sigh of relief, seeing everyone absorbed in their work.

When I turned back to him, I glared at him, but that expression faltered when I saw the soft, adorable smile he was giving me. His lips were slightly parted, eyes twinkling with amusement, and I couldn't resist. My glare melted into a grin, and I shook my head, unable to hide how much I adored him in that moment.

"We would have become tomorrow's headlines if someone saw this," I said, trying to sound serious, but I could already feel the warmth spreading across my cheeks.

Shaurya just chuckled, a low, rich sound that made my heart flutter. His hand reached up and gently pulled at my cheek, making me wince and glare at him—but I couldn't hold the glare for long.

He leaned in, resting our foreheads together, and then brushed his nose against mine in the softest, sweetest gesture. A smile tugged at my lips involuntarily, and all my irritation vanished.

"Don't worry so much, Jaana," he murmured, his voice so soothing. "I've already checked before kissing you."

I couldn't help but smile back, feeling a bit silly for my earlier worry. Of course, he'd be careful. He was always so thoughtful, and his calm presence made me feel like everything would be okay.

I nodded with a soft laugh, the tension in my chest easing.

"I know how the media works," I said, my tone a little more serious now. "They would go crazy if something like this came out. It would cause a lot of problems for both of us—and our families. I'm not ready for paps to be standing in front of my house every day, waiting for something juicier."

He let out a soft sigh, pulling me closer and wrapping an arm around me. "We'll figure it out, Anya. Together."

"Also, send me those pictures, sweetheart." He added, tipping his chin towards my mobile.

The world outside might be chaotic, but here, in this moment, everything felt calm and right.

"Why are you giving me new nicknames every other time?" I asked, raising an eyebrow with a slight frown. He had already given me so many—though I wasn't complaining. I just found it a bit amusing, that's all.

"Well," he said, pausing as if he were deep in thought, "I like all those names, and I only have you to call with all of them, so why not?"

His words brought a smile to my face, and I giggled at his innocent yet thoughtful reply. Only Shaurya could make something so simple sound so charming.

We fell into a comfortable silence, watching the team practice. I leaned into him, savoring the moment. But then, I felt him move away slightly, just enough for me to notice. Coach Sir was walking toward us. I whined internally at the sudden loss of warmth, but I quickly shook it off, knowing this was just one of those interruptions that came with being in a stadium full of busy people.

"How are you, Shaurya?" Coach Sir beamed as he spotted Shaurya, his face lighting up with warmth. Shaurya smiled broadly, bending to touch his feet in respect, seeking blessings.

Sir patted his back and stood him up, his pride clear in his eyes.

"Okay, sir, I will leave now. Bye, Shaurya... sir," I added quickly, realizing Coach Sir was looking at me with the same disappointed expression a father would give a misbehaving child. Shaurya winked at me, his teasing smile barely contained as Coach Sir's back was turned. I couldn't handle the intense gaze from Shaurya, and in an instant, I bolted.

Without looking back, I grabbed my phone and made a beeline for Vansh. I quickly informed him that I'd wait at the nearby café for him, inviting the boys along too. On my way out, I ruffled Sid's hair and playfully patted Ved's head.

I could feel Shaurya's gaze following me as if he were waiting for me to turn around. But he was enjoying the Coach glaring at me, right? Let him enjoy it. I wasn't going to give him the satisfaction of looking back and acknowledging him.

Ananya

I sat in the cafe, the cool breeze brushing against my skin as I absently stirred my cold coffee, the ice cubes gently clinking against the glass.

A phone buzzed with a text, pulling me from my thoughts.

"Anu, please save your handsome friend! Nearly 15 people are staring at me like I'm some criminal in an investigation!"

A laugh bubbled up from my chest as I imagined Bhavin saying those words. I shook my head with a smile.

"Did you already reach?" I sent back, still trying to wrap my mind around how he'd made it to the bride's place in what seemed like 10 minutes. Was he too excited to meet her?

A few moments later, my phone buzzed again with his reply.

"Hmm. The girl lives in the same building."

"Wow, Bhav. You can visit your in-laws and grandparents simultaneously in the future," I shot back, my fingers dancing across the keys as I teased him mercilessly. If there was one thing Bhavin loved more than anything, it was the challenge of annoying me—and now that I had the perfect opportunity, I wasn't going to waste it. He had no idea what was coming.

"Not now yaar! Please help me out. They are boring holes into my body with their stares," came his frantic reply, and I could practically hear the desperation in his voice. I imagined him, sitting in the middle of this bridal meet, surrounded by judgmental aunts and grandmothers, and the mental image was just too much. How would he look pouting in front of all those people?

A laugh burst from me, the sound bright and clear, filling the space around me.

I couldn't help it. His melodrama was always entertaining.

"Are you going to help or not?" he typed again, and by now, I could practically feel the fumes of his anger through the screen. A bit of guilt flickered inside me, but it was quickly squashed by my amusement. This was too good to let go.

I decided to give him a break—for now.

"Fine. What do you want me to do?" I typed, my fingers hovering over the screen.

Seconds ticked by, and I watched the status change back to online. What was taking him so long? Was he distracted?

And then it hit me. No. Don't tell me... I narrowed my eyes at the screen, suspicious now. Could it be?

I shook the thought away, looking down at my phone to text him back, but another message popped up, this time not from him.

Shaurya.

His message was simple, but the way his name appeared on the screen made my heart skip.

"I'm thinking of you, Ananya."

Just five words, but they landed like a warm breeze through my chest, curling around my heart. It wasn't an over-the-top gesture, but something about it made me feel seen. More than seen... understood.

I quickly typed back, my fingers trembling slightly with the warmth of the moment.

"I'm thinking of you too."

I sat back in my seat, a soft smile playing on my lips. There was a certain kind of peace in knowing that someone's thoughts were with you, even when they were miles away. And in that peace, I couldn't help but feel a pull — a deeper connection than I'd ever anticipated.

Just as I was lost in those thoughts, my phone buzzed again. This time, it was a message from Bhavin, followed by a flurry of texts in succession.

"Help! This grandmother of mine is trying to fix me up with every girl here!"

"Tell me I'm not the only one being interrogated by 10 aunts?"

I laughed out loud, drawing curious glances from the people around me.

"Sounds like you're in the middle of a soap opera. "

He replied almost instantly.

"Not now, Ananya! Save me!"

"Okay, Mr. But didn't you fall in love at first sight with that girl? Like those movies?" I sent the text, practically feeling my heart race as I waited.

His reply came almost instantaneously, and the indignation in his tone practically leaped off the screen.

"What the fuck? No!"

I couldn't help but snicker at his denial. Sure, Bhavin, sure.

Then, the next message popped up. And it left me stunned.

"This is the same girl I saw yesterday eating a man's mouth in front of my car."

And just like that, my stomach flipped in laughter. I nearly lost my balance, the laughter bubbling up so uncontrollably that I would have tipped right out of my seat if not for the strong arm that shot out just in time to catch me.

I gasped, barely holding myself together, clutching onto Vansh's elbow for support. His grip was firm, yet gentle, steadying me. I looked up at him through my tears of laughter, and to my surprise, his face was as white as a ghost's, his eyes wide in shock as he glanced between me and my phone like a disappointed father.

"What... what happened?" he asked, still unsure if he should be concerned or amused.

I couldn't stop laughing. How could I? Bhavin's dramatic recount of the scene had me in stitches.

I could barely catch my breath between laughs as I squeezed Vansh's arm, my chest rising and falling with the intensity of the moment. "I swear, Bhavin's life is a soap opera! I'm just waiting for the next episode!" I gasped out, wiping a tear from my eye.

Vansh just shook his head, an amused smirk appearing on his lips as he gently pulled me back into my seat. "I don't even want to know what kind of mess he's gotten himself into this time, Di."

Just as I tried to regain my composure, I caught the curious gazes of Shaurya and the guys from the corner of my eye. Shaurya raised an eyebrow, silently asking what was going on. I couldn't help but give him a tiny shake of my head, discreetly trying to compose myself, my cheeks still flushed from laughter.

And then, the dreaded message came through again.

"Save me!"

"Oye idiot!"

"Are you there?"

"I swear, Anu. I will kill you if you don't call me now."

I quickly dialed his number, amused by his growing desperation. It rang only twice before he picked up. Oh, he was desperate.

"Yes, Mr. Sharma," I heard Bhavin speak, but this time, his tone was colder, almost professional. I pressed my lips together, biting the inside of my cheek to suppress the laughter that threatened to spill out.

I couldn't hold it in anymore. "I didn't know you could speak professionally too," I teased, looking at Shaurya, who was watching me with an amused expression. I mouthed later to him, and he gave me a small nod, his eyes sparkling with understanding.

From the other side of the phone, Bhavin's breaths were sharp, like a dragon trying to stay calm. I could hear the barely contained frustration in his voice, but there was no way he could scold me in front of all those people.

"Sure, Mr. Sharma. I will start immediately." Bhavin spoke in a fake business-like tone, and I could practically see him informing his grandmother about the "emergency" that didn't actually exist.

"Sure, bring me Grandma's papad on your way," I heard him grit through his teeth before the line went dead.

I burst into laughter again, my whole body shaking with it. I couldn't stop, not even if I tried. The cafe around me blurred as I let the sound of my laughter fill the air.

Vansh's gaze was full of questions, the kind of look that asked, What made you laugh so hard? I smiled at him, still struggling to get my breath back. He gave me a look that said What now?

I could also feel the soft warmth of Shaurya's gaze on me as I wiped the tears from my eyes. My fingers trembled slightly, not from the laughter, but from the way he was looking at me as if the whole world faded into the background and all that mattered was this moment between us. The smile on his face was gentle, as if he was silently sharing in the joy that bubbled inside of me.

I pushed the phone into Vansh's hands who was looking at me like I had grown two heads. As he read through the messages, he too burst out laughing.

I straightened up, suddenly aware of the silence that had settled around the table. Sid's puzzled expression and the quizzical look from the others brought me back to the moment, but there was still a lingering warmth, like the glow of a sunset that refused to fade.

"What happened to you both?" Sid asked, his eyebrows knitted in confusion, glancing between Shaurya and me.

I couldn't contain the laughter anymore. It bubbled up from within me, uncontrollable and free, spilling out as I pounded my fists lightly on the table. Just when my head was about to hit the table, I felt a strong, steady hand press gently against it. My head, almost instinctively, landed against Shaurya's palm—soft and protective. The moment was brief, but it felt like time slowed down, and in that single touch, I felt the sincerity of his care, the unspoken bond that was quietly deepening between us.

"One of Di's friends got stuck in something funny," Vansh explained, his voice calm, as though nothing out of the ordinary had happened. His friends nodded, not pressing further, letting the topic slide.

But I wasn't entirely sure how to explain the mixture of emotions running through me—the sudden feeling of warmth from Shaurya's touch, the softness in his smile, the way my heart raced for reasons I couldn't quite pinpoint. It was more than just the laughter from Bhavin's ridiculous predicament. It was the way Shaurya made me feel safe, and understood, like I mattered in ways words could never explain.

I wiped the last of the tears from my eyes with the tissue Shaurya had handed me, my hand brushing against his as I took it. The smallest touch. But in that moment, it felt like the world had stopped, just for a second, to let us exist in this quiet space of shared understanding. I glanced up at him, my heart swelling when I met his gaze. His eyes were soft, his smile even softer, and for reasons I couldn't explain, it made me feel like I was home.

"Hi, sir. I wasn't expecting you here," I said, my tone professional, stretching out the 'sir' with a playful roll of my eyes that only I knew. The slight teasing edge in my voice was hard to miss.

"I invited him," Vansh chimed in, his smirk growing wider as he watched the exchange between us.

I nodded at him, my attention drifting back to the table. The waiter arrived shortly after, placing the orders for everyone while I stayed silent, absorbed in my thoughts. I had already indulged in two pastries and a coffee before they arrived, and now, the last thing I wanted was more food or drink.

As the others enjoyed their meals, I couldn't resist teasing Bhavin further. His threats to block my number if I sent one more text only made me laugh harder. He was too easy to wind up. Eventually, I tucked my phone away, rolling my eyes at him in mock annoyance.

Reaching for my card, I was ready to pay the bill when Shaurya leaned in, his hand stopping mine with a decisive motion.

"I was going to pay," I said, crossing my arms over my waist, and giving him a mock pout.

Shaurya simply shrugged, his smirk widening before he winked at me, sending a shiver down my spine. His wink was always so damn confident, so effortless—and it did something to me that I couldn't quite put into words. My mouth fell open in surprise, and I turned toward the man at the counter to distract myself, my heart racing.

He wasn't just charming, he was dangerous—dangerous in the way he could throw me off balance without even trying. I let out a small sigh, trying to regain my composure. This man... he was going to give me a heart attack someday, I just knew it.

Vansh's friends finally left, bidding us a casual goodbye, and soon after, Vansh excused himself to grab our scooty, leaving me alone with Shaurya. The moment the table felt quieter, the air between us shifted, and I could feel the tension building. Shaurya reached out and grabbed my hand, pulling my attention to him. I instinctively looked around, half-expecting someone to notice, but the cafe was nearly empty—just a couple at the far end, lost in their own world, and the man at the counter, engrossed in a phone call.

I felt Shaurya's thumb rub against the back of my hand, sending an unexpected rush of warmth through me, making me blush furiously.

"It's quite exciting," he said, his voice low, almost teasing. I turned to him, surprised to see that wide grin on his face, his eyes sparkling with excitement, like a kid who had just been handed a secret he couldn't wait to share.

He didn't wait for me to speak and continued, "You know, I always wanted to do things like this—meeting my girlfriend in private, grabbing her hand sneakily, stealing kisses from her, hugging her in a dark corner..." He paused, looking at me with such intensity, like he was imagining it all vividly.

My heart fluttered, and I couldn't help but feel overwhelmed by the depth of his words. I looked around once more to make sure we were still in our little bubble, then, feeling a rush of spontaneity, I leaned forward and pecked his cheek.

Shaurya's eyes widened in surprise, the moment catching him off guard. His grip on my hand tightened instinctively, and I grinned, savoring the playful tension between us. I took a small step back, not wanting to give him the chance to steal a kiss of his own just yet.

Before he could recover from the surprise, Vansh returned. Shaurya released my hand with a final, lingering touch that made my pulse race. I waved goodbye to Shaurya, silently wishing I could have held onto the moment just a little longer.

"Di, you know Shaurya sir is such a down-to-earth person. He played with us and even gave me personal advice about captaincy and everything. Now, I love him even more," Vansh rambled on, his voice full of admiration.

I couldn't help but chuckle at how passionately he spoke about Shaurya, his eyes practically glowing. But in the back of my mind, a mischievous thought popped up. What would happen if Shaurya and I ever got into a fight? Whose side would Vansh take? It was a funny thought, but I pushed it away, not wanting to entertain the idea of any conflict between Shaurya and me.

It was crazy how everything about him made me feel both warm and giddy, even in the most mundane of moments. I hit my forehead gently, almost as if trying to bring myself back to reality.

We reached home soon after, and while Vansh went to freshen up, I took the opportunity to serve lunch for both of us. We ate together, the soft chatter about nothing and everything filling the air. Afterward, we relaxed on the couch to watch TV, enjoying the quiet afternoon.

Vansh left to meet his friends in the evening, and I retreated to my room to read something, trying to pass the time in peaceful solitude. But even in my book, I couldn't escape the warm, lingering thoughts of Shaurya. His words, his smile—everything about him seemed to stay with me, lingering in the air like the faintest fragrance that couldn't be shaken off.

The soft glow of my phone's screen cut through the quiet of the night, pulling me from my deep sleep. Groggy and disoriented, I reached out to grab it from the side table. Seeing Rakshith's name on the screen immediately jolted me awake, and I quickly answered the call, my heart already pounding in my chest.

"Come out with a first aid box. We're on your lawn," Rakshith's voice echoed through the phone, tense and urgent.

I shot up from my bed, panic slowly creeping into my veins. "What happened? Are you alright?" I asked, my voice laced with worry. My mind raced through a million possibilities, each worse than the last.

"I'll explain everything, just hurry," he replied sharply, before ending the call abruptly.

Without wasting a second, I quickly slipped on my slippers and rushed to the closet to grab the first aid kit. My hands were shaking, the fear making it harder to focus. I didn't even consider turning on the lights; my parents were asleep, and the last thing I wanted was to wake them. Rakshith had called me for the very same reason, and I needed to keep everything as quiet as possible.

I snuck out the door, the only sounds around me being the soft rustling of leaves and my own heartbeat, which seemed to echo louder in my ears with every step I took. I quickly scanned the area, my eyes searching for any signs of what was happening.

I spotted Rakshith and Vikram sitting on the chairs on the lawn, their faces pale under the soft glow of the moonlight. My heart skipped a beat when I saw the visible injuries on their faces and hands. Rakshith's usual confident demeanor was gone, replaced by a slight grimace, and Vikram's shirt was torn at the shoulder, the fabric hanging in tatters.

Without a second thought, I rushed over to them. My legs moved faster than my mind, and I quickly grabbed the supplements from my bag, handing them to Rakshith before kneeling down in front of Vikram. I could see the pain in his eyes, but his stoic expression was trying to hide it.

Carefully, I cleaned his knuckles, the roughness of his hands betraying the struggle he'd gone through. With precision, I tied the bandage around his hand, my fingers trembling slightly as I worked. Then, moving to his shoulder, I plastered it with a bandage, the fabric sticking to his skin. Finally, I turned to his forehead, dabbing away the blood and applying a gentle bandage.

I moved to Rakshith next, who appeared relatively unharmed, with just a few bruises marring his skin. I cleaned his wounds with quiet concentration, applying bandages where necessary.

With both of them patched up, I stood up, hands on my hips, my gaze sharp as I glared at the two of them, frustration bubbling inside me.

"Now, explain," I said, my voice firm, though my heart still raced from the shock of what had just happened. I perched on the table in front of them, arms crossed tightly against my chest. "You two are a disaster waiting to happen. You could've called me or Bhavin, you know. Do you realize what stupid thoughts were running in our minds before I found you here tonight?"

They both exchanged a glance, clearly regretting their impulsive actions.

"Sir went to his ex's house after getting drunk, and they held him captive," Rakshith said, glaring at Vikram, who was staring down at his hands, guilt and shame evident on his face. My heart softened at the sight of both of them.

I sighed deeply, frustration mixed with concern, and moved closer to Vikram. I gently took his hands in mine, looking at him with worry and understanding.

"Why did you do that, Vikky?" I asked softly, my voice almost a whisper, as if the words themselves might break him further. "You promised you'd move on, remember?"

I could feel the weight of his pain. He had loved that girl with every part of him, but she had been cruel, cheating on him without hesitation and marrying someone else, leaving him shattered. It wasn't just the heartbreak; he had fought with Rakshith, his best friend, over her. She had left him, and the damage it did was far beyond what anyone could imagine.

"I'm sorry. I wasn't thinking straight," Vikram's voice cracked, and tears welled in his eyes. I immediately pulled him into a hug, my arms wrapped around him tightly as he broke down, the sorrow that had been haunting him pouring out in waves. I could feel his body trembling as he cried against my shoulder, and I gently patted his back, murmuring words of comfort, even though I didn't know how to make it better.

After what felt like an eternity, Vikram pulled back, wiping his face with the back of his hand, his shoulders sagging with guilt.

"I'm sorry. I was so stupid to believe her over you all," his voice was hoarse with regret. "I went there to confront her, but... she told them I was trying to force myself on her."

The shock of his words hit me like a wave. My eyes widened, and I turned to Rakshith, whose anger was now palpable, his fists clenched tightly by his sides. His face flushed with rage, his eyes dark with fury.

"That bitch! I'll kill her!" Rakshith stood up suddenly, shaking in anger. Before he could take a step, I quickly grabbed his arm and made him sit back down with all the strength I could muster.

"Rakshith, stop!" I pleaded, my voice breaking through his storm of emotions. "Whatever happened, happened. I don't want any of you getting involved with her anymore. She's done enough damage, and I no longer want her in our lives. Please... just let it go."

I looked at both of them, my eyes filled with pleading, my heart aching for them. They were my brothers, and I couldn't bear to see them destroyed over someone who didn't deserve them.

After a long moment, they both sighed, their bodies slumping in resignation, the weight of my words sinking in. I reached for them, pulling them into a group hug. We stayed like that for a while, the three of us, silently comforting each other. Finally, after everything that had happened, we shared the first moment of peace we'd had in a long time.

CHAPTER TWENTY-SEVEN

Ananya

Vikram and Rakshith are finally back to their old selves after throwing a few punches at each other—nothing too serious, just the usual. They still have that rivalry, but now it's like the air between them has cleared, the tension replaced with something familiar, something we've all missed.

Bhavin—poor Bhavin—looks like his world's been turned upside down. He's staring at Vikram and Rakshith with wide eyes, clearly baffled by the sudden hug-fest happening in front of him. He's the one who nagged the most about their fallout, and now he's practically in tears, pretending to wipe them away as he teases me. "Explain it to me again," he says dramatically, "I'm not sure my old heart can handle this much emotional chaos." His words pull a small smile from me, despite being very habitual to his dramatic behavior.

A month since that incident, and we're finally back to being a team. A real team. Even Shika and Nithin—always lost in their own little world, going on dates and distracting each other—have returned to the fold, their playful energy lifting the mood, even if just for a second.

I glance at the clock, and my mind automatically drifts to him. The man I've been missing, the man who left for England right after we shared those brief, stolen days together. He left for his overseas tour ten days ago. I can still feel his hands on me, his voice in my ear. He's out there, competing in five tests and four one-day matches. They've finished three tests, and I haven't heard from him since yesterday afternoon. The calls are short, and the texts, well, they are the highlights of my days. We speak, but only for 20 minutes at a time. I pout at the thought, and my heart feels a pang of longing.

"Jai Hind, Sir!"

We snapped to attention as Kulkarni Sir entered the room, followed by Dixit Sir. The air around us thickened with expectation. The tension that always filled the room when they arrived was palpable, like a warning of something big coming. They greeted us back, but I couldn't shake the unease gnawing at me.

Dixit Sir walked forward and handed a thick, sealed packet to Vikram. He took it without question, tearing it open as Kulkarni Sir's voice cut through the air, sharp and commanding.

"You are all going to the UK tonight."

My mouth dropped open in disbelief. England? Tonight? I blinked, trying to process his words. I wasn't the only one stunned. Shika, who'd been sitting next to me, squeezed my hand so tightly that I could feel the bones of her fingers pressing against mine. She was just as shocked as I was.

"Are we really leaving tonight?" Shika whispered beside me, not quite believing it.

Kulkarni sir didn't give us time to ask any more questions before he continued. "We received intel that Wasim is planning something catastrophic. He's embedded his men within Mr. Atul Sisodia's company in the UK. We're certain Mr. Sisodia is aiding them in some way, whether knowingly or not. Your mission is simple: infiltrate the company. Become employees, and figure out what they're planning. We need answers."

I heard the collective intake of breath from the team. A silence settled over us, thick with the weight of what we were being asked to do.

Wasim Akram. The name alone sent a chill down my spine. The face of terror in our country. The reason behind the formation of this team. We'd all been brought together to track him, to bring him down. The thought that we were finally getting so close—so dangerously close—had my pulse racing. This was it. Our moment.

Without hesitation, we shouted out in unison, "Yes, Sir!"

But inside, my thoughts were a whirlwind. Wasim was dangerous. The kind of danger that made your blood run cold. He wasn't just a criminal. He was a mastermind, always one step ahead of us. Every time we thought we'd caught him, he slipped through our fingers like smoke.

And now we were headed straight into his web.

I turned my gaze to my team. Vikram's expression was hard, determined. Rakshith's quiet confidence never wavered, but I could see the flicker of intensity in his eyes. Shika was already pulling out her phone, her mind likely running through logistics. Bhavin was silently nodding, ready to execute the mission, but I could tell he was just as anxious as I was.

I glanced at the packet still in Vikram's hands. Whatever was inside, it was going to change everything. The urgency in Kulkarni Sir's eyes said it all. We didn't have time for second-guessing.

"Get your bags packed," Kulkarni sir ordered, his voice flat but filled with the weight of command. "We move fast. You'll be in the UK by morning. Get ready to act."

"Get to work as soon as you receive the commands," Kulkarni sir says, his voice sharp, final. "I want every lead followed, every detail examined. We move fast, and we move smart. We find him before he finds us."

The room falls into a heavy silence. I know what's coming next. The hunt.

"You can take a half day and pack your bags. Your fake IDs and passports are in that cover. Mr. Murthy will help you settle into the company. You'll receive his contact details once you land there. Also, one of our agents will hand over a few more details to you once you land there. One of you personally visit him and collect the information." Dixit Sir ordered us, his tone professional but laced with the urgency of the task at hand. We nodded sharply, taking in every detail. This was real now. The mission was no longer just a plan; it was happening.

We saluted them and walked out of the office, our minds already shifting to the next phase.

As the team dispersed, I felt the familiar surge of adrenaline coursing through me. I wasn't just going to the UK to gather intel. No, this time it was personal. Wasim had taken so much from us already—so many lives, so many families ruined—and now it was time for him to pay.

I straightened my back, a fierce determination lighting up inside me. We were going to find him, and this time, we weren't letting him slip away.

The hunt had just begun.

"Our flight is at 9," Vikram announced as we stepped into the cool evening air. I glanced at my watch—3:00 PM. The minutes were slipping away too fast. My stomach churned with a mixture of excitement and anxiety.

I groaned in frustration, slumping against Bhavin's shoulder. The reality of packing hit me hard. He flicked my forehead, making me yelp in pain. I glared at him, rubbing the spot where his finger had made contact, but he was already grinning at my reaction.

"I will just keep a suitcase packed from now on," I muttered, shaking my head in disbelief. The thought of packing always made me feel like I was forgetting something important. No matter how carefully I checked, there was always something I'd miss. It was a pattern. My mom would inevitably scold me for weeks afterward for not packing properly.

Vikram and Rakshith's laughter filled the air, their hands wrapping around my neck in a familiar, playful grip. They knew me too well, knew how much I despised packing. Vikram nudged me lightly with his shoulder.

"Come on, Ananya. We'll help you," Rakshith teased, raising an eyebrow with a grin. "We can get everything ready for you."

I shot them both a look. "I'm not going to let you pack my bags. I'll probably end up with half my clothes missing." I sighed, trying to suppress the rising irritation. It wasn't just about packing. The reality of what we were about to do—the stakes—hit harder every second. But I couldn't show that. Not now.

I took a deep breath and shook my head, forcing my mind back to the mission. We were about to go after Wasim. The weight of that hung heavy on my shoulders. This wasn't just another job. This was personal. Every move counted.

We rushed back to our respective places, the clock ticking faster than I could keep up with. Kulkarni sir had told us we could be gone for a month or so, and my mind scrambled to pack everything I might need for the unpredictable days ahead. I packed efficiently, but my mom's watchful eyes never let me off the hook as I packed my clothes and other toiletries. She went through my bag with the precision of a soldier inspecting supplies before giving me the green signal.

"You're all set, beta," she said, her voice thick with the mix of concern and pride I'd grown so accustomed to. Her worry was a constant, but she knew better than to try and hold me back.

Before leaving, I sent a quick transfer to Vansh's account. He gets his match fee and salary, but that idiot still loved spending my money like it was water. And, as usual, I couldn't help myself. I loved spoiling him. He was my little brother, after all.

Vansh came to the airport to drop me off, his face a mixture of teasing and affection. He gave me the most dramatic goodbye, full of exaggerated waves and ridiculous hugs that made me roll my eyes, but deep down, I cherished every second of it. I knew he'd be fine, but a part of me always hated leaving.

Once the announcement for our flight came, he finally left, his last words lingering with me: "Stay safe. Don't get too caught up in the mission, okay?

I'm your priority."

I chuckled and waved him off. He always had a way of making things feel lighter, even in the middle of a serious mission like this.

At the airport, we gathered together as a team. There was something about being around these people—my teammates—that grounded me. We all went through the security checks without any issues and made our way to the gate.

The flight from Delhi to Heathrow would take nearly 10 hours, plenty of time to prepare mentally for what lay ahead. We reported in to Kulkarni sir before takeoff, making sure everything was set. His words were brief but sharp: "Keep your guard up. This is bigger than anything you've faced."

The gravity of his words settled in my chest like a heavy stone, but we had our orders.

Shika and I sat together, with Nithin beside her. Watching the two of them interact—their subtle smiles, the light touch of their hands, the way they seemed so in tune with each other—it was enough to make me feel like the odd one out. The lovebirds, as I liked to call them, were in their own world.

I shoved my emotions aside. I wasn't about to let a couple make me feel single, especially when the weight of Wasim and our mission was bearing down on me. So, I did what I always did when I needed to focus: I opened my book.

The quiet hum of the plane and the rustling of pages lulled me into a state of concentration, but somewhere along the way, my mind betrayed me. The exhaustion from the day's rush, the overwhelming sense of purpose and urgency... it all caught up with me. I don't know when sleep took over, but before I knew it, I was leaning against the side of my seat, my book forgotten in my lap, my eyes closed in a deep, uninterrupted slumber.

We landed in London a while ago, the cool air of Heathrow hitting me like a welcome slap to my face. The airport's noise, the chatter of people in a dozen different languages, and the feeling of foreign soil beneath my feet—everything felt new, different. But the mission was still the same. Mr. Murthy was already waiting for us, his face as serious as always. He handed us a few documents and assured us that everything was set up—our stay, our fake identities, the details we'd need to get jobs in Mr. Sisodia's company, and left after wishing us luck.

Our plan was clear: blend in, gather intel, and stay focused. We have to join our jobs the day after tomorrow, but for now, we have a bit of freedom.

I was busy chatting with my team as we made our way out, laughing at something Shika said, when I felt a familiar presence in the air. My heart skipped a beat as my eyes unconsciously flicked to the entrance. There they were—Shaurya, Akshith, and Yuvaan, making their way through the crowd with their usual swagger.

I couldn't help but smile, my eyes locking with Shaurya's. The intense look in his eyes made my pulse race, though I tried to keep my composure.

I gave Shika a quick look and rolled my eyes. "What are they doing here?" I muttered under my breath, just loud enough for her to hear.

"Well, I don't know, but someone looks quite pleased to see them," she teased, nudging me. I shot her a quick glare, but I could feel my cheeks warming up. I am happy seeing Shaurya here, but there is a lingering fear inside about him finding out our identity.

Shaurya was already walking toward us, and before I knew it, his arm was around my shoulders, pulling me into a side hug. "Well, well, if it isn't my favorite troublemaker," he said, his voice low and warm, and I couldn't help but feel a little breathless.

I leaned back into his embrace, my heart fluttering. "What are you doing here?" I asked, trying to keep my tone light, but I could feel the doubt slipping into my voice.

He gave me that devilish grin of his. "We came to collect some package for Akshith. But what brings you to London? You didn't even mention it earlier."

Before I could respond, Rakshith jumped in, his voice dripping with mock seriousness. "We're here for some very important work." He paused, trying to hide our truth behind his dramatics, glancing over at Akshith and Yuvaan for added effect. "Official government work at the Indian Embassy. Can't give out too many details, you know how it is."

Rakshith's acting was on point, making Shaurya and others roll their eyes. I decided to play along, keeping the act going. "Yes, exactly," I said, my voice dropping into something more serious. "PMO work and all that. Very secretive business."

Akshith raised an eyebrow, clearly not buying it but playing along anyway. "I'm sure it's all very secretive," he said, his gaze lingering on us for a moment, and then he smirked. "I guess we all have our official duties, huh? But Secret and Ananya in a single sentence doesn't seem convincing!"

My eyes widened at his statement. I scowled at him, ready to give him a fitting reply, but Shaurya didn't give me any chance to speak as he kissed my temple, leaving me stunned at his sudden display of affection.

Yuvaan snickered softly. "Well, I'm not sure about top secret, but it's good to see you guys."

Shaurya chuckled, his eyes still locked on me, sending a little shiver down my spine. "For whatever reason, you are here, it feels amazing to have you around. How long are you staying?"

"We'll be here for a bit," I said, my lips curving into a teasing smile. "But you better be careful, Shaurya. You never know what kind of trouble I could get you into if I'm around."

His eyes darkened just slightly, the mischievous grin never leaving his face. "Trouble is the last thing I'd worry about when it comes to you."

I couldn't resist; I leaned in just a little, my voice a soft whisper. "Oh, I'm sure you would love to worry about me, but we'll see."

His gaze softened, and it was like the world around us disappeared for a brief moment. There was just him and the unmistakable pull between us.

"Well, I guess we'll have to make the most of it while we're both here," he said quietly, and my heart fluttered again.

Just then, Rakshith coughed loudly, bringing me back to reality. "I'll let you two get back to your 'top secret' romance later," he said with a wink. "But it was good running into you all."

As our team began to head toward our respective gates, my eyes stayed on Shaurya, and I could feel the tension still crackling in the air between us. There was something undeniably magnetic about him, and I had to fight to keep the smile from spreading too much.

"Take care, Shaurya," I called, my voice low and teasing. "Don't get too lost in London."

He gave me one last lingering look, and I saw his lips twitch into a smirk. "I don't think I could get lost, not with you around."

Once Shaurya, Akshith, and Yuvaan were out of our sight, we glanced at each other, the same thing going on in all our minds. Meeting someone from the ICT right after landing was nowhere in our plans. We didn't want them to know about us being here. That was why I didn't mention it to Shaurya, but now we are here, and they know about it.

"Let's try to keep our work away from the team without them getting suspicious," Vikram said, his voice filled with conviction.

Though it seems to be an easy task, it wasn't. Now that Shaurya and others know that we are here, it will be a hard way ahead. And, if my seniors get to know about our relationship, I would be left with no option but to choose between my profession and Shaurya. A choice I am not ready to make. Not now. Not ever.

After getting the keys to the apartment Mr. Murthy had arranged for us, we retired to our rooms to rest for a while before starting with our duty. The apartment was cozy and surprisingly spacious—three bedrooms, a kitchen, a living room, and even a balcony that offered a stunning view of the city's skyline. I couldn't help but appreciate the quiet beauty of the place, though the noise of our mission was never far behind in my mind.

Shika and I decided to share a room. We were always on the same wavelength when it came to anything, and I was more than happy to have her beside me. We left the boys to figure out how they'd divide the remaining two rooms.

Unpacking didn't take long. It never does when you know you're moving quickly and on the go. But the tech setup... that took some time. We worked in sync, pulling out cables, plugging in devices, and making sure everything was ready. The hours passed before we finally took a break.

"We'll be living here for a while, so we might as well make it feel like home," Shika said as she folded up the last of her clothes and placed them in the closet.

I nodded, glancing around the room. It felt like we were setting up for real life, but I knew it wasn't going to be. The next part of our mission was just beginning, and everything was about to get a lot harder. Still, for the next few hours, I pushed that thought aside.

Once we were finished, we ordered food from a local spot—simple, nothing fancy, but comforting in its familiarity. We ate together, joking and chatting like we always did. It was normal, easy. The kind of carefree moment we couldn't afford once the mission truly started.

Afterward, we all agreed to sleep for a while. We still had time before we went out to meet the agent Dixit Sir talked about, and I could feel the exhaustion in my bones. It wasn't just from the long flight; it was the emotional toll that this kind of life took on you.

Being in a new place, under new identities, with a new mission... everything was shifting, and I could already feel the weight of it all pressing down on me. But for now, I let myself close my eyes, knowing that tomorrow, everything would start moving faster.

"Anu, you go meet the agent and collect the details. We'll check the locality for possible escape routes," Vikram said, brushing his fingers through his trousled hair as we all regrouped after catching some rest.

"Alright," I nodded, slipping my phone out as Mr. Murthy forwarded me the location and table reservation details.

We left the apartment together and split up, each of us walking our path with one goal in mind. My cab ride was quiet, the city passing by like a blur outside the window.

The café was tucked in a corner, charming and peaceful. The golden evening sun spilled through the glass walls, casting a soft glow over the tables. The warm smell of coffee and freshly baked brownies wrapped around me like a blanket—too comforting, too deceiving.

I found the table. Sat down. Kept my head low. Everything felt... normal. People laughed around me, sipped on lattes, shared stories. I was just a part of the background.

Ten minutes passed.

I felt someone walk up behind me.

Assuming it was the agent, I turned—ready to keep things short, professional.

But the moment I saw him, something inside me stopped. Like literally froze.

Standing there, wearing that smug grin and his usual lazy outfit, was the man I never expected to be an agent.

I blinked once. Twice. What? What is he doing here?

"Akshith?" I said his name like I didn't believe it myself. My voice barely came out. It sounded like a question—but even I didn't know what I was asking.

He just grinned wider. Like he knew exactly what was going on.

And I?

I had no idea what the hell was going on. Was it some kind of joke? How can Akshith be here? How can he be an agent?